WAKING SLEEPING DOGS CAN BE MURDER

He stuck a cigarette between his lips and lit it, tossing the match over the boat's railing.

"So," he said, "what would you do, Peggy, some gal comes and wants you to help her find her baby after twenty years?"

"Why would she come to you?"

" 'Cause I talked her into selling the kid to some people who wanted a baby but couldn't adopt one—the agency didn't think they was suitable. She could use the money, and I make a little on the deal too, of course," he added with a chuckle. "Sort of finder's fee, you might say."

"It's going to come as a big shock to everybody involved, " I said.

"Let sleeping dogs lie, huh?" Steadman George said with a chuckle . . . his small bright eyes watching me behind the dirty lenses. His voice became dreamy as he added, "It wouldn't make much of a story that way . . . "

Other Peggy O'Neill Mysteries by
M. D. Lake
from Avon Books

Midsummer Malice

A PEGGY O'NEILL MYSTERY

*Merry Christmas
to Marion,*

M. D. LAKE

md lake

AVON BOOKS ◆ NEW YORK

This is a work of fiction. Names, characters, places and incidents either are the product of the author's imagination or are used fictitiously. Any resemblance to actual events, locales, organizations, or persons living or dead, is entirely coincidental and beyond the intent of either the author or the publisher.

AVON BOOKS
A division of
The Hearst Corporation
1350 Avenue of the Americas
New York, New York 10019

Copyright © 1997 by Allen Simpson
Published by arrangement with the author
Visit our website at **http://www.AvonBooks.com**
Library of Congress Catalog Card Number: 97-93747
ISBN: 0-380-78759-8

First Avon Books Printing: December 1997

AVON TRADEMARK REG. U.S. PAT. OFF. AND IN OTHER COUNTRIES, MARCA REGISTRADA, HECHO EN U.S.A.

Printed in the U.S.A.

WCD 10 9 8 7 6 5 4 3 2 1

This is for Pat Hayner, who not only told me everything I know about beads and findings and how to sell them from an old school bus, but also produced a daughter who's made me a grandfather twice.

Prologue

It began innocently enough, when Steadman George, the piano player on the Showboat, asked me if I'd like to hear a story. I hesitated before answering. I lie awake at night sometimes wondering what would have happened if I'd said no. It's not a pleasant thought.

I'm a campus cop and I take the dog watch whenever I can. That's most of the time, since most cops prefer the day watches. The night's a dangerous place for a woman, which might be why I've always loved it, but since it's rapidly becoming a dangerous place for men now too, they'll probably find some way to abolish it soon.

It helps, of course, that I'm carrying a pistol I know how to use and a walkie-talkie that keeps me in contact with the dispatcher at the campus police station and with cops patrolling other parts of the campus.

My assignment that night was the Old Campus, my favorite part of the University. I like the lawns that surround the old ivy-covered buildings and the giant oaks that shade them. The New Campus, on the other side of the river, is mostly naked steel, glass, and concrete put together on the orders of cost accountants. No grass grows over there and not many trees, a reflection, I think, of the minds of the people who run our universities now.

My only problem with the dog watch that night was that the campus was too quiet, which gave me a lot of time to brood. I was brooding on the fact that I was in the process of losing my lover, Gary Mallory.

Gary and I had met a couple of years ago and we'd gone together for a while. Then he'd grown restless—he wasn't fond of modern civilization—and so he'd moved to Belize, which, if I remember correctly, is somewhere in Central America, a continent or subcontinent that teems with life-forms unfamiliar to me. He'd wanted me to go with him, but I'd shuddered at the thought and declined politely. For better or worse, I belong here, in the city, surrounded by modern life in all its complexity and disarray. I'm also very fair-skinned and burn easily. Gary's dark, and doesn't.

I thought that was the end of our relationship, but it didn't take Gary long to discover that Belize wasn't the answer he was looking for: the eco-friendly, off-the-beaten-path tour buses from the States were making too much racket, I suspect, or else he couldn't get parts for the computer he needed to write his books and articles on the beauties of the simple life lived close to the soil.

Whatever the case, he came back here and got a job as a feature writer on the local newspaper and moved in with me.

That only lasted a few months. I have a nice apartment, but if I'm in it, it seems to be only big enough for one. Every time I turned a corner, there Gary would be, coming the other way. Once he even padded up behind me as I was taking my first swallow of morning coffee and planted a clammy kiss on my neck. I jumped a foot and, for a terrifying moment, imagined I was living in Belize and something from whose bite there's no cure had plopped down on me from the high jungle canopy.

Luckily, he sensed what was coming and moved out. Perhaps the months of living in Belize had forced him to develop senses that the rest of us, lulled by the softness of our unnatural civilization and culture, had let atrophy. He moved in with a friend of mine, Lillian Przynski, an elderly widow who's no longer physically or financially able to keep up her home. Gary's good with his hands and likes fixing things, so it was a nice arrangement for both of them. It was nice for me too and, I thought, for Gary's and my relationship.

We continued to spend many of my nights off together, and I thought things were going well, but then, last week, he announced that he'd been offered the chance to buy a newspaper in someplace called Loon Lake.

I masked the effect of a heavy stone dropping into my belly with sarcasm. "*A* newspaper?" I said. "How many could there be in a place called Loon Lake?"

"I know the owner," he said, ignoring the sarcasm. "He's a friend of my dad's. He's getting ready to retire and wants me to take over the paper. There's only the one."

"Where is Loon Lake?" I asked.

"About three hours north of here. It's a small, thriving community with lots of lakes and forest."

"And loons, I imagine," I said.

It occurred to me that running a newspaper in a little town called Loon Lake was just what Gary was born to do, since it would combine his desire for a simpler, less complicated life with what he does best, write.

"I'm going up to case the joint," he said casually. "Tomorrow. I don't suppose you'd like to come with?"

"You'll be busy," I replied, "casing, as you say, the joint. I'd just be in the way."

"Yeah, maybe," he'd agreed reluctantly.

And so Gary was out of town and I was walking my beat in the night and brooding on relationships.

A little after midnight I stumbled on someone trying to break into a car in a faculty parking lot using a bent piece of wire. It turned out to be a literature professor who'd locked his keys in his car—not an unusual occurrence around this place. Since I knew the man, I got the door open for him and then continued my patrol. A university campus isn't exactly the mean streets of L.A. Not yet, anyway.

Around two A.M., I crossed the mall and made my way down to the Mississippi River below the Old Campus, where I strolled along the path on the riverbank, shining my flashlight into the shrubbery. Contrary to what some of the students we find down there think, the campus cops don't get a kick out of surprising lovers in the bushes, chewing them out, and shooing them away; we just want to be sure both partners are there willingly. Once we've established that, then we chew them out and shoo them away.

The path ended at the parking lot for the old Showboat, another favorite spot for lovers. That night, though, the parking lot was as empty as the bushes had been.

As I approached the Showboat, a big stern-wheeler docked there in the summer and used for theatrical productions, I saw the glow of a cigarette from the upper deck at the stern, and a dark figure silhouetted against the sky, his white hair and beard a phosphorus glow in the moonlight.

I knew who it was: Steadman George, the pianist for this summer's play.

"You're up late, Steadman," I called to him from the shore.

"Yeah. But it's hard to sleep, Peggy O'Neill, when you got a lot on your mind."

"What's the problem?"

"Ghosts."

"The Showboat's haunted?"

"Nah—I don't believe in them kind of ghosts!"

He didn't say anything for a moment, and I was about to go on my way, when he suddenly asked: "What would you do if a gal who'd sold her baby some twenty years ago was to come back and ask you to help her find it?"

"*Sold* her baby?" I repeated.

"Yep."

"It sounds like the premise of a melodrama."

"Maybe it is," he said, with the ragged chuckle of a man who's done a lot of drinking and smoking in his time. "You want to hear about it?"

"Sure."

Why not? I usually spend my breaks with one of the other cops on the dog watch, but the only cop besides me patrolling the Old Campus that night was Floyd Hazard—known to all of us who loathe him as "The Hazard of Being Male"—and I'd rather have a root canal than spend time with him.

I stepped over the chain across the Showboat's gangplank and walked onto the boat, then climbed the outside stairs to the upper deck. I'd spent my breaks with George a couple of times before when he'd been up and about that late, so I knew the way.

He led us over to the river side of the boat, since he knew I hate the stench of cigarettes and the breeze is stronger there, and we made ourselves comfortable in folding chairs, with me upwind. Below us the dark river flowed silently by and a half-moon hung over the city in the distance.

Steadman George was short and heavy, with a belly that hid his belt, and he wore his white hair in a long ponytail. He'd been a fixture on the local jazz scene for years. I'd never heard him play jazz because I don't go to bars unless it's to hear a musician or comedian I like a lot, but I'd attended last year's Showboat production and knew he was a talented pianist and a crowd favorite. I hadn't had a chance to attend this summer's play yet.

He shot me a look. "Ain't you gonna ask me how it's goin' with my drinkin', Peggy?"

"I wasn't planning to," I replied, "but since you brought it up, how's it going with your drinking, Steadman?" He'd asked me to call him Steadman a few nights earlier when I'd stopped to talk to him and he'd told me he was trying to quit drinking.

He chuckled, shook his head. "Tough love, eh? Well, I'm still hangin' in there. Been two weeks now."

"I know how hard it can be," I said, keeping my voice neutral. My father had been an alcoholic. I wasn't going to let George think he'd hooked me into his struggle for sobriety.

He stuck a new cigarette between his lips and lit it, tossing the match over the boat's railing. "So," he said, "what would you do, Peggy, some gal comes back and wants you to help her find her baby after twenty years or so?"

"Why would she come to you?"

" 'Cause she don't know where the kid is, that's why."

"But you do?"

"Maybe."

"Why'd she sell her baby in the first place?"

He shrugged. "She was just a kid. Sixteen when she got pregnant, seventeen when she had the kid. What was she gonna do?"

"She could've put the baby up for adoption," I said, "or had an abortion."

"She was gonna have an abortion," he replied, "but I talked her out of it. I knew some people wanted a baby but couldn't have one themselves, and couldn't adopt one either. I talked her into selling the kid to them—she could use the money. I made a little on the deal too, of course," he added with a chuckle, "sort of a finder's fee, you might say."

He shot me a hard look. "This is only a story we're talkin' about, now, remember," he added. "Moonspin, my ma would've called it."

"Sure," I said, feeling a slight revulsion at a man I knew had sold a baby—at least one—to a couple who couldn't legally adopt a child. I asked him why they hadn't been able to adopt.

He shrugged. "I guess the adoption agency didn't think they was suitable. The guy'd been busted for having some marijuana, back in the sixties." He laughed his gravelly laugh. "That was a big deal back then, y'know."

It probably still was in adoption circles. There were enough people out there wanting babies who hadn't been busted for narcotics possession.

I asked him how the sale had been managed.

He gave me a smile full of secret mischief, like a degenerate department store Santa. "*If* it really happened," he said, "here's how I'd do it. I'd have the *real* mom pretend to be the woman who's gonna buy the baby, see. That way, everything's in her and her husband's name, especially the birth certificate. Simple as that. No court records sayin' the kid was adopted, even. And after twenty-some years, where's the witnesses? The doctors? The nurses? All pregnant women look the same, right? All babies look alike too."

"But surely this woman remembers the name she used in the hospital, doesn't she? Why does she need your help finding the child now?"

" 'Cause it was so long ago, Peggy," he answered, as if speaking to a child himself. He sucked smoke, blew it out noisily. "A lot can happen to a family in twenty years, y'know. They can move away, for example, or the parents get divorced—or die even. Maybe if Bernie tried hard enough, or hired a private detective, she could find her kid, but somethin' tells me she don't have any idea how to do the one thing, or the money to do the other."

"Bernie?"

His nicotine-stained teeth glittered in a grin in his unkempt beard. ''Somethin' like that,'' he said, with all the slyness of a backhoe.

''So there's just you to help her,'' I said.

''Yep. You think I should?''

I thought about it awhile. I'm never sure of myself when two people's needs, equally pressing, meet head-on, which is why I'm glad I'm not God or a judge. It's bad enough, sometimes, just being a cop.

''I suppose you'd want to ask the child's permission before telling this Bernie where to find her,'' I said. ''Or him.''

George smiled mysteriously. ''I suppose you would,'' he said.

''Boy or girl?'' I asked.

''That make a difference, Peggy?''

''No. It's just easier to talk about if we know the sex.''

He nodded and pursed his lips as though giving it some thought. ''Call her a girl, then,'' he said.

A thought struck me. ''She knows the truth about her birth, doesn't she, Steadman? That her parents got her illegally?''

George smiled and shook his head. ''Doubt it. Why should they tell her? The birth certificate don't say nothing except that the stork dropped her right down the old chimney, fair and square. If it was your kid, Peggy, would you tell her? It'd be kinda hard to do, wouldn't ya think, tellin' a kid she was bought 'n sold, like a calf or a lamb?''

''I suppose it would,'' I said, ''but I'd tell her anyway.''

I think it's foolish of people not to tell their kids they're adopted, since secrets that big have a way of coming out, usually at a bad time. In this case, though, it hadn't been an adoption: the child had been sold. But even so, if I was the child, I'd want to know the truth about myself, and be outraged if I discovered I'd come into the world with a false passport.

''Why, after all these years, does the birth mother want to find the child now?'' I asked.

He shrugged and smoked a minute, watched a string of barges glide silently by out in the middle of the river.

''Who knows how women think?'' he answered finally.

"Bernie was a strange bird back then and most likely she's a lot stranger now—the soulful type that can't wipe the past out and move on, I guess."

"Do you know how the child's getting along now?"

The old stern-wheeler began rocking gently in the wake of the barges as George nodded, stroking his beard. "She's doin' just great," he said. "Raised in one of them white bread neighborhoods like that TV family from the fifties, the Muppets or whatever they was called."

"How do you know?"

"How?" He turned and gave me an indignant look. "On account of I keep an eye on her, that's how! I told ya, Peggy, if it hadn't been for me, Bernie would've got an abortion, so her kid's as much mine as the people who bought her, ain't she, when all's said and done?"

"What about the father?" I asked. "The biological father, I mean? Does he play any role in this melodrama of yours?"

"Never knew who he was," George said. His cigarette arced over the side of the boat like a kamikaze firefly.

"Of course," he went on after a moment, "Bernie might not know for sure who the father was herself. She wasn't beautiful by a long shot, but she was young and innocent and all alone in the big city. That's just as good as looks sometimes, y'know." He gave me a smile that was mostly a leer, his eyes challenging me to say something morally disapproving.

I didn't want to start a quarrel with the old lecher and it was too late, in more than one sense, to teach him anything anyway.

"I don't know what to tell you, Steadman," I said, getting up. It was time for me to get back on patrol.

I could imagine this woman suffering for a choice she'd made many years ago when she'd still been only a child herself—a runaway, pregnant, with even fewer social services available to her than exist today. But we all have to take the consequences of how we play the cards we're dealt, learn from them, and move on. That's always easy to say to others—but it's been my experience that people who don't either whine a lot or cause a lot of trouble, or both.

"It's going to come as a big shock to everybody involved," I said, "Bernie's showing up suddenly like this after such a long time. You might consider assuring her that her child's doing fine, and ask her to think about the possible consequences of telling her about it now—I mean, if you really think the child really is doing fine."

That sounded feeble to me—and I was sure it wasn't what I'd want for myself if I were the child—but it was the best I could come up with on a showboat in the middle of the night.

"Let sleeping dogs lie, huh?" Steadman George said with a chuckle, his small bright eyes watching me behind the dirty lenses. He fumbled in his shirt pocket for another cigarette, stuck it in his mouth and lit it, tossed the match over the side of the boat.

"That's probably what I'd do too," he said, "if we was talkin' about something that really happened. But this is only a story, Peggy O'Neill, and it wouldn't be very interesting that way, would it?" His voice became dreamy as he added, "It wouldn't make much of a story that way at all."

MONDAY

One

Bernie, with Gideon, her black Lab, asleep on the floor beside her in the old school bus, arrived in town Sunday night. She followed the directions her friend Swallow had given her to the Riverview Campgrounds, about ten miles north of town. She introduced herself to the manager, an old friend of Swallow's, and rented a spot under a large oak tree close to the river, where she unhitched her trailer from the bus and hooked it up to the water, sewer, and electricity. Then she took Gideon to the river and let him explore the woods that lined the bank while she stretched her own legs.

She'd played in woods like these as a child in Pine City, the town seventy miles north of here where she'd grown up. She'd sat and rested against oaks like these too, while slapping mosquitoes and listening to the river lapping softly on the shore at her feet. The Mississippi didn't run through Pine City, of course, but there'd been a river anyway—the Snake, it was called—and it was as good a river as any, if you hadn't seen another.

She remembered the last full day she'd been in Minnesota, almost exactly twenty years ago. She'd had the baby two days earlier, cradled her to nurse but otherwise didn't hold her more than she'd had to, to keep the nurses from wondering. After she'd handed the baby to the man who was going to be her father to carry out of the hospital, she'd never touched her daughter again.

The man and his wife had offered her a lift to wherever she wanted to go, but she'd said no. Still sore from the stitches, she'd walked back to the room she'd lived in near campus until the baby was born. Then she'd packed and taken a bus to the Greyhound station, where she'd taken another bus to California, a thousand dollars in a pouch around her neck from the people she'd sold the baby to and another four hundred from the baby's father for the abortion she hadn't got.

She'd had the baby only those two days. That was a short time to stay in the hospital back then, but if she'd stayed any longer, she might have changed her mind about giving the baby away.

Not *giving* her away, she corrected herself: she'd *sold* her baby. She said it aloud, her wide mouth thinning in disapproval. Bernie worked hard to try not to make herself seem better in her own eyes than she was.

She remembered the fullness of her breasts, the baby's sweet smell, and the hard, determined suck of her tiny mouth. That was the part that had almost made her change her mind about selling her baby, when she'd seen and felt the fierce desperation with which the baby sucked and the determined way her tiny fingers crawled on her breast, like the fingers of a blind person thrown out of a familiar world into one where all the rules had changed.

She drove into town the next morning, parked the big yellow bus on the street in front of a pay phone, and tried to look up the people she'd sold her baby to. She wasn't surprised or discouraged to discover that there was over a page of Walkers, twenty-seven of whom were Robert or Bob, and no Linda.

She couldn't remember the name of the man who'd arranged the sale, so next she looked up the woman who'd introduced her to him: Sue Ann Maslowski. There weren't many Maslowskis in the phone book, but none of them was Sue Ann.

As a last resort, and reluctantly, she flipped through the phone book in search of her old boyfriend, Geoff Seaton. She found his name and stared at it a long time, surprised at the hurt and anger it could still arouse in her. He'd never had any idea she was pregnant—she'd broken up with him before that happened—but he'd known Sue Ann. She dropped a coin in the slot and dialed his number.

"Geoff Seaton," he said crisply, all business, and the sound of his voice, almost unchanged after all this time, plunged her back into the past like the sickening drop of a roller coaster.

When she told him who she was, there was a long pause and then he said, "Bernie! You're kiddin' me!" She recognized the false enthusiasm in his voice. It hadn't changed either.

"No, I'm not," she said. "I'm really Bernie."

He laughed. "Okay—I'm convinced! 'Really Bernie' after all these years! How're ya doin', sweetheart?"

She saw him in her mind's eye as he'd looked in the seventies: dark complexion and curly dark hair, a little stocky and an inch shorter than she. He had a slow crooked smile, a smile she no longer trusted in anybody—not right off the bat, anyway—and sleepy dark brown eyes.

"I'm fine, Geoff," she replied. "How about you?"

"Not too bad, not too bad. What're you doin' back in town, sweetheart?" he asked, his voice suddenly wary.

She didn't want to tell him about the baby she'd given up, so she said she was here to sell beads and jewelery at an art fair at the Riverton Mall.

"The Riverton Mall, huh? One of those hippie fairs they put on there in the summers, now that the mall's folded? You still a hippie, Bernie?"

"No," she said. She'd never been a hippie—he knew that as well as she did. "What I called about," she went on, anxious to get the call over with, "was I was wondering if you knew what happened to Sue Ann Maslowski. You remember Sue Ann?"

"Sure, I see her occasionally at the club." He didn't explain what he meant by that, and she didn't ask. "Isn't she in the phone book?"

"I couldn't find her," Bernie said.

"Oh, well—she's married. Was, I mean. Her name isn't Maslowski anymore, it's—lemme think. Naylor—Sue Ann Naylor. Hold on a sec, I'll see if she's in the phone book."

After a moment, he gave her the number and address.

"Maybe I'll drop by the fair one of these days," he added. "How long you gonna be in town?" Again she heard wariness in his voice, wondered why.

"Just through Sunday," she said, "when the fair ends." She couldn't afford to stay any longer than that.

"I'll try to make it. I'll spring for a beer and a brat and we'll talk over old times." His laugh sounded nervous to her. She wondered if maybe he thought she'd called to borrow money or something.

"Great," she said, putting as much feeling into the word as she could, just to be polite.

She doubted she'd see him again, though. She had no interest in talking over old times with him and she was sure he felt the same way.

Two

She called the number he'd given her and got a recorded woman's voice that told her only that she'd dialed correctly and to leave a message if she wanted to. The voice was female, low and cultured, as different from Sue Ann's twenty years ago as Maslowski is from Naylor. She couldn't think of what to say to an answering machine, so she hung up.

She drove back to the trailer park and let Gideon out for a run, then brought out a folding chair and table and placed them under the oak tree that shaded her trailer. She began making a necklace, with Gideon dozing at her feet.

Bernie made her living selling beads and findings—"hardware for jewelry" was her answer when people asked her what findings were—at Indian powwows, rock and gem shows, and art fairs all over the Southwest. She'd removed all but the first row of seats from the school bus to make room for her stock and the equipment she needed to set up her booth and display her wares. On both sides of the bus she'd painted BERNIE'S BEAD BUS BEADS & FINDINGS, and she spent ten months a year—from February to November—on the road.

She spent the worst of the winter months parked in a friend's yard in Arizona. There she repaired the bus and trailer—out of necessity she'd become a pretty fair mechanic—ordered new supplies from her wholesalers, made beads herself from stones, shells, and bleached wood she picked up in the desert, and rested up. She also made jewelry when she had nothing else to do—which wasn't often, since she needed to sell beads and findings to live, and to do that she had to be on the road.

Then, a few months ago, her friend Swallow, a professional tarot reader and psychic, had given her a hard look and said she could see that Bernie had some unfinished business to attend to in Minnesota. That had startled her at first, but she convinced herself that Swallow could have been influenced by her knowledge of Bernie's past. It would be a pretty safe bet to tell a person who'd run away from home at sixteen that she had unfinished business to take care of!

Besides, Swallow wanted Bernie to come to Minnesota, and she wasn't above using her psychic abilities to try to get her way. Swallow came here every summer to work the various fairs. She believed Minnesota was a good place for "alternative spirituality," she said; it wasn't overrun with charlatans, the way the warmer parts of the country were.

The Riverton Art Fair wasn't due to start until Thursday afternoon, but Bernie had arrived four days early to try to find out what had become of her daughter. If she couldn't find her in four days, that would probably mean she wasn't meant to, since she couldn't afford to stay away from her regular routes in the Southwest any longer than that.

For most of the years since she'd left Minnesota, she hadn't given her daughter more than a fleeting thought. However, she'd occasionally met people who'd been adopted, and some of them wanted to know who their birth parents were, and not because they were unhappy with their adopted parents either. They wanted to learn their family health histories, for example, or wanted to meet somebody who looked like them, after living in families where they didn't resemble anybody.

Whenever she heard talk like that, Bernie wondered if her daughter ever thought about her or wanted to find her. She wouldn't be able to do it through the normal channels, of course; she'd have to do it the same way Bernie was, except go the other way.

Then, five or six months ago, she'd read a chilling story in a magazine about a birth mother who'd discovered years later that the adoptive mother had murdered her child. Bernie hadn't been able to sleep for a long time after reading that.

She'd replayed in her mind the time she'd spent with Linda and Bob Walker, trying to recall if there'd been anything about them that might have indicated they'd be abusive parents. She didn't think so. But then, the murderous adoptive mother must have seemed okay to the adoption agency, which was supposed to know how to weed out bad prospective parents from good ones, wasn't it? It hadn't weeded that one out!

Her daughter began to occupy her thoughts more and more. She could be having a few beers with friends, or playing cards, or working on her accounts, and without warning she'd remember her baby as she'd last seen her—or, just as often, the car that was taking her away to her new life as it disappeared around a corner, its turn signal winking.

As Bernie thought about the past, she worked on the necklace, occasionally returning to the bus to rummage through cases in search of a particular color or shape or texture of bead, until she noticed that the necklace was becoming something unusually beautiful as it grew in her hands. She often felt the things she created unconsciously were better than those she created with her conscious mind. Some of her friends even claimed she created poetry in beads and wished she'd do more of it.

She'd started out making the necklace thinking she'd give it to Sue Ann, but now she decided it really belonged to her daughter. She hoped that someday, somehow, she'd be able to give it to her.

Three

At six o'clock that evening she drove to the address Geoff had given her for Sue Ann. She'd made up her mind to arrive at her door unannounced since, in Bernie's experience, it was harder to turn somebody away in person than over the phone. When she arrived, though, and saw the wrought-iron gate in a high wall, she almost changed her mind and drove to the nearest drugstore to call. On the other side of the gate she could see streets lined with town houses that all looked exactly alike, right down to the hedges and trees in the tiny front yards.

Resolutely, she pulled the bus up to the gate, got out, and studied the list of names in a glass-encased box. Next to each name was a button. She pressed the button next to NAYLOR and after a moment a loud, metallic voice, coming from nowhere, asked, "Who is it?"

Figuring it was a system of the kind they use in drive-up restaurants, Bernie hollered her name, adding, "We knew each other back in the seventies. You worked in a used clothing store and I—"

"Bernie! Sure! Hey, what's up? You don't have to yell, by the way."

Bernie started to explain what she wanted when suddenly the gate in front of her began to swing open and somebody in a car behind her leaned angrily on his horn, making Bernie jump.

Sue Ann heard it too and said, "Oh, shit, Bernie, you're holding up traffic! C'mon in." She gave directions and Bernie, smiling as pleasantly as she could at the indignant man in the expensive-looking sports car behind her, climbed back into her bus, shifted into low, and nosed cautiously through the gate.

Sue Ann opened the door and held out both hands—to grasp Bernie quickly by the upper arms and hold her at a distance. Bernie smiled and tossed her head back in the direction of her bus. "Is it okay to park it there?"

Sue Ann's gray eyes widened slightly as she peered around Bernie and saw the old yellow bus sprawled across three parking spaces. "Sure, the neighbors can probably handle it—for a little while, anyway."

The first thing Bernie smelled when Sue Ann stood back to let her in was marijuana, which surprised her. She knew people who smoked it, but she didn't realize that people who lived in places like this did. A long, thin, expertly rolled marijuana cigarette was balanced on a heavy glass ashtray sitting on the arm of a white leather sofa.

"Can I roll you one?" Sue Ann asked, following her glance.

Bernie shook her head. She'd never liked dope; it just made her dizzy.

"How about a drink, then? I've got beer too."

"A beer would be great."

Sue Ann got it for her and then curled into the white leather sofa, her small body almost disappearing in its expensive-looking softness. "How'd you find me, Bernie?" she asked as she relit her cigarette.

"Geoff Seaton," Bernie said.

"Geoff? Oh, yeah. You've seen him, huh?"

Bernie shook her head. "No," she said, "just talked to him on the phone for a couple of minutes."

"He's a stockbroker now," Sue Ann said. "Just sits at home and lets his computer buy and sell for him. Must be one hell of a smart computer, considering the way he dresses and the car he drives. Last I heard, he still wasn't married—maybe you broke his heart!" Her laugh sounded like a small window breaking.

Bernie forced a smile.

Sue Ann looked Bernie over critically. "You haven't changed much at all, have you?" she said. "A little older, maybe—wiser too, I hope."

She remembered Bernie the way she'd looked the last time she'd seen her: a gawky child with large dark eyes in an oval face, dark hair parted in the middle and falling down her back almost to her waist, a wide mouth and large teeth. She remembered thinking that if it wasn't for her big feet, Bernie might just float away, like smoke. She still had those same big dark eyes and the same wide mouth, but she'd put on weight that looked like muscle and her skin was rough, as though she worked outdoors. Her hair was short now and looked like she cut it herself.

Bernie gave Sue Ann an embarrassed smile. Sue Ann hadn't really aged, Bernie thought, she'd just become a cleaner, sharper image of what she'd been in the seventies, as if she'd been burnished by one of those stones Indian women used on their pots. Her hair was reddish brown and short, cut to emphasize her shapely head and delicate features.

"You've done well for yourself," Bernie said as she let her eyes dart around the room.

"Yeah," Sue Ann said with a deprecating smile, "I guess I have come a ways since we both toiled in the grubby aisles at Rags to Britches. It's Raggs now, with two g's, you know—the old name didn't fit the image we want to project—and I'm the head buyer. Big deal, huh? You mean you haven't been in any of our stores, Bernie?" she teased. "They're in all the better malls."

Bernie was wearing faded khaki pants, a well-worn denim shirt, and work boots—an outfit, Sue Ann reflected, she could have gotten from Rags to Britches twenty years ago.

Bernie shook her head. She wasn't sure she'd ever been in what Sue Ann meant by a "better mall."

"So what are you up to these days?" Sue Ann asked. "What's that old school bus all about—'Bernie's Bead Bus'?"

Bernie explained while Sue Ann smoked and listened.

"And you can make a living that way?" she asked when Bernie had finished.

"Sure."

"What about health benefits, retirement? You makin' enough to put some away?"

"I have a health plan," Bernie said. "It just pays for the basics but I'm lucky, I almost never get sick, knock on wood."

She added that she sometimes bought annuities, when she had a little money left over. She figured that those, together with Social Security, would be enough for her old age.

"Social Security!" Sue Ann snorted. "Right!"

"I've never needed a lot," Bernie added.

"Takes all kinds, doesn't it?" Sue Ann said, her eyes darting around her living room nervously, as if to make sure it was still there. She tried to imagine giving it all up—telling her boss what she could do with her job—buying an old school bus, going on the road . . .

She laughed the thought quickly out of her head. "You're not married?" she asked.

Bernie shook her head.

"Lucky you!" Sue Ann said. Then she fixed Bernie with the expectant half-smile that said the pleasantries were over. "So what brings you back?" she asked.

"I want to find my daughter," Bernie said.

"Your—?" For a moment Sue Ann looked puzzled. Then: "Oh, God—of course! I'd forgotten all about that. Why?"

Bernie shrugged. "It's hard to explain," she said. "I just want to know how she's doing, make sure she's all right. But I can't remember the name of the man who arranged it—the sale, I mean. I was hoping he could help me locate the people I sold her to. Of course, he could be dead now, I guess."

Sue Ann laughed harshly. "Men like Steadman George never die," she said. "You sure know how to stir up the memories, Bernie, don't you? You're like a time capsule."

She uncoiled herself from the sofa and padded out into her kitchen. She came back a few minutes later with a margarita, a cordless phone, and a directory that she began flipping through.

"He's not here. I wonder where the old lecher could be hiding. . . ."

She paused a moment, thinking, tapping an elaborately

manicured fingernail on the phone. "Oh, sure—Vicki Layne!"

As she turned pages, she explained to Bernie that Vicki had been a jazz singer twenty years ago. She'd sung in some of the groups George had played with and then they'd made music in the same bed. "Mine," she added dryly. "Ah, here she is."

As she dialed the number, she said: "I didn't blame Vicki, of course. Back then, the girls flocked around Steadman like flies on—hey, Vicki, it's Sue Ann, remember me?" She laughed. "Yeah, it has been a while, hasn't it? How're ya doin'?"

She winked at Bernie as she listened to Vicki's answer, then went on: "Well, a friend from the Stone Age—or was it 'stoned age'?—just dropped in out of the blue. She knew Steadman back then and wants to get in touch with him."

She listened a moment, then laughed. "No, she's not crazy. It's a long story, Vicki, and you don't wannna hear it, believe me. Let's just say there's no accounting for taste, and let it go at that."

She listened some more. "The Showboat? My, old Steadman must've got respectable since we booted him out! Don't you have to be sober for that kind of gig? What— he's *living* on the old tub? Be damned. Hold on a sec, let me get a pencil."

Sue Ann drifted back to the kitchen, where Bernie could hear her finishing the conversation.

"Steadman's got a gig playing the piano for the University's Showboat," she said when she returned. "They do plays in the summer—you know, melodramas, where the audience gets to boo at the villain and cheer the hero. Wholesome, all-American fun. Vicki says they're letting Steadman live on the boat in return for keeping an eye on it at night. Kind of like letting the fox watch the henhouse, in my opinion, but maybe there's nothing on it worth stealing. Here's the number."

Bernie thanked her for her help and, after a few more minutes of stilted conversation, got up to go. Sue Ann followed her to the door.

"Good luck in finding your daughter," she said. In spite of herself, she was moved by Bernie's quest, which she thought was hopeless. Two decades was a long time.

"Thanks," Bernie said. Then she dived into her battered leather shoulder bag and dug out a necklace she'd chosen from some she'd made to sell.

"I thought you might like this," she said with a self-conscious laugh as she held it out. "I remember how much you loved jewelry with heavy stones back in the old days."

Sue Ann took the necklace and stared down at it without saying anything for a moment. Bernie stifled the urge to offer to take it back.

"You made it?" Sue Ann asked, and when Bernie nodded, she added, "It's lovely." When she looked up at Bernie, her eyes were full of tears. "It's just how I was twenty years ago," she went on. "You got that right, Bernie. Thanks."

"You're welcome," Bernie said.

Bernie tried the number Sue Ann had given her for Steadman George at the first pay phone she came to but got no answer, so she drove back to the trailer park and tried again at regular intervals until, at a little after ten that night, a man finally answered. "It's your quarter," was all he said.

She told him who she was and what she wanted.

After a long silence he said, "I'll be damned!"

"Can you help me, Mr. George?" she asked, when he didn't say anything more.

"Well," he went on, speaking slowly, as if thinking, "I'll see what I can do for ya, Bernie. I'll see what I can do." Then he laughed. "You free tomorrow night?"

"You think you can find out where those people are by then? The Walkers?"

"I can't promise nothin'," he said, "but I'll tell you what, I'll leave a ticket for you at the ticket window on the boat. You see the play and we can talk afterwards. How's that?"

"That's fine," she said.

He gave her directions for how to find the Showboat and then added, "The play starts at eight sharp. Don't be late!"

"I won't be," she promised.

She fell asleep that night smiling, feeling that, one way or another, she was on her way back to her daughter.

TUESDAY

Four

The next night she drove to the University and followed the signs on the river road to the Showboat parking lot. An attendant directed her to a field next to the lot, where other buses were parked that had brought groups to the performance, and then she joined the crowd going up the gangplank onto the boat, ablaze with light, like a strange birthday cake. Following Steadman George's instructions, she told the young man at the ticket window who she was, and he handed her her ticket, smiled, and said, "Enjoy the show!"

Bernie did enjoy it, although it was pretty silly, she thought, and she had her mind on something else entirely.

Between acts, there was something the program called "oleos"—comic skits with songs and dances performed by the actors in the play. Bernie enjoyed them more than the play, because she didn't have to concentrate, and because the actors looked like they were having a good time along with the audience.

Steadman George accompanied the singers on the upright piano below the stage during the oleos and also provided background music during the play that heightened the emotions of whatever the scene was, like the background music in movies and television shows. He was wearing a black fedora hat, red suspenders, and a garter on the sleeve of his white shirt. Bernie wouldn't have recognized him after so long a time if she hadn't known who he was. He was clearly an audience favorite and when he stood up to doff his hat and take a bow at the final curtain, the audience cheered.

After the performance, the actors lined up on the shore by the gangplank to greet the audience as it filed off the boat. Steadman George was at the end of the line, surrounded by fans, talking and laughing boisterously, basking in their praise. He didn't recognize Bernie, of course. When she introduced herself, he just nodded and told her to wait for him over by the refreshment tent. He was clearly more interested in talking to his fans than to her.

After the crowd had gone, he waved to her and then led her up a flight of steps to the upper deck and back to the stern of the boat. He paused at a door, looked both ways in an exaggeratedly cautious manner, then slid up a window, reached in, and opened the door from the inside.

"Lost the key," he explained in his raspy voice.

He ushered her into his cabin, which took up the entire back end of the boat. Through a half-open door, she could see a little bedroom, the bed unmade.

"It's like a little apartment," she said, looking around.

"Yeah," he said. "It's okay, if you don't mind the rockin' when the barges come by."

He went over to a door in the back wall and threw it open. "Those stairs lead right down into the theater. That's so's I don't have to go outside in the rain when it's show time." He chuckled. "They're afraid I might catch cold. The show couldn't go on without Steadman George, y'know."

He closed the door, then went over and sat down in a rocking chair, gestured to a lumpy overstuffed chair with a faded green flower pattern for her to sit in. "I use this thing on account of after playin' the piano all night, I need to rest my achin' back. I ain't as young as I used to be," he added, giving her a hopeful grin.

"Me either," Bernie said.

She'd only met George a few times but she remembered that he'd been a clean-shaven man back then with long dark hair. He'd put on a lot of weight since then, and his belly protruded over his heavy wide belt, but he still had all his hair, which he wore in a ponytail, and a wild white beard that concealed most of his face.

He asked her what she'd been doing all these years and she answered patiently, not wanting to offend him in any way, but hoping she could soon bring the conversation around to her daughter's whereabouts.

"Sorry I can't offer you a beer or anything," he said. "I quit a couple weeks ago—doctor's orders." He grinned as he picked up a bag of marijuana on the table next to him. "The doc didn't say nothin' about dope, though."

As he rolled a fat joint, he looked Bernie up and down. After he'd talked to her the night before, he'd called Sue Ann to find out what he could about her—not for any specific reason, just that he liked to know what he was getting into.

She'd told him that Bernie had hardly changed at all, just gotten tougher and wiser, she thought. "She'd have to have," she added dryly, "to have survived this long."

"She have any money?" he'd asked.

She'd told him no and added that he didn't seem to have changed any either.

"You know who the kid's father is?" he'd asked.

"No."

"Maybe she don't know herself."

"Oh, I'm sure she does," Sue Ann had replied. "Bernie wasn't the type to sleep around." She laughed. "She was even babysitting for one of the chaplains at the U, so she was probably the religious type."

"A chaplain, huh?" He chuckled. "They're horny devils, some of 'em."

"Oh, Steadman!" she'd said in disgust, and hung up.

When he finished making the cigarette, he lit it and inhaled deeply, then offered it to Bernie.

She shook her head, wondering where these people—first Sue Ann, now George—had been the past two decades.

"C'mon, it's good shit," he said, inhaling the words to keep in the smoke. He shoved it at her, his little eyes staring at her unblinkingly.

She didn't want to get him mad, so she took it and took a quick shallow hit, then handed it back.

"That's better," he said.

They made small talk for a few minutes. Then he said, "So, you're unhappy on account of you let your baby go."

"I worry about her," she told him. "I can't get her off

my mind, so I decided I had to come back and try to find out if she's okay.''

"And you'd be sad if you didn't find out."

She wondered where this was leading. Was he going to demand money? "Yes," she said.

He took another drag off the cigarette and handed it to her. She took it and put it to her lips, sucked noisily, pretending to inhale. She could feel the effects.

"So, you liked the play, huh?" he asked.

"Yes," she replied. "Thanks for the ticket."

"What did you think of the acting?"

"The acting? I liked it."

"You think any of the actors were particularly good?"

She thought back, her brow furrowed. "I guess I thought the heroine was the best."

He grinned, nodded approvingly. "You remember her name?"

"Florence?"

He laughed loudly. "No, I mean her real name."

She shook her head, wondering what this was all about.

"Greta Markham," he said. "Used to be Walker before her mom got remarried."

It took a moment to register. Then her eyes widened. "What are you saying, Mr. George?" she whispered.

"What do you think I'm saying, Bernie?"

"You mean she's—she's my *daughter*?"

He nodded, looking pleased with himself.

An image of her daughter in her elaborate Victorian costume, surrounded by the other actors as she took her bow on the brightly lit stage as the applause swelled, came into her mind.

"Oh!" she breathed. "Oh—she's beautiful!"

George chuckled. "Well, I wouldn't go that far," he said, "but then, I ain't a mother either. Besides, you only seen her in makeup. She's not ugly or anything," he added quickly, realizing he might have been guilty of tactlessness. "In fact, she looks kinda like you, Bernie, under all the paint and fiddle-faddle."

"She must've taken after her parents, though," she said. "I mean, the people who—the Walkers. They were actors."

He nodded. "*He* was an actor and a pretty good one too. She just thought she was. She never really took to the life and as soon as they got Greta, she stayed home and took care of her. Bob's dead now and Linda's married again—to a dentist, this time. She learned her lesson, I guess."

He pulled a piece of crumpled paper out of his shirt pocket and handed it to her. "Here's the address, in case you're plannin' on droppin' in on 'em and sayin' hello. They live in one of them suburbs that weren't here in the seventies."

"Thanks," she said, eagerly taking the paper.

"Greta don't live at home now, though," he added. "She lives around campus someplace."

Bernie was sorry to hear that Bob had died. She'd liked him more than Linda, who'd seemed a little cold, although that might only have been on account of the awkwardness of the situation. She'd seen more of Bob too, since he'd brought her to the obstetrician's office as his wife for checkups, been in the waiting room while she had the baby, and fussed over her in the maternity ward to fool the nurses. Even the kisses he'd given her, the way a husband would, had felt genuine. But then, he was an actor.

"When did Bob die?" she asked.

He shrugged. "Ten years ago, maybe. Cancer. He went real fast."

"Is she happy? Greta, I mean."

George pinched the cigarette into a paper clip, then tried to suck smoke out of it. "Who knows? She's got a boyfriend, a dental student and a prick, in my opinion, but there's no accountin' for taste, right? Greta's parents—or step-parents, whatever you wanna call 'em—want her to be a dentist too."

"How do you know?" Bernie asked.

"I hear the kids talkin' during rehearsals, and sometimes I join 'em for coffee at one of them expresso places that've popped up all over the place, now that I'm off the sauce. You know how actors are, they talk at the top of their lungs, don't care what they say or who's listenin'."

"Do you keep in touch with Greta's mother too?" Bernie asked.

"You kiddin'?" He snorted contemptuously, tossed the

dead roach into his ashtray in disgust. "Not since Bob died. Like I said, Linda's remarried and lives in the 'burbs somewhere. She never felt real comfortable around me, knowin' I know what I know. But I never told nobody the story and I never will," he added righteously.

He chuckled. "I thought of calling her and warning her that you're back, but she'd probably have a fit and beg me not to tell you anything. Might even offer me some money to keep my mouth shut—tell you Greta's in Alaska or Timbuktu."

Bernie's brow furrowed. "You don't think she'd want me to see my—see Greta?"

"I don't think Greta knows the story," he said. "Leastways, they hadn't told her by the time Bob punched out, and I don't suppose Linda's had any reason to spring it on her since."

Steadman George's words sank into Bernie like a big rock. In spite of herself, she felt diminished by the knowledge that she might not exist even as a question mark for her daughter, as somebody her daughter thought about sometimes, if she didn't have an actual burning desire to meet her.

"So now what?" George asked, touched in spite of himself by the confusion on her face. "You gonna tell her?"

Bernie's eyes roamed all around the cabin, as if searching for an answer. "I don't know," she said. "If you were me, what would you do?" In her experience, it was safest to act as though you looked up to men like Steadman George, if they had power over you.

"Me? If I was you, I wouldn't give a damn." He grinned. "But I'd like to see the look on Greta's face when you tell her who you are!"

"If I tell her," she said, as if speaking to herself. "I'm going to have to decide by Sunday."

"Why's that?" he asked, curious, as he dug a pack of cigarettes out of his pocket and lit one.

"I can't afford to stay any longer than that," she said. She told him about the Riverton Art Fair and how she earned her living.

She wanted to leave now, to be alone and think things

over, but she thought she'd better stay a little longer, for politeness's sake.

"What about the father?" George asked, after a few minutes. "I seem to recall he don't even know there is a Greta."

"Yes," Bernie said uneasily.

"Well, if you tell Greta you're her mom, she's gonna wanna know who her daddy is too, right?"

Bernie hadn't thought of that. "I suppose so," she said.

"Would you tell her, if she asked?"

"I'd have to."

"You know his name?"

"Yes!" she flared, turning crimson.

He laughed suddenly. "I remember now!" he said. "You took his money for an abortion and then turned around and sold the baby. Am I right?"

"I was *going* to get an abortion," she said, glaring at him. "That's why I told Sue Ann I was pregnant—I wanted her to help me find a good doctor. But then she asked me to talk to you and you talked me into selling my baby instead—and I couldn't go back to Ted and tell him I wasn't going to get an abortion."

"Why not?" George asked, storing "Ted" for future consideration.

"I didn't want him to know I was going to have the baby."

"Why?" he asked again.

She shook her head, bewildered. She didn't know why—it was too long ago. Had she been afraid of how he'd react, of what he might do? Or was it that she didn't want to share the knowledge of the child, of the child's existence, with him? Or was it just that she didn't want to have to give him back his money? Four hundred dollars had seemed like a fortune to her then, along with the thousand dollars Steadman George had given her.

"I don't know," she repeated.

Steadman George rocked back and forth for a minute in his chair, a smile making his little teeth glint through his beard as he watched her. After a minute, he said, "Sue Ann mentioned you was babysitting for a chaplain at the U back then." He watched her turn pale, her eyes widen and slide quickly away from him. "Did you talk to him about your troubles?"

She couldn't say anything, just shook her head.

He laughed. "That's what they're for, ain't it? To tell your troubles to."

"I didn't," she managed to say.

He nodded, pleased about something. "Well, I guess I'm more of a father to Greta than your 'Ted' is, ain't I? Huh, if it wasn't for me, there wouldn't be any Greta."

"I know that," she said, "and I'm grateful to you, Mr. George." And she was, even though she might have preferred a nicer agent for whatever good power had decided to spare her daughter's life.

"Call me Steadman," he told her. "All my friends do."

She thanked him for his help and got up to go, asked him what she owed him.

He stayed where he was, rocking gently in his chair, squinting up at her through smoke. Then he laughed. "You don't owe me nothin', Bernie," he said. "Old time's sake. And besides, the answer was right here on the Showboat all the time, wasn't it? Think you can find your way ashore by yourself or do I have to get up?"

She said she could find her way.

WEDNESDAY

Five

It took George about a minute the next morning to find out who Greta Markham's biological father was. He'd spent most of his adult life playing piano around the University and knew a lot of people who worked there. One of them was a woman he'd been involved with for a time who worked in the reference room of the library, Sally Pyne. They'd stayed on friendly terms after they'd split up, a tribute more to Sally's forgiving nature than to George's charms. She was a bit too long in the tooth now for George's taste, but there'd been a time when she'd known more than the Dewey Decimal System—at least when she let her hair down and took off her glasses.

He called her and asked her to find out the last name of a chaplain back in the seventies who'd answered to the name of Ted. Without any hesitation, she said, "What're you trying to pull now, Steady?"

"What do you mean?" he asked, surprised.

"I mean everybody knows there was one chaplain here back then named Ted: Ted Mason, better known today as 'Pastor Ted.' "

It took George a moment. "You mean the guy on cable who's always running for mayor?"

"Governor. Are you trying to tell me you didn't know?" she asked suspiciously.

Jesus! Jackpot! George thought fast. "Damn, I just lost ten bucks," he said. "I bet a guy that 'Pastor Ted' wasn't at the U twenty years ago."

"Well, you got suckered, Steadman."

"I don't read the papers much," George said. "All I

know about him is that he's one of those right-wingers who's against homosexuals and abortion and women giving sermons. 'Mr. Family Values,' right?''

"You got it. He wrote a book on morality for co-eds when he was here too—a best-seller. The University newspaper had a big interview with him a while ago. The way they described it, it's about how boys are shameless seducers of innocent girls and so girls have to keep them at a distance until they marry them—after which they're supposed to submit to them as Sara submitted to Abraham.'' She laughed. "Sounds like something you might've written, Steady, if you'd thought of it.''

George laughed too, and not just at Sally's attempt at humor.

"I suppose Pastor Ted was married at the time he wrote the book, huh?''

"Yep. He claims he wrote the book while babysitting one kid for his wife, who was pregnant with another and going to school.''

"Amazin'!'' George exclaimed, trying not to laugh. "Listen, Sally, thanks. I guess I should say, thanks for nothing, since you cost me ten bucks.''

"Don't blame me, Steady,'' she retorted. "Blame your ignorance of current events.''

George roused himself and left the Showboat. It was only nine-thirty, as early as he'd been out and about in years. He walked up from the river to the campus, crossed it to the library, and with the help of a librarian got the books Mason had written. The librarian also showed him how to do a computer search for articles on the man.

He skimmed the books. The first, the one Sally had told him about, was *Morality and U,* a big soft-cover book printed on glossy paper that featured on the cover a wholesome-looking young woman standing in front of a generic university building. She was dressed in what the publisher must have thought was a typical co-ed outfit twenty years ago—oxfords, a pleated skirt, and a sweatshirt with a big U on the front—and she was carrying textbooks and smiling a smile that showed perfect white teeth. Standing slightly behind her, a young man was ogling her with cynical bedroom eyes, his hands stuffed deep in the pockets of his jeans. George noted with satisfaction that the book had been published the year after Bernie had sold her baby.

In addition to many articles, Mason had written two more books, both indicating his growing interest in issues beyond the campus: *Main Street/Mainstream: Morality versus the Media* and *Home Restoration: A Do-It-Yourself Guide for the Family,* which had come out last year and was described as Mason's prescription for the ailing American family.

Next George skimmed some of the articles that had been written about Mason. After graduating from a small midwestern Bible college, he'd accepted a position as chaplain at the U and held that job for five years, at which time he'd been called to a church of his own that he'd quickly built into one of the largest in the city. About ten years ago, he'd started to involve himself in politics and soon made a name for himself as an articulate and passionate spokesman for the religious right. A year ago, he'd started his own program on cable television—*Pastor Ted's Fireside Hour*—which was a mix of preaching, political commentary, and wholesome Christian music.

Mason was now in his second term on the city's school board, where he'd distinguished himself by fighting against sex education in the schools and in favor of school prayer. He'd narrowly lost a bid to be the Republican candidate for governor in the last primary and was considered a sure bet to run for governor again.

Steadman George left the library and sat in the early afternoon sun on the steps in front of the library, smoking and thinking and paying no attention to the heat, the humidity, or the students giving him dirty looks as they went around him.

The question was, how was he going to make money out of the situation? He was as sure as the summer days were long that Bernie was going to tell Greta Markham who she was and who her father was too. And he'd seen and heard enough of Greta and her friends to know they didn't share Pastor Ted's values. He could easily imagine Greta pointing to Mason and saying, in her most passionate and melodramatic voice: "That man is my father!"

At which moment, Pastor Ted's preaching and politicking days would be over. But what Bernie and Greta did or didn't do wasn't really important. What was important was what he, Steadman George, could convince Mason they would do.

The clock in the bell tower on the Old Campus across the river struck the half hour: twelve-thirty.

George jumped up, dropped his cigarette butt on the library steps, and left it smoldering there to annoy the students as he strode purposefully back to the Showboat. He looked up the Reverend Mason in the phone book and found only a listing for the church. He dialed the number and when a woman answered he told her he'd like to speak with Pastor Ted.

"May I ask the purpose of your call?" she asked.

"Personal," he said.

"Pastor Ted's a busy man," she told him, still pleasant. "I'm his secretary. Perhaps it's something I could help you with."

"Doubt it. It's about a babysitter he had back in the seventies, when he was a chaplain at the U. Bernie, her name was. I'm tryin' to find her and I thought maybe she'd kept in touch with him. They was on pretty good terms, I guess you could say, and I think he'll want to help me with this matter."

"That's a long time to remember a babysitter, isn't it?" she said with a laugh. "She must've been a very good one."

"Yeah, she was," George agreed. "Pastor Ted'll remember her for sure. Put him on."

There was a brief pause. Then: "Your name, please?"

"George. Just George."

A very long minute later, a man's voice said, "This is Pastor Ted."

"I'm not gonna beat around the bush," George began, "so first tell me one thing: is this line secure?" He'd got that from watching television.

"What do you mean?"

"I mean, can anybody listen in?"

"No. No, of course not. What do you want?"

"You probably remember a kid named Bernie," George said. "Twenty-some years ago you knocked her up and then you paid her to get an abortion."

He waited for Mason to say something. When he didn't, he continued: "Well, guess what, Pastor Ted? Bernie didn't get the abortion, she had the baby. I bet that's a load off your mind, ain't it, considering how you feel about abortion now."

"I don't have the faintest idea of what you're talking about," Mason said.

"Maybe not, but just in case you wanna know how the story ends, the upshot is that Bernie sold the kid to some friends of mine and now you and I are the only people in the world—besides Bernie, of course—who know you're the daddy. How valuable is it to you for me to keep the secret in the family?"

"I don't know what you're talking about," Mason said again, "but I do know something about the laws pertaining to extortion."

"So hang up, then." George waited, holding his breath.

"I'm not going to hang up," Mason said. "I'm curious to hear just how low my enemies can stoop to try to destroy me."

"*Try* to destroy you?" George said with a laugh. "And with Bernie and her daughter—*your* daughter—out there, you don't need enemies. You got family, as in 'family values.'

"I know Bernie," he went on, his voice suddenly harsh, "and she don't look nothin' like the gal on the cover of that book of yours, *Morality and U*. When the world finds out what you was doin' when you was writin' it, Pastor Ted, you're dead, as in Rest in Peace."

"You really believe what you're saying, George, don't you?" Mason said, struggling to sound incredulous.

"We both do," George said crisply.

There was a long pause. George waited it out, enjoying himself now. He had nothing to lose and, possibly, a lot to gain.

"Look, George," Mason said finally, a wheedling tone creeping into his voice, "I think we'd better talk. In person, I mean. We can't discuss things of this nature over the phone."

"No dice, Ted—I like bein' anonymous. But I know what you're thinkin', you're thinkin' maybe I'm recording this conversation, aren't ya? Why would I bother? Bernie and her kid are a lot more real than any tape I could make.''

There was silence while Mason thought that over. "What do you want?" he asked, now almost whispering.

"I could say I want for you to stand up in front of the world and confess what you done," George said.

"I may just do that," Mason said bravely. "If I have to," he added, weakening the impression somewhat. "It depends on what you want."

"Money," George said. "What do you think I want? Your prayers?"

"I won't pay you anything until you give me some assurance that it would do me some good," Mason said. "How do I know that even if you keep silent, this woman and her daughter will?"

George was ready for this question. "On account of Bernie don't know where her daughter is, for one thing," he replied, "and on account of her kid—your kid—don't know who you are for another. That's why."

"What do you mean, Bernie doesn't know where her daughter is?"

"She sold the baby right after she was born and then left town. Now she's back and she comes to me and asks me to help her find the kid. Without me, she can't do it."

"I see. And you know where the child is."

"Yeah—and she ain't exactly a child anymore, either. Just to give you an idea, she drives a car with a bumper sticker on it that says, 'Keep your laws off my body.' ''

"How do I get hold of this—of Bernie?" Mason asked.

"You don't. And if you pay me ten thousand dollars in cash, she won't have no reason to get hold of you either."

"Why not?"

"Because," George explained patiently, "without the kid she don't have no proof you knocked her up, does she? And without me, she can't find the kid. You're payin' me not to tell Bernie where to find her kid."

Mason had two more questions. One was the age-old blackmail question: what assurance would he have that one payment would be all this man would ask for? The other, more frightening question was, once he'd paid George ten thousand dollars, how could he be sure George wouldn't turn around and tell Bernie where her daughter was anyway? But these weren't questions he intended to ask, since he knew George could give him no assurances he could believe about either one.

"Ten thousand dollars is a lot of money," he said. "It'll take me a while to get it. As a public figure, I'm closely watched. It would look very suspicious if it was discovered that I'd abruptly drawn that much money out of my bank account."

"Let's say the day after tomorrow, okay?" George said, speaking in the tones of a loan shark with whom he'd once had frightening dealings. "Friday. Bernie's impatient to see her kid again and she's pesterin' me something awful. I don't want to torment her any more'n I have to. But if I don't get what I want from you, Ted, she gets what she wants from me."

"But what could you tell her that would keep her from looking for the child through some other agency?" Mason asked.

"I'll tell her I talked to her kid but she don't wanna see her mom. Bernie's poor. She told me she can only afford to stay in town through Sunday. If she don't find her kid by then, she'll give up and go back where she came from."

"All right," Mason said. "I'll work something out. Where shall I send the money?"

George hadn't thought that far ahead. "I'll get back to you tomorrow with the details," he said. "Nice talkin' to you, Pastor Ted," he added. "Almost makes me feel like I've been to church."

He hung up feeling he was on top of the situation. The only thing that wasn't perfect was that he'd told Bernie where to find her daughter before getting the money from Mason. That was too bad, but how could he have known there'd be money in it to keep quiet until he'd found out who the father was? Besides, what difference did it make? He would have told Bernie where to find Greta anyway, sooner or later.

He laughed when he remembered Mason asking how he could get hold of Bernie. If Mason could get to her, he might be able to buy her silence, because if she denied that

Mason was the father, George wouldn't be able to say a thing.

The laugh froze on his face as another thought occurred to him: if Bernie was dead, Mason would be home free. Nobody would believe George if he claimed Greta was Mason's daughter.

It was a good thing he hadn't told Mason where he could find Bernie, he thought. How far would a man—even a man of the cloth—go to preserve his reputation, his career, maybe even his family?

George laughed again. He'd met a few people in his time who were capable of murder and had probably committed a few, but Pastor Ted Mason wasn't anything like those characters! Amateurs only commit murder in the old black-and-white movies he watched sometimes on television.

He was glad Mason didn't know where to find him, though. You can never be too careful when you live alone on an old showboat and hold a man's future in the palm of your hand.

Six

Mason sat at his desk for a few minutes after George hung up, white-faced, staring at the phone. Then he shook himself, got up quickly, and went out to the secretary's office and asked her for the number of the last call. "He forgot to give it to me," he explained.

"It's a University extension, Pastor Ted," she said as she copied it for him off her Caller ID display. "That Bernie must've been some babysitter," she added.

He forced himself to return her smile. "Yes, she was," he said.

Back in his office, he sat with the number in front of him on his desk and stared at it as if it were a death warrant—his death warrant. Then he shook off the spell and reached for his phone. He hesitated a moment, glanced up at the copy of *The Last Supper* that hung on the wall opposite his desk, a gift from one of his congregation, a painter, and quickly away, then dialed his brother Stan, praying he was home. He was.

"I need to talk to you," he told him. "Can I come over?"

"Sure. What about?" Stan replied, surprised. It had been a long time since his brother had sought him out.

"I'll tell you when I get there," Mason said, and hung up.

He told Marcie to cancel his appointments for the rest of the day—he wasn't feeling well, he said, and was going home—and drove over to his brother's apartment, an efficiency in a lower-middle-class neighborhood on the north side of town.

Seven years ago Stan had retired—probably involuntarily, but Ted had never looked into the matter—after serving twenty years in the Army as an enlisted man. Before that, as a teenager, he'd been in and out of trouble with the law, until a judge gave him the choice of enlisting in the military or going to jail. He'd never really found a foothold in civilian life since leaving the Army. He'd tried a variety of jobs, but failed at them all, or quit out of boredom or disgust, and now he was living on his Army pension.

"C'mon in," he said, holding the door open for his brother. "You look like you could use a beer." He was tall and thin, with a long, lined, narrow face, thick gray hair, and a thin mouth. He looked older than his forty-six years.

"Thanks, no," Ted said. He went over and sat down on a shabby couch, clasped his hands together on his knees.

Stan got himself a beer, then came back and spun a chair around and straddled it, waiting for Ted to explain what he wanted. He hadn't seen his brother so obviously upset since they were kids and he'd gotten himself in some kind of jam and turned to Stan to get him out of it.

"I—" Ted began, then stopped, tried again. "I got a phone call a little while ago," he said. "A blackmailer."

"Blackmail!"

Ted hesitated, wondering if he was doing the right thing in telling Stan about it. Then, before he could change his mind, he said quickly, "Back in the seventies, I got a girl pregnant."

Stan thought, You! but said nothing, and his face showed none of the strange sense of joy he was feeling. He was a good poker player.

"She was babysitting for us while Patricia was pregnant with Matt," Ted went on, hurrying to get the worst over with. "She told me she was going to get an abortion, but she didn't, she sold the baby instead. Now she's back and wants to find it."

He told Stan everything George had said to him on the phone, ending with the demand for ten thousand dollars. When he finally ran out of words, he looked up to see his brother's reaction.

Stan's face remained expressionless. "How old was the girl?" he asked.

"Sixteen. Seventeen. I don't know."

Stan shook his head in disbelief.

"I was vulnerable!" Ted cried. "Patricia wouldn't let me touch her those last two, three months of her pregnancy. I don't blame her," he added quickly.

"That's nice," Stan said softly. "A less Christian man might easily blame his pregnant wife for what happened."

Ted winced. "Please, Stan—you've got to help me! My entire career, all I've worked for! Besides, Bernie was no angel! She might've been just a kid, but she'd been living with a man! She'd found him in bed with another girl and was upset about it. I tried to comfort her, but she—she seduced me—probably to get back at him."

"I guess she didn't read that book of yours on what can happen to a girl on a university campus," Stan said. "Except you hadn't written it yet, had you? But it wouldn't have helped her anyway, would it, since I don't suppose you warned girls against the college chaplain."

Stan was surprised at the mixture of contempt for his brother and pleasure at his dilemma that he was feeling— Ted had always been the perfect son, the son their parents boasted about.

"How many more Bernies are there out there, big brother?" he continued. "How many more little bombs just waiting for the right moment to go off?"

"None, Stan," Ted said. "None, I swear it! When Bernie disappeared and didn't come back, I thought she'd been sent by God as a warning to me: never again! And I never did anything like that again—ever."

To get away from his brother's eyes, he got up and began pacing the small, untidy apartment.

"I even think about the abortion I paid for sometimes," he went on quietly, "and feel a great sense of guilt."

"At least you don't have *that* on your conscience anymore," Stan remarked dryly.

"I've paid an enormous price in spiritual agony," Ted said, "and I've grown from the experience. I truly believe it made me a better pastor, a better husband and father—a better man! What am I going to do now, Stan?"

"You know your congregation better than I do," Stan said, "and the voters. Maybe if you came clean?"

Ted slumped back onto the couch. "They'd crucify me."

Stan nodded, barely suppressing a smile.

"So what should I do? Pay the man? He's given me until Friday to get the money."

"It's possible the kid doesn't really exist," Stan said, "that this woman—Bernie—got the abortion after all. It's even possible that she and this George character are in it together, trying to scare money out of you."

Mason hadn't thought of that. "You think I should call his bluff?"

"You don't call a bluff until you know something about the man who's making it," Stan answered. "It's too bad you don't know who he is."

Mason dug out the scrap of paper on which he'd copied down the telephone number, hesitated a moment, then handed it to his brother as though it were hot and could burn his fingers. He explained how he'd got it and where the call had come from.

"The University, huh," Stan said. "That's interesting." He folded it carefully and put it in his shirt pocket. "If he calls again, stall him. Tell him you're having trouble raising that much money so fast. I'll try to find out something about him, maybe talk to him and see if I think money'll keep him quiet—and if the woman really couldn't find her kid without him, assuming it even exists. If I think he's unreliable—well, then you can consider repentance and confession."

"Don't do anything to make the situation worse, Stan," Mason said.

Stan smiled at his brother. "How could I?"

Seven

Linda Markham shielded her eyes from the early afternoon sunlight as she peered from the woman standing on her front stoop to the big yellow bus parked in the brick driveway behind her: Bernie's Bead Bus. The woman was a stranger to her, but there was something familiar about her too.

Bernie told her her name. That meant nothing to her, so Bernie added awkwardly, "I'm your daughter's mother. I mean—" She turned crimson, because that wasn't how she'd meant to put it.

Linda Markham's tanned face went as white as her tennis costume and she gripped the doorframe so tightly that her knuckles turned white too. "Oh, God!" she blurted out. "What do you want?"

When she saw how stricken the woman was, Bernie almost regretted coming. She took a step back, then realized it was too late. "I'm sorry," she said. "I'm not here to do you any harm."

"Then . . . ?" Mrs. Markham paused, her eyes unconsciously running over Bernie from her old work boots to her faded but clean and newly pressed khaki pants, her flowered shirt, and the heavy necklace and earrings.

Her switch into hostess mode was quick and fluid. She smiled and invited Bernie in.

"Is Greta—your daughter, I mean—here?" Bernie asked, still outside. "I wanted to talk to you alone, before—"

Mrs. Markham shook her head. "No—it's all right. Greta doesn't live at home anymore—she has a little apartment over by the U."

The home's air-conditioning was in sharp contrast to the hot and humid day outside, but it was cold to Bernie in other ways too. The living room ceiling was high and sloped, crisscrossed with beams that looked unnecessary and didn't even look like real wood to her. The decor was all muted colors that balanced one another perfectly—somewhat boring, in her opinion.

Her eyes fell on a glass-topped coffee table supported at only one side by a squat pillar that looked like marble. She knew that, if she owned such a thing, she'd gash a leg on one of the sharp corners every time she passed it. The thick white wall-to-wall carpeting that covered the floor came right up to a large fireplace. Pure white birch logs were stacked in the fireplace, as if ready for next fall and winter.

"The carpet must be hard to keep clean," she blurted, thinking of how messy fires can be.

"Oh, it's not a real fireplace," Mrs. Markham said with a bright little laugh. "Here, let me show you."

She picked up something that looked like a television remote control and pointed it at the fireplace. The logs burst silently into flame. She looked expectantly at Bernie.

Bernie didn't know what to say, just smiled because she didn't want to disappoint Mrs. Markham entirely. Mrs. Markham pointed the device again and the fire—if that's what it was—went out, leaving the logs as white as they'd been before. Bernie wondered if what she'd just witnessed had been real or television or some other kind of thing entirely.

"Let's sit on the porch, shall we?" Mrs. Markham said, and led the way across the living room to a glassed-in porch that ran the length of the back of the house. It wasn't what Bernie thought of when she thought of "porch." Beyond it Bernie could see a large, beautifully manicured lawn and a flagstone patio with a little white table surrounded by wrought-iron chairs.

"Could we sit out there?" she asked. Where she spent her summers, she could go a long time before seeing as much grass as there was in the Markhams' backyard.

Mrs. Markham thought it was too hot and humid outside didn't say so. She agreed and asked Bernie if she would like iced tea or lemonade. Bernie chose lemonade and Mrs. Markham hurried to get it, letting Bernie out into the backyard first.

A little waterfall trickled down from an arrangement of stones against a fence, then meandered through neatly arranged flower beds. Bernie knew the waterfall was manmade but wasn't sure about the rabbit nibbling the grass around it. It could have been activated by some kind of remote control device too, like the fire.

"Well," Mrs. Markham said breathlessly when they were seated with their glasses in front of them, "this is quite a surprise!" She laughed nervously. "In fact, it's the shock of my life, next after learning Bob had cancer and only a few months to live, of course."

Bernie was amazed at how little Linda Markham had changed since she'd last seen her. She had to be in her fifties now, but she looked much younger. Her hair was ash blond, her arms firm and her hands were still as lovely as Bernie remembered them. Twenty years ago, she recalled, Linda Markham had earned money as a hand model. She probably still could, if she had to.

"I was sorry to hear about your husband," Bernie said. "I saw a lot of him when I was seeing the doctor and in the . . ." She paused, wondering if it would be bad manners to remind Mrs. Markham of how she'd given actual birth to Greta. "Maternity ward," she finished. Because she *had* been there and Mrs. Markham hadn't.

"It was just like he was the baby's father and I––I was his wife," she continued. "He fussed over me a little, even brought me flowers." Her laugh was strained. "Of course, he was only pretending, but I think he really was kind."

"Oh, yes," Mrs. Markham replied, "Bob was very kind. He'd give anybody who asked the shirt off his back. If it was a woman in need, he'd convince me to give her mine." Her eyes stayed on Bernie, curious, wary, waiting.

"I just got to thinking about—about Greta," Bernie said. "You hear all kinds of stories, you know, about kids wh are messed up by their adoptive parents—even murde sometimes. Or else they want to find their birth parer see what their family looks like—their biological fai mean, of course—or to get their medical histories. So I thought I'd come back, just to . . ." She stopped, didn't know how to go on.

"That's really commendable, Bernie," Mrs. Markham assured her warmly. "I hope I can convince you that Greta's had a wonderful life with me—with us. The years with Bob were lean at times, of course, and unsettled too, but we survived. We were a team, I guess you'd say, Greta and I." She gave a brave laugh.

"She's in very good health too," she went on. She looked concerned. "Is there something in your medical history we should know?"

Bernie didn't think so, she said, although she hadn't had a physical in years. "I'm hardly ever sick," she added.

"There, you see!" Mrs. Markham said. "And, of course, Greta doesn't know she's not mine by blood, so she can't be wondering about your family. And her aunts and uncles and cousins have always accepted her without question. Nobody suspects a thing—least of all Greta."

"How come you never told her the truth?" Bernie asked.

"I suppose it was a mistake not to," Mrs. Markham said with a sigh. "But we didn't know how. We kept it secret from everybody at first, of course, because the authorities would have taken her away from us if they'd found out. Later they wouldn't have taken her from us, we knew that. But . . ." She shrugged, gave Bernie a helpless look.

"How'd you fool people into thinking you were pregnant?"

"Oh, that was easy!" Her face lit up at the memory. "Both Bob's and my families lived in the East, so they didn't see much of us. And we were doing a lot of regional theater that year, so none of our close friends here saw much of us either."

She laughed. "We came back into town a couple of times and Bob would dress me up to look pregnant—he was good at costume design too—and I played the role to ᵗe hilt. I wasn't a very good actress, but I have to say I ᵈ fine with that role."

ʳer face grew solemn. "I enjoyed it. I was never able ⁿerience the real thing—what you experienced, Ber-
She laughed again, softly this time. "People com-

mented later on how lovely I'd looked pregnant and after a while I began to think I really had been.'' She looked down at her hands. ''After putting on such a good show, we couldn't bring ourselves to tell anybody that's all it was.''

She looked at Bernie with her large eyes, reached across the table, and took her hands.

''Oh, Bernie,'' she exclaimed, ''I can't tell you how grateful I am that you were willing to give up the baby— *your* baby! I'm sorry if you regret it now, but I just want you to know how happy you made me, and Bob too.''

There were tears in her eyes and Bernie knew she was telling the truth, even though what she was doing was also making a shameless appeal. Unconsciously, she looked down at Mrs. Markham's hands, noticed that they weren't big enough to cover her own.

Bernie freed one of her hands to take a long swallow of lemonade, because suddenly her throat was very dry. ''She seems to be taking after Bob,'' she said. ''After her father, I mean,'' she added. ''I saw the play last night. She has a lot of talent, doesn't she?''

Mrs. Markham sat back in her chair and took a deep breath. ''I suppose so,'' she said. ''To be honest, Loren and I—Loren is my husband—hope this acting thing is just a phase, a kind of sentimental gesture to her father—to Bob—that she'll wake up and realize is not very sensible.''

She lowered her voice and, speaking as one mother to another, went on: ''Greta's very, very bright, Bernie, and we hope she'll go into dentistry. It would make Loren so happy. He has a wonderful practice, you know, and would dearly love to have her as his partner.''

''But is she interested in dentistry?'' Bernie asked.

Mrs. Markham waved the question away with a pretty hand and an annoyed look on her face. ''She has a talent for it, Loren says. She worked for him summers, all through high school, with filing and such. She's got a double ma jor—biology and theater—so she's well positioned to st right in in dental school.''

''Or theater,'' Bernie said.

''I certainly hope not,'' Mrs. Markham said. ' everything I went through with Bob, I'd be a damn mother if I wished that for my daughter! You have no idea of the hardships and uncertainties and heartbreak of an actor's life.''

Bernie thought of the hardships and uncertainties of her own life, but didn't say anything about that. Instead, she asked Mrs. Markham if her husband knew Greta's real history.

"No!" Mrs. Markham said, shaking her head vigorously. "And he'd be very upset if he found out I'd kept a secret that big from him all these years! Loren's a very moral man, Bernie. It would be a blow against our marriage from which it might never recover. More lemonade?"

Absently, Bernie held out her glass. She didn't see anything wrong in Greta wanting to be an actress. Of course it would be risky, and Bernie knew enough to know that the chance of success was not very great even if Greta was good. But some people succeeded, didn't they? There wouldn't be any movie and television stars otherwise! You just had to be willing to take risks, as Bernie herself had when she'd quit her secretarial job and used the money she'd saved to buy the bus and go on the road. The first years had been lean—she didn't have the trailer then, she'd lived in the bus—but she was doing just fine now, wasn't she?

There was something about her daughter becoming a dentist that rubbed her the wrong way. She had nothing against dentists—she was even planning to see one herself one of these days about some loose fillings and a cavity or two—but she found it hard to visualize her daughter as one and living in a house like this, where you couldn't be sure what was real and what wasn't. She glanced over at the waterfall, saw that the rabbit was gone, and wondered if a timer had turned it off.

It was so hard to know what to do. Again she thought of her friend Swallow. It would be nice to talk it over with er, hear what she had to say. At least she'd have some as for her to consider. Swallow was full of ideas.

'Does Greta have friends?'' she asked.

riends? Of course she does!'' Mrs. Markham ex-
d. "She's always been popular. In fact, she was the
he musical the high school put on her senior year.

And she's very serious about a boy she's known forever—well, since I married Loren, anyway. Rick is Loren's partner's son. The plan is that Rick'll take over his father's share in the practice someday. Wouldn't it be wonderful if Greta took over Loren's share? They could merge the two practices!''

Bernie smiled politely, wishing she could work up enthusiasm for this plan. Despair settled over her suddenly, like a wet blanket fallen from the sky: what Greta did or didn't do was none of her business.

Anxiety flooded back into Mrs. Markham's voice at Bernie's silence. "What are you going to do, Bernie?"

"I don't know," she said, getting up slowly.

Mrs. Markham got up too. "You gave up your baby because you couldn't care for her," she said, her voice urgent. "You should be happy about how well she's turned out, and you mustn't do anything to disturb it, Bernie! Who knows what it might do to her—to us—if she finds out the truth."

"I know," Bernie said. "But shouldn't she—I mean, doesn't she have the right to know the truth about her life?"

"She *does* know the truth—*this* is the truth!" Mrs. Markham cried, gesturing around her. "*I'm* her mother, Bernie!" she went on. "*I* stayed with Bob all those years after I got sick and tired of the life we were leading. You can't imagine what it was like, living hand to mouth while waiting for him to get parts, waiting to hear if the play would succeed or fold, living and dying on the reviews of people we knew were fools—and waiting for him to come home, only to leave again. I stayed with him because he loved Greta so much, I worked hard to make our home life as normal as possible for her. And now I've got all this—and Greta's got all this too. Oh, Bernie—we've earned it!"

Bernie said: "It wouldn't be taking anything away from her, or you, Mrs. Markham, if she knew about me. Would it?"

Mrs. Markham started to say something, her eyes running over Bernie again, and then she started to cry. "I don't know, I don't know! Oh, why . . . ?" She left the question unfinished.

She followed Bernie back into the soft light and

the house. Passing through the living room, Bernie banged her leg on the glass coffee table.

She turned and gave Mrs. Markham an anguished look. She said, "I don't know what I'm going to do. Talk to a friend about it, I guess, to hear what she has to say. She's a—"

She stopped, realizing that telling Mrs. Markham what Swallow was wouldn't be reassuring to her. "I'll let you know by Sunday," she continued, "or Monday morning at the latest. The Riverton Art Fair ends Sunday night."

"The Riverton . . . ?"

Bernie explained. She smiled encouragingly into the distraught woman's face and went on, hoping to make it better: "Why don't you think about it yourself? Who knows, maybe Greta would like knowing about me. Maybe she'd admire you for what you did to get yourself a daughter."

Mrs. Markham shook her head, the tears streaming down her cheeks. "But what if she didn't, Bernie? Back when Bob and I were trying to adopt, I read a lot about adopted kids. Sometimes they're hurt when they discover they were their parents' second choice, adopted only after they'd tried and failed to have children of their own."

Bernie's mouth fell open. She'd never thought of it that way before. "But you never treated Greta like she was your second choice, did you?" she asked.

"Of course not! We loved her as though she were our own daughter—and she was, she is! I told you, Bernie, after a while I forgot she wasn't my own child!" She started to cry uncontrollably now.

Bernie patted her awkwardly on the shoulder for a moment longer, then turned and left the house, almost fled from it, feeling the blood trickling down her leg and into her shoe. She started up the bus and shifted into low, grinding the gears, and drove around the curved driveway back onto the street lined with lovely, expensive homes.

Eight

As she drove back to the trailer park, Bernie's head was full of conflicting emotions and thoughts. She was sorry she'd upset Linda Markham, but angry too when it also occurred to her that Mrs. Markham hadn't asked anything about *her* life at all! Apparently the old bus and Bernie's appearance had told her everything she needed to know. That wasn't very nice, was it?

Then she wondered if maybe she wasn't just starting to build a hate-case against Mrs. Markham so she could justify to herself telling Greta who she was. That wouldn't be a good reason for doing it. She had to resist thoughts like that, had to think about it calmly and decide what to do solely on the basis of whether or not it would hurt Greta.

She decided she wanted to see the play again, now that she knew who her daughter was. She thought of redoing the necklace she'd made for her, to better match the elaborate Victorian dress Greta wore in the play, but then she remembered that the dress was only a costume and she had no idea what Greta was really like. Her feelings about her daughter that had gone into the making of the necklace were more reliable, she felt. It was a fairly heavy necklace, but Greta was a tall woman like herself. She might very well look good in a necklace like that, depending, of course, on what she wore it with.

Bernie arrived back at the University at seven-thirty, nosed her bus down to the river, and parked it again in the field next to the parking lot, among other buses. She we on board the Showboat and bought a ticket and, since seats were not reserved and she was early, she found a seat in the middle of the first row.

Once the curtain rose and the performance began, she had eyes only for her daughter. Now that she knew who she was, she could see more clearly the features they had in common: the shape of their heads and noses, the large wide-set eyes and the wide mouths. It didn't add up to beauty in Bernie's case, she thought, but it did in Greta's. When Greta danced and acted in the skits between acts, Bernie was awed by how talented she was; she laughed and cried simultaneously, wiping her eyes and blowing her nose more than once, unconscious of the amused glances of the people around her.

Again she felt a tremendous desire to get to know her daughter; not to be her mother, exactly—she knew she could never be that—but to be acknowledged as having given birth to her. Why should Linda Markham, who had so much, get the credit for everything, even the one thing she hadn't done?

When the performance was over, she stood in line with other members of the audience who wanted to tell the actors how much they'd enjoyed the play. As Bernie slowly approached Greta, her heart was thumping so loudly she could hear it, and her hands were sweaty. Close up, Greta was even more beautiful than she'd been on stage, with a dazzlingly warm smile that Bernie was sure couldn't be faked. As her turn came, she was afraid she was going to faint.

Greta looked at her, an expectant smile on her face, a smile so dazzling to Bernie that it almost blinded her. She held out her hand and, after a moment's hesitation, Greta took it. Suddenly, as clearly as if it had been just a moment ago, Bernie remembered the last time she'd held her daughter's hand, when it had been a tiny thing with fingers that played over her breasts like a cool breeze.

Bernie's eyes filled with tears, her face starting to crumble, and she knew that, if she stayed a moment longer, she'd make a dreadful mistake. She saw how Greta's smile had begun to freeze, so she did what she'd come there to what she'd planned to do all afternoon. She pulled the ace out of her jacket pocket and, before Greta could flinch away, draped it—almost flung it—clumsily over her head.

"I made this for you," she managed to blurt out, her voice choked. She wanted to add, "I hope you like it," but couldn't. Instead, she turned abruptly and walked quickly away.

Greta stood there a moment stunned, then recovered from her surprise enough to start after the fleeing woman.

"Wait," she called, "I can't accept this!" But when Bernie turned, the look on her face was so full of dismay that Greta stopped in the act of pulling the necklace off and let it fall back over her head. She forced a smile. "Thank you," she said. "It's beautiful."

When she returned to the receiving line, the actors on either side of her were laughing.

"Who was that, Greta," one of them teased, "your mom?"

She shrugged, embarrassed, and laughed when the next well-wisher apologized for not bringing a gift too.

Steadman George, surrounded by his fans as he always was after the play, hadn't noticed the little scene between Bernie and Greta, but he saw Bernie striding quickly across the lawn toward her bus. She looked as though she were fleeing from something. With a stab of fear, he wondered if she'd changed her mind about talking to Greta right away.

"Hey, Bernie!" he called after her, but by then she was too far away to hear. He glanced down the line of actors to see what Greta was doing. She was chatting with a couple of members of the audience as if nothing out of the ordinary had taken place.

Stan Mason, coming across the field from the refreshment tent with a beer, witnessed the strange scene between Bernie and Greta too, but it made no sense to him. Then he heard George call Bernie's name and, swearing under his breath, he dropped the beer cup and set off after her with long quick strides, struggling to get through the crowd of people making its way to the parking lot.

He looked for her in vain in the lot among the cars parked there or driving out, then ran up to the river to look for her on the sidewalk there. He didn't pay any attention to the old yellow bus that pulled out of the parking lot behind him and disappeared down the road in the opposite direction.

Nine

That night Steadman George was so excited about the potential gold mine he'd stumbled upon in the guise of the Reverend Ted Mason that he couldn't sleep, so he stood on the Showboat's upper-deck porch and smoked, leaning over the railing and watching the dark river flow slowly past below, working out how he'd get the money from Mason without leaving a trail anybody could follow. Since Mason wouldn't know him from Adam, he didn't have to worry about wearing a disguise, or trying to hire a go-between, he could—

"Permission to come aboard, Cap'n!" a voice behind him said.

He almost jumped overboard. He turned and saw a man standing at the top of the stairs on the other side of the boat, bathed in moonlight.

"Jesus Christ!" he said, still breathless. "You scared the shit out of me. Can't you read the sign on the gangplank? 'No trespassing'? Get off the boat!"

"Sorry," the man said, raising his hands, in one of which he was holding a paper bag. "Didn't realize anybody was living on the boat. I just thought it'd be a nice place to sit and watch the river pass by as I sip a little of this whiskey—Wild Turkey."

George took a closer look at the intruder. He was about forty-five, tall and lean, clean-shaven and neatly dressed in gray slacks and a dark short-sleeved sports shirt. He had a long face, thick gray hair, and his wide thin mouth was open in a friendly grin.

"What're you doin' out here this time of night?" George asked.

"I'm at the U for a conference," the man said, "staying at the conference center down the road a way."

"Yeah, but that still don't explain what you're doing on my boat in the middle of the night."

The man chuckled. "The wife and I got in a little fight after we got back to the hotel from seeing the play, so I took my bottle and brought it down to the river. I didn't know anybody would still be on the boat this late—Say, aren't you the piano player?"

George nodded.

"Man, you were fantastic! You *were* the play, in my opinion—and I overheard other people saying the same thing!"

He waved the sack he was holding again and turned to go back down the stairs. "Sorry to disturb you. I'll just take my bottle upstream a way and do my drinking there."

George hesitated. He liked company when he couldn't sleep. He wouldn't have to drink any of the man's whiskey, he could smoke a joint instead, that'd be just as good.

"The mosquitoes'll eat you alive down there," he said. "I've got a fridge with an ice tray, if you like your whiskey over ice. I've got a glass too," he added.

"Two glasses, I hope," the man said, as he followed George into his cabin and settled into the old overstuffed chair George offered him.

"Snug!" he said, looking around. "Like a little apartment."

George filled a glass with ice from his refrigerator and brought it out to the man, who gave him a questioning look. "What are you, a Mormon?"

George laughed. "I'm tryin' to quit," he said. "Doctor's orders."

"What do doctors know?" the man asked. "I get to ask that question," he added with a chuckle, "because I'm one myself." He poured whiskey over ice and took a sip. "Smooth stuff for being a hundred and two proof. How come you're living on the boat?"

"They let me live on the tub in exchange for keepin' an eye on it. Keep the kids off, mostly."

"Nice duty!" the man said. "Skoal!"

"Cheers," George said without much enthusiasm. He rummaged in a drawer for his bag of marijuana and brought it out.

"Try this instead," the man said, and offered him a bag he pulled from his pocket. "Medically approved," he added with a grin.

George was happy to use somebody else's—especially a doctor's. It ought to be better than the crap he had. "Thanks," he said, and rolled himself a fat one.

"Name's Dave," the man said, "Dave Brown. And you're Steadman George, of course—who keeps the actors on their toes!"

George growled a modest laugh. "You can call me Steadman," he said.

It wasn't hard to get George talking about his musical career and all the famous musicians he'd known and played with.

"Must get lonely out here," the man said after a while. "I'm surprised you don't have one of those cute young actresses keeping you company."

George chuckled. "Ten, twenty years ago, I would've," he said, inhaling smoke, "but now they treat me like I'm their father."

"Come to you for advice, do they? Tell you all their little secrets?"

George shook his head. "That wasn't what I meant," he said, suddenly feeling a little uneasy under the man's expressionless gaze. Close up and in the light of the cabin, there was something a little unsettling about him—he had a cruel mouth and eyes with no humor in them. George had seen eyes like those before in his life. They'd belonged to people he'd learned to keep away from.

"What kind of doctor are you?" he asked.

"A pediatrician," the man replied. "A baby doctor."

George nodded, inhaled more dope. It was good—better than his own by a long shot. He offered the cigarette to Dave, but he said no thanks, tonight he preferred whiskey.

"The kids either ignore me or treat me like I'm about to

kick the bucket," George went on. He growled a laugh. "They don't got any notion how people are who're over thirty—they think we've got one foot in the grave."

"So you don't get to know anything about their personal lives, huh? Theater students were a pretty wild bunch when I was a student. I'll bet they're even wilder these days, with all the drugs and sex."

"They don't do any drugs around me," George said. "But I get the idea there's a lot of foolin' around. Hell, they're young—who can blame 'em? I just play the piano and keep my nose clean and my mouth shut." He laughed again—he hadn't enjoyed an evening like this in ages. He was having a wonderful time.

The man stood up suddenly, asked if he could get more ice for his drink.

When he came back, he had two glasses, one of which he set down on the table next to George. "Speaking as a doctor," he said as he went back to the overstuffed chair and sat down, "one drink won't kill you."

"But you're just a baby doctor," George said with a grin. "What do you know about livers?"

"Babies have livers too, don't they?" the man replied as he filled the two glasses.

George threw back his head and roared at that.

"I'm not much of a theatergoer," the man said, "but a couple of the kids seemed pretty talented to me. The boy who played the American cousin, and the female lead especially. I forget their names."

"Greta Markham," George said, "and Paul Boone."

"Yeah, whatever. I'll bet they'll go far if they stick with it. But what do I know?"

"Yeah, they're good, all right," George agreed. He picked up the whiskey and held it under his nose, sniffed it as though it were good brandy.

"I wanted to be an actor when I was a kid," the man said, reminiscing. "Get to pretend to be somebody you're not." He laughed, shook his head. "But my parents discouraged it. Dad wanted me to be a lawyer like him, Mom wanted me to be a doctor. It's important to have parents who encourage you, don't you think?"

"I suppose," George said, taking a small swallow of whiskey.

"I suppose they come from showbiz families?" the man asked.

"Who?"

"This gal, Greta, and Paul What's-his-face."

George chuckled, more to himself than to Dave. He had a story to tell, but knew he couldn't tell it. It was worth too much money not to tell it. But, on the other hand, it was nice to know things other people didn't—and especially nice if they knew you knew. "I don't know about Paul," he said, "but Greta does. Her dad was in the business." He sipped some more.

"Was?"

"He's dead now. Her mom's remarried."

"That's too bad. That her dad's dead, I mean, not that her mom's remarried."

"Yeah, it is," George said. They sat awhile and drank whiskey. The man kept George's glass full. After a while, he said, "You said 'her mom' in a kind of funny way. What'd you mean by that?"

"Huh?" The question made no sense to George.

"We were talking about that actress, Greta something," the man said, enunciating carefully. "You said that after her dad died, her mom remarried. You said 'her mom' in a kind of funny way. For that matter, you said 'her dad' in a kind of funny way too."

George felt the blood drain out of his face. "I did?" He glanced over at the man and then away quickly. "No, I didn't. I mean—why would I?"

The man shrugged. "I don't know," he said. "You tell me."

"You tell me what?" George said. "I mean, tell you what?"

The man didn't reply, just sat in the old chair with the faded flowers, some kind of smile on his face. George thought he looked like a wolf peering at him through shrubbery.

"You're at the U for a conference," George said. "What's it about?"

"Pediatrics. I told you, I'm interested in babies."

Why'd he laugh when he said that? What was funny about being a baby doctor?

"There was a woman out there tonight," the man went on, "from the audience. After the play, she went up to this Greta gal and draped a necklace over her head—almost threw it. Didn't you notice?"

George shook his head. "No," he said. "Why'd she do that?"

"As she passed you," the man said, "I heard you call her 'Bernie.' Didn't you say that was the name of Greta's mom?"

"Nah, Linda's her mom, Bernie's—"

He stopped. Something had gone wrong with the night, the room, the conversation. Something terrible, but what it was, was just out of reach of his mind. Dope did this to him sometimes, made him wonder if he was crazy or the person he was talking to was. And the booze. He'd been dry for over two weeks, and Wild Turkey's strong anyway, stronger than he was used to.

He didn't know why this man was asking him these questions, he just knew he couldn't answer: there was money riding on not answering—and more than money, a lot more than money. He knew that clearly, he just didn't know what that "more" was, but fear closed around his heart anyway like a gloved hand.

"I knew Bernie a long time ago," the man went on dreamily. He was mostly a brutal grin to George now, and a voice that spun from it like the web of a busy, poisonous spider, and a pair of cold eyes that went in and out of focus, too close to George's face for comfort.

He said, "You knew Bernie?"

The man nodded. "I'd like to see her again. I missed her in the crowd after the play. She called me earlier in the day, but I wasn't home."

He wasn't home when Bernie called, George thought. He was in town for a conference, a conference for pedi—pedia—for baby doctors. The two things didn't add up.

"She called you, huh?" George said, his mind working furiously, trying to inch its way out of a deep, dark hole.

"Uh-huh. I'd really like to see her again."

"Too bad," George said. "She's gone now. She was here tonight, to see—"

"To see what? Her daughter? Greta?"

Steadman George was a tiny creature, little Georgie Steadman, Georgie Porgie, pudnin' pie, kissed the girls and made 'em cry, crawling out of the hole and up one thick, sticky-green vine after the other. Climbing, climbing, his entire life he'd been climbing to get out of a hole, like Jack and the beanstalk.

He knew there was danger, terrible danger, and he had to crawl out of the hole. Fe, fi, fo, fum, I smell the blood of a Christian man—but this man wasn't Pastor Ted. Who was he and what did he want?

"Where's Bernie staying?" the man asked, his voice suddenly as sharp and clear and hard as glass.

George tried to collect his wits. "How the hell should I know?" he said, much too loud and blustery to be convincing.

"I'll pay you to tell me."

George looked up quickly, and suddenly it dawned on him that this man had been sent by Ted Mason—Pastor Ted—to try to find Bernie and pay *her* to keep quiet! George's story wouldn't be worth shit without her to back it up. That was it!

No, wait! If he told the newspapers, the TV, about Pastor Ted and Bernie and Greta—Bernie could deny it till she was blue in the face, they'd still believe him. They always believed the dirt—it's just human nature. And if it came out, Bernie wouldn't deny it. Bernie wouldn't lie. Bernie wouldn't take money, either. Not now, not anymore. Steadman George knew that about her.

And then George got it: this man, this Dave Brown, had come from Mason and he wanted to kill Bernie. Maybe he wanted to kill Greta too, George realized, the horror growing in his confused brain. Greta!

No, they wouldn't kill her! A man of the cloth wouldn't kill his own daughter, for Christ's sake!

A man of the cloth! A man of straw, you mean! Besides, he thought as he peered at the man sitting across from him, this man would kill anybody who stood in his way. He'd seen men like this before, he knew the type, he'd always kept out of their way—you learn that fast in his line of work.

He'd kill Bernie and that would be the end of it. If Bernie couldn't talk, Ted would be safe.

"A thousand dollars, Mr. George," the man said quietly. Then he brought out an envelope, held it over the table between them, and let hundred-dollar bills fall from it.

George stared at the money for a moment, then took a quick swallow of whiskey. Then he looked at the man across from him and saw something on his face that almost sobered him up. He told himself it was the dope and the booze—they'd made him paranoid before, he'd imagined some pretty frightening things in his time—but he struggled to his feet anyway, knocking the whiskey bottle over.

"Get off my boat!" he shouted. "I ain't telling you nothin', I don't know where Bernie is. She just come here tonight to see the play like everybody else—that's all! Now get off my boat, you hear me?" He tried to gather up the whiskey-soaked money, throw it at the man, but it fell at his feet.

He left it there as he staggered toward the man, tripped, and fell. The man caught him and straightened him up. He smiled down into his face and said, "Hey, take it easy, Cap'n! You'll be okay—you're just having a bad trip. I'm leaving now, okay? I'm leaving. Let's don't make a fuss about it."

Don't make a fuss! George thought. They're tryin' to kill Bernie and maybe Greta too, and he says don't make a fuss! He didn't want to go with the man, but the man wouldn't let go of him, and maybe it was for the best: he wanted to make sure the man really did leave his boat anyway.

The man shoved him to the door and out of the cabin, then down the stairs to the main deck. He looked up and down the dark shore in front of the boat and then pushed George across the gangplank.

As they reached the shore, George tried to jerk himself free, but the man turned and gave him a violent shove and George fell backward into the river. He tried to cry out, but before he could, his back hit the water and his head and shoulders struck the shallow sandy bottom, knocking the wind out of him.

Panicked, eyes wide, he tried to raise himself up, saw the man wading toward him, and imagined for a desperate moment he was coming to help him, but instead the man bent down, grabbed his ankles, and lifted, thrusting George's head back into the river. His mouth and nose filled with water, he couldn't cry out, he could only gasp, thrash left and right trying to hold his head out of the water as long as he could as he stared up at the man holding his ankles at the level of his face.

Then the man was kneeling in the water beside him, holding him out of the water by the shoulders, staring down calmly into his face.

"Where is she, Mr. George? Where's Bernie now?"

Coughing, gasping for air, George said, "I don't know! I swear, I don't know! She didn't tell me, I didn't ask."

"That actress she gave the necklace to—that was her daughter, wasn't it? You lied about that to Ted Mason. You did tell Bernie where to find her daughter, didn't you?"

"That's not true!" George whispered, panic on Greta's behalf almost replacing his fear for his own life because Greta was *his* daughter too, wasn't she? If it hadn't been for him, she wouldn't have even been born! He'd given Greta her life, he couldn't take it back now—could he?

"Bernie," the man said then, whispering. "Where is she, Mr. George—Steadman? I know you know. Tell me and I'll let you live and you can have all that money in the cabin too."

George had played a lot of poker in his life and he knew he was holding a bad hand. He stared up into the man's face, desperately searching for a clue as to how to play it, but there was nothing there.

"She's . . . she's—" He coughed and gagged, tried to think of someplace he could convince the man Bernie would be—anyplace but at the Riverton Mall—but his tormented mind could come up with nothing.

"Tell me," the man repeated.

"I don't know," George gasped. "I don't know! I'd tell you if I did. Honest I would!"

Stan Mason had heard all he had time to hear. Swearing angrily under his breath, he stood quickly and jerked George's legs up again, high into the air, and, his muscles trembling with the strain, finished what he'd begun. It didn't take long, and then he shoved the body out into the river and went back onto the Showboat to remove any traces that he'd been there.

Ten

After roll call, I walked out of the campus police station with my friend Lawrence Fitzpatrick, who had one of the squad cars that night. We agreed we'd meet for our middle-of-the-watch break at the old river willow a little way downstream from the Showboat, and then I set out on my patrol.

The first part of the night was reasonably calm—the campus was turning out to be an unusually tranquil place that summer and I hoped it would continue. Not every night was like that, or every summer.

About an hour after I'd started my patrol, around midnight, a female graduate student called the dispatcher from her office in one of the buildings at the end of the Mall. A man was loitering outside the building's entrance and she was afraid to leave it to go to her car.

I was close by, so when I got there, the man was still where she'd seen him—a professor who'd stepped out of the building to get some air and clear his head.

The woman apologized for taking up my time and I assured her that was what my time was for and that I hoped she'd do it anytime she was working late and saw somebody she was uncertain about lurking.

"I wish I could wear what you're wearing," she said to me angrily as we walked to her car, looking at my two-way radio, my nightstick, and my gun.

I agreed with her that that would be another way women could take back the night.

Since I was almost there, I walked down to the Showboat parking lot, half hoping I'd find Steadman George hanging over the side of the boat again, as he'd been two days before. I was curious to know how the story he'd told me had ended, the one about the woman who'd sold her baby and was now back wanting his help in finding it again. I was also curious to know how he was making out in his struggle to stay sober, although I wouldn't let him know it for the world. If he wanted to talk about it, though, I'd listen.

A light was on in his cabin and I heard the faint sound of his phlegmy laugh. As I stood watching, somebody inside came out of what I knew was the cabin's kitchen—or galley, as they'd call it on a boat. I only saw his profile, but he wasn't George.

As I walked away, I heard George laugh again. I didn't like the sound of it—I'd heard laughs like it before in my life. I caught myself hoping he wasn't drinking, and quickly squelched it: I'd had hopes like that dashed many times before too; I didn't need to carry them around with me now for an old man I hardly knew.

A little later Lawrence called to ask me to help him arrest a trespasser in the Medical School, Denny McClure. Denny's well-known to the campus cops, although he usually only comes out when there's a full moon. He's convinced that his missing dog's somewhere in the building being used for research. He could be right that that's where the dog ended up—they don't ask questions in the medical school—but if so, he'd be long gone now.

Denny's a large man with a tendency to be violent, especially if he's forgotten to take his medicine, but he was docile enough that night. I put the handcuffs on him—he's a gentleman and doesn't resist women cops—and helped Lawrence get him into the squad car's cage, and we drove him downtown to the county jail. By the time we got there, he was muttering about Lawrence's striking resemblance to an SS officer and Nazi experimentations on human subjects.

Lawrence does bear a striking resemblance to the Aryan ideal of manhood, which is why it took me a long time to warm to him, but he differs in several significant ways: he's sweet and gentle, and he's engaged to marry my friend Paula Henderson, who's black. Not something you find in Nazis in good standing.

As we drove away from the jail, Lawrence said, "Still want to go sit under the old willow?"

"Sure. It's break time, isn't it?" I don't feel good about taking some people to jail. Denny McClure was one of them.

It was about two A.M. when we got back to campus. Lawrence parked in the Showboat's parking lot and we walked down to the river. I noticed as we passed that except for a light still burning in George's cabin, and the warning lights at either end, the Showboat was dark. It was about this time Tuesday morning that I'd last talked to George. I looked for the glow of his cigarette but didn't see it and figured that if he was still up, he was probably over on the river side of the boat.

Lawrence and I made ourselves comfortable, our backs to the tree, our feet almost touching the water lapping at the sandy shore, and drank the coffee we'd bought at an all-night café on the way back to the U from downtown. After a while, Lawrence cleared his throat and asked me if Gary was back from Leech Lake yet.

"Loon Lake," I corrected him. "No, he won't be back until Sunday."

"Does it sound like he likes it up there?"

"Yes."

"Think he might want to move up there?"

"I'd be surprised if he didn't," I said, swatting a mosquito that had just landed on my arm.

"Would you go with?"

"No."

"Well," he said after a thoughtful pause, "it's only a couple of hours' drive, right? It's not like when he moved to Belize."

More than distance separated Gary and me, I thought, but didn't say it. Instead, I pointed upstream at the Showboat and asked Lawrence if he and Paula would be interested in seeing the play some night with Gary and me, after Gary got back.

Paula's in law school, but now that it was summer, she had more time for a social life. Sam Allen, the director of this year's play, is a friend of mine.

"Paula and I saw it a couple of nights ago," he said.

"Oh." Thud.

I recovered quickly and asked him what it was about. He said it involved a heavily mortgaged English country estate, a villain who held the mortgage and wanted the heroine in exchange for it, and an all-American hero who saves the day with a sterling character and a great deal of inherited money.

"Just like real life," I said. "Was the heroine tied to a railroad track too?"

"No, and the villain doesn't try to feed her into a buzz saw either. He wants her body in one piece."

"How old-fashioned," I muttered moodily, and smacked another mosquito.

"It's the play Lincoln was seeing when he was shot," Lawrence went on. "Do you know what the last words he heard were?"

I confessed I didn't.

" 'You sockdologizing old mantrap.' "

"What's that supposed to mean?"

"Who knows? It was what the hero was calling a woman who was trying to marry her daughter off to him. The line always got big laughs, which was what Booth was waiting for, to cover the sound of the shot."

"It probably wouldn't get a big enough laugh to cover the noise a semiautomatic makes," I said.

"It's strange, isn't it?" Lawrence went on as if I hadn't spoken. "Your brain just registers a ridiculous line like that, you start to laugh, and then something moves in the darkness beside you, a blur you register out of the corner of your eye. You start to turn. Maybe you see the flash, hear the shot, feel pain, hear your wife scream—or maybe not, maybe you don't see or hear or feel anything. But the rest of the country feels the pain forever."

I turned and looked at him a long time as he stared out at the river. Sometimes I can't see what Paula sees in him, and sometimes I can.

I felt a little hurt that they hadn't invited me to go with them. Although I see Lawrence often enough at work, I hadn't seen much of Paula since she started law school. Before that we used to do a lot of things together. Is this the fate of unmarried, unpartnered women, to be deserted by their married friends? Is that what drives us to marriage?

As though reading my mind, Lawrence said, "The people next door couldn't go. Their kid got sick at the last moment so they gave us their tickets."

Oh.

I asked him how the piano player was.

"Steadman George? He's great. He's like the sound track in a movie, with ominous rolls and chords and stuff and sweet music when the heroine's on stage being courted by the hero. Plus he accompanies the singing and dancing and has a solo of his own that brought down the house. I'd give anything to be able to play the piano like that! He lives on the Showboat and sometimes I talk to him when he's out on deck when I come by."

"Me too," I said. "In fact, I spent my break with him Tuesday morning about this time. He told me a story about a woman who sold her baby a long time ago and now she wants his help finding her, or him. George claimed he knows where the kid is, and wanted my opinion about whether or not he should tell the mother."

Lawrence nodded. "He's told me some whoppers too," he said. "Mostly about the great jazz musicians he's known and played with. You think Gerry Mulligan ever played the Getaway?"

"Probably," I said. The Getaway was a bar across the river that used to be known for good jazz, before it fell on hard times ten or fifteen years ago.

"Lately," Lawrence said, "he's been talking about how hard it is to stop drinking. To hear him talk, he used to drink pretty heavily."

"A doctor told him he had to quit," I said. "His liver was starting to act up." I thought about the laughter I'd heard in George's cabin, hoped it wasn't what it sounded like.

When we'd decided we'd loitered long enough on the river, we got up, ready to get back to work.

A string of barges in the middle of the river glided swiftly by like something from the past, eerie and silent, as though everybody on them had died a long time ago. Before the wake reached us, it reached something else, a patch of darkness darker than the water around it, and set it bobbing. Something white reflected in the moonlight caught my attention.

"Lawrence," I said, pointing, "what's that?"

"A bunch of weeds."

Then he saw what I'd seen.

As I called the dispatcher, Lawrence stripped to his underpants and swam out to pull in the body. I recognized Steadman George as soon as Lawrence brought him ashore. His eyes were open and they stared up at me with all the expression of a dead fish. His color was that of a dead fish too.

My friend Ginny Raines arrived ten minutes later. She's a lieutenant, and the officer in charge that night. She's in her mid-thirties, short, dark, and tough.

I filled her in on how Lawrence and I had found George and what we knew about him. Ginny said she knew who he was too, she'd heard him play in nightclubs.

Bonnie Winkler, an assistant medical examiner I've met before in the line of duty, arrived twenty minutes after Ginny. She knelt and gave George's body a cursory once-over, then stood up.

"No visible signs of trauma," she said, "and the foam"—she meant the froth that had appeared around George's mouth soon after Lawrence had brought him ashore—"makes it look good for a drowning."

An odd way to put it. I told her who he was and that he'd lived on the Showboat, a couple of hundred yards upstream. She wanted to take a look at his cabin, so she, Ginny, and I walked up there and I led the way up the stairs to his cabin. The door wasn't locked.

The cabin reeked of alcohol and marijuana. A nearly empty bottle lay on the ratty piece of carpet covering the floor and a glass sat on a table next to the rocking chair, along with an ashtray overflowing with ash, cigarette butts, and the mashed butt of a roll-your-own cigarette.

"This pretty much tells the story, doesn't it?" Ginny said grimly.

She nosed around looking for a suicide note while Bonnie checked the cabin for medicines.

I wandered around too, looked at the padded old oak

rocking chair and the shabby overstuffed chair with the faded flowers, glanced into the bedroom with the unmade bed, opened the door that I knew led down into the theater beneath us. It was obvious the place hadn't been burgled—it's not hard to tell a cluttered room from one that's been ransacked.

There was an empty plastic tray of microwaveable food in the sink and a dirty fork beside it. In a cupboard next to the sink, a couple of glasses and a few cups and plates were scattered around. Steadman George had not died surrounded by much in the way of worldly goods.

I felt infinitely sad. He'd been trying to quit drinking but had failed and it had cost him his life. I wasn't sad only because he'd died; mostly I was sad because I believe people should die feeling they'd done the best they could.

I went back out into the living room, looked around some more.

"No sign of a struggle," Ginny said, "and no notes of any kind, not even a grocery list."

Bonnie came back from the bathroom with a couple of medicine bottles in an evidence bag. She looked at me, a wry smile on her face. "Something bothering you, Peggy?" she asked.

I shrugged. "He was trying to quit drinking," I said. "When I talked to him two days ago, he was still on the wagon."

"It doesn't take long to fall off," she said. "Besides, what's the alternative? You think someone arranged the cabin like this, maybe even forced booze down his throat, to make his death look like an accident? Why?"

"No," I said, "I don't suppose anybody had to force booze down Steadman George's gullet tonight." I told them about the man I'd seen in the cabin with George a couple of hours earlier.

Bonnie gave me an expectant smile, waiting for my point.

"So where's the other glass?" I said.

"What other glass?"

"There's only one glass on the table," I said. "If that one's George's," I said, pointing, "where's the other guy's?"

"You saw him drinking?" Bonnie asked.

"No."

"Then maybe he was a teetotaler. Or he was the one smoking the dope and George was doing the drinking—or vice versa."

Sure, it could've been any of the above. I went back to the kitchen and took a closer look at the two glasses in the cupboard. "Come here," I said, "I want to show you something."

Ginny and Bonnie came into the kitchen. I pointed to the glasses. "That one's kind of grimy and there's dust on it," I said, "and this one's sparkling, as though it's just been washed."

"So what?" Bonnie asked.

"So maybe whoever was in here with George washed and put away his glass," I said. I turned to Ginny. "Could you send these glasses—and the bottle and the ashtray—to the state crime lab for fingerprinting?"

She rolled her eyes, but didn't argue. She knows you don't have anything to lose by overprocessing a crime scene, a lot to lose if you underprocess it.

I asked Bonnie how soon she could tell me if George had been drunk when he drowned. I was pretty sure he had been, but I wanted to be sure.

"I could probably do that right now," she said, "if I had a pocketknife and if they hadn't already taken the body away."

She looked at her watch. "Unless there's something more urgent waiting for me, I can do the autopsy as soon as I get back to the hospital. Will that be soon enough for you?"

I said sure. I'd never attended an autopsy, but I knew enough about them to know that when you open somebody up who's been drinking heavily, it smells as though he was breathing on you.

Bonnie stomped away to her car. I sometimes think she chose to become a medical examiner just to work against the fact that her name's Bonnie Winkler and she looks like Shirley Temple having a bad hair day.

"Don't expect results from the crime lab that soon,

though," Ginny told me as we walked off the boat. "Unless Bonnie comes up with something surprising, this isn't going to be high priority. It's probably not a murder at all. You of all people shouldn't be surprised that an alcoholic has a relapse, Peggy."

"I'll wait for the autopsy results," I retorted, "before I stop being surprised."

The sky was getting light by the time we drove out of the Showboat parking lot and across campus to the station.

"How does Gary like it up at Moose Lake and when's he coming back?" Ginny asked.

"Loon Lake," I said. "Sunday," I added garrulously.

"Why don't you go home after your shift's over, Peggy, and take a long cold shower, then drive up and spend your three days off with him? It'll do you good."

Ginny likes Gary a lot and wishes we'd get married. She comes from a small town, grew up on a farm, and still has a lot of the traditional values in her.

"Why don't you?" I snapped. "Pickle some peaches or can some watermelon pickles for him or something." I didn't know what watermelon pickles were, but they sounded like something a woman who lived in a place like Loon Lake would can for her man.

"Touchy, touchy!" Ginny said with a laugh. "And don't think the thought hasn't crossed my mind. The trouble is, the poor fool only has eyes for you."

At the police station I got myself a cup of last night's bitter squad room coffee and sat down to write my report.

As Ginny headed back to the office, she said, "See you around noon?"

"Yeah."

On our campus, the police work a six-days-on/three-off rotation and this was the end of both Ginny's and my six days on. Some of us who regularly take the dog watch always try to stay awake the day following our last night of duty so we can get into the rhythm of our friends who think working days is the natural thing to do—as though sitting in an office wheeling and dealing is natural. There's no point in being rested and ready to go just when all your friends are getting ready for bed. So Ginny and I had agreed that I'd spend the afternoon at her place working in her garden, and then we'd order takeout pizza and watch a scary video to keep ourselves awake until bedtime.

THURSDAY

Eleven

Stan slept well but woke up angry. He spooned instant coffee into a mug, poured hot tap water over it, and took it into the living room, where he sat and brooded.

He'd thought it was going to be so easy, once he'd called the number Ted had given him and, pretending it was a wrong number, conned the unsuspecting George into telling him where he was. But then he'd learned that George had lied when he'd told Ted that Bernie didn't know where her daughter was. That was too bad, because it meant Bernie would have to die too.

Of course, he'd planned to kill her anyway. She was a loose end otherwise, somebody he and Ted would have to worry about the rest of their lives if she were allowed to go on living.

The scene he'd witnessed in front of the Showboat last night had been puzzling: Bernie had draped a necklace over her daughter's head and then run off. The girl had just stared after her, surprised. Stan wasn't sure what Bernie's intentions had been with that, but it was clear the girl didn't know who Bernie was. Not yet, anyway.

He drank coffee, and wondered if Ted really thought he was just going to talk to Bernie. Talk about what? Her views on abortion? The possibility of giving her a job working for Ted? How much she would accept for keeping her mouth shut?

Stan laughed silently, shaking his head at his brother's naïveté—if that's what it was.

He admired Ted for his success in getting where he'd set his mind to go. He envied him too, and didn't try to hide that from himself. That was one way in which he differed from his brother: *he* wasn't afraid to look at the darkness in his own soul.

Stan envied Ted for how lucky he'd been, for luck had been a part of his success, there was no doubt about that. He hadn't had to go to Vietnam because his number hadn't come up, and when he'd knocked up Bernie, she hadn't blown the whistle on him, which would have ended his career before it even got off the ground.

Ted had lived a charmed life—up to now. And with Stan working for him, his life would continue that way.

He smiled as he looked around at the shabbiness of his small apartment. Once he'd taken care of the loose end called Bernie, he and Ted would be on a more equal footing. In fact, Stan would be able to call himself Ted's right-hand man with complete justification, since Ted would owe him his career.

Unless he had to, Stan wouldn't tell Ted what he'd done for him, for Ted had no stomach for reality. He'd never had a stomach for it, even when they were kids. Stan had always been the physically stronger of the two of them too, which meant he'd had to fight more than one bully who was after Ted.

Well, wasn't that what brothers were for, to help each other? Stan would help Ted now and, as soon as the danger posed by Bernie had passed, Ted would help him.

Ted called what he believed in "family ties," and that sounded very nice. What Stan called it was something a little closer, he believed, to the truth: ties of blood.

Twelve

Swallow, carrying a steaming cup of herbal tea, came knocking at Bernie's trailer door around eight Thursday morning. She'd arrived the night before, while Bernie was at the Showboat. Swallow traveled light and, when she was on the road, usually lived in a tent.

Gideon sniffed her suspiciously through the screen on the window before giving her a bark of recognition. It had been Swallow who'd found the old Lab abandoned in a motel room—hence his name—and forced him on Bernie, claiming he would be good company for her as well as protection against rapists and burglars. Bernie had owned a dog for most of the years she'd been on the road, but when he'd died she hadn't gotten around to getting another until Swallow showed up with Gideon.

"Sorry if I woke you up," Swallow said, not looking particularly sorry. "I thought you were an early riser."

It had taken Bernie a long time to get to sleep the night before, so she'd slept in. She made coffee for herself in her old percolator, then she and Swallow sat at a picnic table next to the trailer and talked while Gideon explored the brush and trees along the riverbank. Birds and squirrels in the trees gossiped about him. It was a cool summer morning.

"Welcome back to Minnesota," Swallow said. She was a short chunky woman with dark eyes stuck like raisins in a large round face, curly brown hair and a wide-brimmed blue felt hat. "It's about time."

"You think so?" Bernie said.

"You're here, aren't you?"

Bernie laughed. It was hard to argue with that. Swallow maintained that everything that happened, happened for a purpose or else it wouldn't have happened. The best anybody could do was try to figure out the significance. Everything was significant to Swallow. They'd had a lot of discussions about that over the years they'd known each other.

"Why do I need protection," Bernie had asked at the time Swallow was insisting she take Gideon, "if everything happens for a purpose? If I get robbed or raped, it'll be for a purpose, won't it?"

"That's true," Swallow had replied. "But I was the one who found Gideon at that motel, and that must have been for a purpose. And since I don't have a nice big bus and trailer the way you do, but only a tent, I can't keep a dog. You, on the other hand, don't stay at motels, so you could never have found Gideon. Therefore, I must have been the means through which Gideon was sent to you, because you didn't have the sense to get a dog yourself."

Bernie'd just rolled her eyes. She wasn't sure that the "why" of why things happened didn't depend a lot on who was answering the questions, and would vary from person to person depending on her beliefs or interpretation. Take for example the way Swallow had gotten her name.

She'd gone on what she called a "vision quest" in Mexico with a group of other women. They'd fasted for several days, chanted and beat on drums, then taken the name of the first creature they'd seen when they stepped out of their tents on the morning of the third day. Swallow had wanted a bird name, so she'd resolutely tilted her head to the sky as she emerged from her tent.

She'd seen a loggerhead shrike. At first she'd tried to convince herself it was a mockingbird—they look a little like shrikes—but no, the hooked bill and black mask left no room for doubt: the bird was the ferocious shrike, totally unlike Swallow.

"So what did you do?" Bernie had asked her.

"Tried again the next morning," she'd answered.

"And you saw a swallow."

Swallow shook her head. "I didn't see anything. The sky was empty."

"Then how'd you get the name Swallow?"

"I decided that the empty sky was God's way of telling me to look inside myself and pick a name. Barn swallows were my constant companions when I was a child and so that's the name I took."

Bernie, smothering a grin, had suggested the empty sky might have meant God was angry with her for rejecting the name He'd chosen for her.

Swallow shook her head. "I couldn't believe in a God who wanted me to be called Shrike," she'd replied.

Now she asked Bernie if Bernie was planning to do some soul work while she was here.

"Soul work?"

"Oh, so it's not soul work you're here for, eh? You're only here because I told you how eager people at the fair would be to buy your turquoise and feathers."

Bernie laughed, shook her head.

"You didn't come back on business," Swallow said. "You came back to find a lost piece of yourself."

So then Bernie blurted it all out, about Greta and how she'd sold her and gone away and tried to forget, and she had forgotten for a lot of years, but then it started to come back and wouldn't leave her alone.

"You've found her, haven't you?" Swallow said.

Bernie nodded.

"Is she doing well?"

She nodded again. "I think so. She looks happy, anyway. She's an actress and I think she must be very talented."

"Then what's bothering you? You found what you came for—or didn't you?" She cocked her head, swallowlike, and waited for Bernie's answer.

"She doesn't know she was adopted—bought, I mean," Bernie said.

"Well, well," Swallow said quietly. Then she burst out laughing. "So now you feel a double loss. You not only gave up your baby—she doesn't even know you exist!"

Bernie turned red, looked miserable.

"Do you really believe in the appearances of things, Bernie?"

"What do you mean?"

"Your Greta's parents did her a great disservice, not

trusting her with the truth about her life, and so now she's living a lie. She thinks she's one thing, but she's something else. As long as there are people out there who know something important about her that she doesn't know, her life's fictitious. You understand what I'm saying?''

Bernie nodded, unconvinced.

"I don't see how anybody can be happy," Swallow plowed on, "who's grown up among people who're letting her live like that. It makes her less than they are, because they know something important about her that she doesn't know. And they're trying to live this lie too. They're all fictitious characters!''

"You think I should tell her about me?''

"You want to, don't you?'' Swallow said, darting her a look.

Bernie stared out at the rows of campers and trailers and tents in the park, a couple of children playing on a swingset. "Yes, but that's not a reason for doing it.''

Swallow finished her tea at a gulp and stood up. "We need to talk about this some more,'' she said. "Your daughter has brought you back here for a reason and we have to try to find out what it is. One of these nights we'll do a tarot reading. The tarot's good for clarifying difficult matters, you know. Now let's go off to Riverton Mall and start setting up.''

Thirteen

By the time I'd finished writing up my report on Steadman George's drowning, it was too late to go back out on patrol, so I went home. When I got there, I decided I needed a nap, so I set my alarm clock for ten and went to bed.

I didn't sleep very well. Images of George's dead eyes staring out of his bearded face alternated with images of his cabin with the bottle on the floor and the glass on the table and his chuckle as he'd told me the story of the woman who wanted his help in finding the child she'd sold. "Call me Steadman," I remembered him telling me, as though bestowing an honor on me.

I finally turned off the alarm and got up and took a long cold shower, then drank a couple of cups of coffee and tried to read the paper. The phone rang.

It was Gary, calling from Loon Lake.

"I know it's the start of your three days off," he began, "and you're trying to stay awake. So I thought I'd help."

"Thanks," I said with a laugh. I told him I was just drinking coffee and reading the paper, and asked him how things were going up there.

"Great," he said, his voice full of enthusiasm. "Kermit's in a hurry to sell the paper. He and his wife have been bitten by the travel bug and they've already bought tickets to Italy for September. If I don't buy it—or somebody else doesn't soon—they're just going to shut it down. They'll let me have it at a fair price and I can pay them in installments at really low interest, Peggy."

Kermit? "It sounds like a wonderful opportunity," I said brightly. I hadn't heard Gary so excited about anything since he'd talked to me about his plan to move to Belize several years ago.

What had I hoped to hear him say? That the situation was impossible and he was coming home as soon as he could?

"It's really beautiful up here too," he went on. "Land's still pretty cheap, even on the lake."

"I should hope so," I said. "Anyway, I don't want to have to do the things that women do in small towns: wear calico, learn to spin and weave, play the dulcimer, sing through my nose."

He laughed. "You wouldn't have to do any of those things! You could help me run the paper. With your insatiable curiosity, you'd make a good reporter."

I tried to visualize Gary wearing a green eyeshade and bent over a press with his sleeves rolled up as I come running in hollering, "Stop the press! Methodist picnic rained out."

"Well, nothing's definite yet," he said finally, when the silence had stretched out far enough. "Anything new going on there?"

"Steadman George apparently fell off the Showboat this morning and drowned. Lawrence and I found his body."

"That's too bad," he said. "I remember you telling me he was trying to quit drinking."

"Yeah. But it looks like he was drunk when he drowned."

"Sorry to hear that," Gary said. "I know you were rooting for him."

"The thing is," I went on, "I talked to him Tuesday, just two days before he must've died, and he was still on the wagon."

Before Gary could tell me the same thing both Bonnie Winkler and Ginny had told me, that drunks fall off wagons and nobody should know that better than I, I told him about how we'd found only one glass in George's cabin on the boat, even though I'd seen another man with him a few hours before Lawrence and I had found him.

The silence when I'd finished went on for a while.

Finally he said, "So you think he was murdered, huh? The guy you saw with him force-fed him the whiskey and then drowned him. There would've been signs of a struggle, in that case. Were there?''

''No. And no visible marks on his body either, as far as we could see.''

''And what's the motive for this murder, Peggy?'' he went on, his voice neutral.

''I don't know. Anyway, I didn't say I thought he was murdered. But I'd like to know what happened last night to make him start drinking again, if he did.''

''Why?''

''Why?''

''Why do you want to know that?''

I sighed. Gary knew about my father, of course, the charming drunk who'd finally ended up blowing his brains out with a shotgun outside my bedroom door, and he has an unpleasant habit sometimes of trying to psychologize me.

I think psychology has gone too far, myself. We started out asking who God was and what he wanted and we've ended up asking who we are and what we want. I don't see that the world's improved much by trading in the big questions for small ones.

To avoid a quarrel, I decided to change the subject. I asked him when he was coming back.

''I don't know, exactly,'' he said after a pause. ''Sunday sometime, I guess.''

''I have to go back to work Sunday night,'' I said, ''but how about coming over for dinner first, if you get here early enough?''

''Sounds good. But why don't you get in your car right now and drive up here and spend your time off with me? Don't you think you could use a change of scenery?''

Ginny had suggested that too—I wondered if they were in cahoots. It didn't seem like such a bad idea, actually—and it would only be for a couple of days, after all. Then nobody—meaning Gary, Ginny, Paula, and Lawrence and about ten other people who claimed to be my friends—would be able to say I hadn't given it the old college try.

So I said, ''How about tomorrow? I'm too tired to make a long drive today. Besides, I promised Ginny I'd help her in her garden this afternoon.''

"Okay, then," he said. "Tomorrow. Bright and early."

"I don't guarantee early."

I called the Medical Examiner's Office, identified myself, and asked if Bonnie Winkler had left a message for me about the autopsy on Steadman George. The secretary asked me to hold a sec. When she came back on, she said, "Dr. Winkler's note says, and I quote, 'Sorry, Peggy, but he had to've been drunk as a coot. It's too soon to know what else might be in his blood. No signs of physical trauma anywhere. In my opinion, Steadman George got drunk, fell off a boat, and drowned.' "

I thanked the secretary and sat and stared angrily at the phone a few minutes. That's what drunks do, who live on boats, I thought. First they fall off the wagon, then off the boat. What had I expected, after hearing George's drunken laugh on the Showboat? That he'd died sober and proud?

As a child I'd lain in bed and listened to my father laugh like that, and hoped it didn't mean what experience had taught me it always did.

Then a question occurred to me: if Steadman George had decided to start drinking again, where had he gotten the booze?

I reached for the yellow pages and looked up the listing of liquor stores by location. There were four within easy walking distance of the Showboat. George had once mentioned to me that he hadn't owned a car in years.

I called the liquor store nearest campus, identified myself as a cop, and asked the clerk if the name Steadman George meant anything to her.

"He's an old customer," she said, "if that's what you want to know."

"Have you see him recently?"

"Saw him yesterday, right around this time. Why?"

"He's dead," I said. "He drowned."

"Oh, yeah?" She sounded shocked. "Geez, that's too bad. He was a real nice guy. How'd it happen?"

I told her. "It looks as though he'd been drinking," I went on, "and I'd like to find out where he bought it. Wild Turkey."

"He didn't buy it here," she said. "At least not from

me, and I'm here most days from the time we open till six. Wild Turkey wasn't Steadman's brand anyway.''

"But you said he was in yesterday. What'd he buy?''

"Just cigarettes. He could've got them anyplace, of course, but like I say, he's an old customer, he liked to come in and talk. Get some exercise too, he said. Funny, he claimed he was trying to quit drinking. Course, with a guy like Steadman, that don't mean much. But he seemed pretty jaunty yesterday, like he wasn't having a problem with it. Wild Turkey, huh? Must've got it from one of the other stores around here. I never sold him any of that.''

I asked her if she'd check with the other people who worked in the store.

"Sure," she said, "I'll ask 'em, but if he'd bought it here, I would've seen him—at least until I left at six. He would've said something to me, even if I wasn't the one who waited on him. He liked to flirt, you know.''

She was in the store until six yesterday and George had been sober until then and apparently still planning to stay that way. Since the play started at eight and liquor stores here close at ten on weeknights, he would have had to buy the whiskey sometime between six and about seven-thirty, to give himself time to get back to the Showboat. That didn't make any sense.

He'd either bought the whiskey somewhere else, already had it, or the man I'd seen on the Showboat had brought it with him.

I called the other three liquor stores within a reasonable walking distance of the Showboat. One of the clerks I spoke to knew who George was but said he wasn't a regular customer and he hadn't seen him in he didn't know how long. The other two didn't know him at all.

Of course, George could have bought the Wild Turkey—even if that wasn't his brand—anyplace and at any time. It could have been in his cabin and he just happened across it last night and couldn't resist temptation.

A more likely scenario, it seemed to me, was that the man I'd seen with him had brought it. But why?

And why didn't he have any himself or, if he did, why did he wash his glass and put it away? Or did he drink straight from the bottle?

I wasn't convinced that Steadman George's death was anything other than what it seemed to be; I just wanted to do what I could to make sure it wasn't anything more.

I also thought about the story he'd told me about the woman—Bernie—who'd just arrived in town wanting George's help in finding the child she'd sold some twenty years ago. It was an unusual story—and about twenty-four hours after telling it to me, George was dead. Bernie's story didn't have to be related to his death in any way and it probably wasn't, even if his death turned out not to be an accident. But I don't like coincidences.

I'd suggested that he might try to convince the woman to leave well enough alone. He'd chuckled at that and said there wouldn't be much of a story in just letting sleeping dogs lie. I wondered if he could have awakened one, and it bit him.

Of course, there'd probably been a lot of sleeping dogs in Steadman George's life, any one of which could have awakened, for any number of reasons.

It was still early in the day and I had a lot of time to kill, to try to stay awake until I wanted to go to bed—around nine or ten P.M. I decided to spend some of that time trying to learn more about Steadman George and how he lived and died.

Fourteen

Before she and Swallow left for the Riverton Mall to set up their booths, Bernie introduced Gideon to the trailer park's manager, an old friend of Swallow's from her many trips to Minnesota, who'd agreed to let Gideon stay with him while Bernie was at the fair. Then Swallow led the way to the Mall in her pickup and Bernie followed in her bus. They were allowed to park on the cobbled street that ran along in front of the Mall long enough to set up their booths.

Swallow had arranged it so that she and Bernie would have adjoining booths. They went looking for another friend of theirs, a furniture maker named Fred Foster whom they'd gotten to know over the years at fairs in the Southwest. They found him down the street a way, his furniture already displayed in and around his booth, and he came back with them and helped them set up their booths.

Swallow didn't have much setting up to do, since all she had was a small striped tent with a pointed roof, a card table with two folding chairs, a sign giving her prices, and four or five decks of tarot cards.

Bernie's setup took much longer—about three hours. Her booth was a tent of blue canvas with silver stripes. Plain blue canvas was cheaper and she'd made do with that for years, but last year had been a good one and since her old canvas was faded and tattered, she'd treated herself to the new, more expensive material. She kept the sides rolled up except when it rained and when she closed up for the night. Setting it up went a lot faster with Fred's and Swallow's help.

She formed aisles under the tent's roof with the cases that held her beads and silver and then hung pegboards from the tent's frame for displaying her jewelry. At night, she took the silver and some of the more expensive jewelry back to the trailer park with her. Lids with locks covered the bead cases.

When she was set up, Bernie, accompanied by Fred, drove her bus into the parking ramp behind the Mall, leaving Swallow to keep an eye on her booth.

Since it was too early for fairgoers, and the Mall—as Geoff Seaton had told her on the phone the other day—was dead, the parking ramp was almost deserted. After she parked the bus, she and Fred cut through the Mall to get back to the fair, their footsteps echoing eerily in the emptiness.

"I'm glad you came," Fred said. "Swallow must be very persuasive—or was it her cards that convinced you to come?"

Bernie didn't say anything to that, just smiled. Fred was very tall so that even she had to look up when she talked to him.

His face became serious. "I've decided to stop traveling around," he went on. "I'm going to get a shop of my own around here someplace, if I can. Maybe just do a few fairs somewhere where it's warm in the winter."

Fred had been born and raised in Minnesota, and when he wasn't traveling around the country to fairs he lived here with his brother, Jim.

"Jim's found a house he thinks I might like," he went on. "It's zoned both residential and small business, so he thinks I could live upstairs and use the downstairs both for a workshop and showroom. I'm going to check it out tonight, after the fair closes. It's time I settled down," he added. "I'm getting too old to be driving all over the country."

A shadow passed over Bernie's face at hearing that. She'd miss Fred a lot.

"You want to come with us tonight, see what you think of the house?"

"Sure," she answered, and gave him another of her big

smiles—two in the same minute, perhaps a record for Bernie, he thought.

They paused on the plaza outside the Mall to look over the fair, which extended down the cobbled street in both directions and around the corner to their right. They could see Bernie's booth about halfway down the street. It looked like some kind of exotic southwestern mirage with the sun glittering on silver and glass beads, shimmering on the pheasant hides, and splintered and refracted by the crystals.

"Don't you ever get tired of driving that bus and trailer all over the Southwest?" Fred asked Bernie. He'd often tried to get her to talk about her childhood in Minnesota, but she wouldn't. She was quite a mystery woman to him.

"Of course I do, but it beats a lot of other things I could be doing to earn a living," she answered as they walked back down to the street and joined Swallow. She'd done a lot of things since leaving Minnesota: been a secretary, a bartender, worked in day-care centers and driven a school bus, among other things, until she'd gotten into the bead business.

She was surprised to discover that she didn't like the idea of not seeing Fred the four or five times a year their paths crossed. It gave her something else to think about.

Could she live in Minnesota, she wondered, knowing her daughter was here, and not tell her?

Fifteen

I called Sam Allen, the director of the Showboat production, at his office in the Theater Arts Department and asked him if I could come over and talk to him about Steadman George.

"You think there's something fishy—excuse me, that was a poor choice of words, wasn't it?—something suspicious about his death, Peggy?" he asked.

I told him I didn't know, I just had some questions I wanted to ask him about George.

"Well, you're not alone."

"Oh?"

"A reporter for the *Tribune*'s doing a feature on him. He called a while ago to ask me if I knew George's last address before he moved onto the Showboat. He also wanted to know if I knew him personally and might have some good stories to tell about him. I disappointed him, I'm afraid. Steadman George and I were not cronies," Sam added, unnecessarily.

That was pretty fast work for the *Tribune,* I thought.

I wondered who the reporter was. Through Gary I knew all the feature writers on the paper. It didn't surprise me that a reporter was interested in George, though, since he'd been a well-known local musician for a long time and his life would make a pretty colorful story.

Sam said he was about to go over to the Showboat to rehearse the cast in the songs and dances of the oleos, since he was going to have to play the piano himself until they could find a replacement for George. He said he could meet me after they were finished. We agreed to meet at four at the Boardinghouse, an old coffee house that's a popular all-night hangout for University students, faculty, and cops.

I biked over to Ginny's house and we worked in her garden a couple of hours. When I told her I'd have to leave in time to get over to the University to talk to Sam, she asked me why.

I told her. She sat back on her haunches—she was thinning the marigolds she'd planted around her tomatoes to keep the aphids away—wiped a muddy hand across her sweaty face, and looked at me sternly. She said my concern for the late Steadman George was touching, then asked me again why I didn't spend my three days off with Gary at Loon Lake, just to give country living a chance.

"I promised him I'd drive up tomorrow," I told her. "I'm too tired to drive up there today."

She gave me a disbelieving look. "But you're not too tired to chase after a dead man today," she pointed out.

"I'm never too tired for that," I snapped, just to shut her up, and because there was some truth in what she said.

It was a bright, warm summer afternoon as I biked to the University, cut through it, and then crossed the bridge that connects the Old and New Campuses. I dodged students walking or on Rollerblades who clogged the streets, oblivious to their surroundings as they listened to music on their headsets or talked and laughed or fought with each other either in person or over their cellular phones. I wondered if they knew the difference anymore, and what the world was coming to.

The Boardinghouse is on one of the little side streets just off Central, within walking distance of the University theater. It started life around World War One as a real boardinghouse, offering cheap, possibly even nutritious meals to students coming to the big city from the country, but the fast food industry stole that business and now it's a coffeehouse. On weekends, local writers come in to read from their work on a little stage in the back. A sign on the podium warns, WE DO NOT WANT TO HEAR ABOUT YOUR VICTIMIZATION, which keeps away a lot of the local poets.

Sam was already there when I arrived, pouring chocolate and cinnamon and God knows what else on a large coffee concoction. I got a latté and joined him at his table.

Sam's in his early thirties—tall, heavyset, with a face that looks as if it had been carved out of his curly black beard and thick wild hair. I'd met him last fall and even played a small role in a play he directed. We hit it off and now we get together for dinner sometimes with his lover Christian and their friend Pia Austin. The four of us share guilty knowledge of a murder too, but that's another story.

"Did you know Steadman George was trying to quit drinking?" I asked him when the preliminaries were over.

"Yes—everybody who knew him knew that. He said he was determined to quit and apparently thought it would help if he told us all instead of trying to do it in secret." Sam sighed. "It's very sad," he went on. "The last time he mentioned it to me—a couple of days ago—he said he'd been on the wagon for two weeks. Apparently his liver was starting to act up and his doctor told him to quit, or else."

I asked him if he'd spoken with George the night of the performance.

"Of course. Why?"

"How'd he seem?"

Sam thought about it, staring down into his coffee. "Hm. Well, now that I think about it, I guess I'd have to say he seemed a bit preoccupied, as though he had something on his mind. It wasn't one of his better nights at the keyboard, either."

"Could he have been drinking?"

Sam shook his head. "I never got close enough to George to smell his breath, of course—nobody would—but I don't think so."

"Drugs?"

Sam rolled his eyes. "I wouldn't know. I suspected he smoked a little dope in the cabin—I could smell it sometimes, on the rare occasions when I had to go up there to talk to him about something—but a lot of people smoke the stuff. I certainly wasn't going to make an issue of it. I never saw him acting as though he were high. What's this all about, Peggy?"

I told him about the man I'd seen with George last night, and the things I thought were suspicious about his cabin on the Showboat.

Sam laughed and waved them away, as Bonnie Winkler and Ginny had before him. "I'm sure the old reprobate had lots of company on the boat," he said. "He wasn't a hermit, Peggy, after all! And who knows why there was only the one glass? Maybe his pal didn't drink!"

"In which case, where'd the Wild Turkey come from?"

"Wild Turkey," Sam said with a shudder. Sam drinks some kind of exorbitantly expensive scotch that smells like damp wool. "It could have been in George's cupboard for months or years," he suggested, "or his guest could've brought it."

"A guest who didn't drink? And people who're sincere about trying to quit don't keep booze in their cupboards. No," I went on, "either George went out sometime yesterday afternoon and bought that whiskey or his visitor brought it. I'd like to meet the guy to find out what went on last night."

"He probably doesn't even know Steady's dead yet," Sam said, stirring his grotesque coffee drink with a vanilla wafer, "since it happened too late to make the morning paper. It's always possible he'll go to the police and tell them all about it, once he finds out."

"Not if he was the one who brought the booze," I said darkly. "It's not very nice, bringing booze to somebody who's trying to quit."

Sam gave me his gentlest smile. "Is that what this is all about, Peggy? You just want to find the guy and give him a piece of your mind for not keeping Steady sober—or do you think he forced the sauce down his gullet and then shoved him overboard?"

"I just want to know," I said.

"If it was the latter," Sam said, "what might his motive be? Do you have one in mind?"

I sighed, told him the story George had told me about Bernie and her child.

"Oscar Wilde did those misplaced baby stories brilliantly," Sam said when I'd finished. "Next summer, we should do one of them on the Showboat—*Lady Windermere's Fan*, perhaps."

"I doubt Steadman George read Oscar Wilde," I said.

"Why do you think this story is true? Everybody tells me he was an accomplished storyteller."

"You'd have to have been there, Sam," I said wearily. I was tired. My lack of sleep was catching up with me.

He gazed at me a long time, a little smile darting in and out of his beard. Finally he said, "I only wish I'd found a part for you in the play, Peggy. It doesn't seem to me you have enough going on in your life these days. You and Gary aren't having problems, are you?"

"I don't want to talk about it," I snapped, which seemed to be my mantra for the week.

"That *does* make it serious!" he said.

I asked him to tell me how George had gotten the job as Showboat pianist and ended up living—and dying—on the boat.

"I hired him last year," he said, "towards the end of the season, when the regular piano player left without warning. One of the actors suggested I check him out, so I made a pilgrimage to the Getaway—a grogshop a couple of miles down the river—to hear him play. You wouldn't believe the kinds of lowlife that frequent the place: faculty, students—even administrators, Peggy!"

The Getaway had gone downhill, but it wasn't as bad as Sam made it sound. It still brought in good enough jazz musicians occasionally so that even I went there, and I don't drink.

"Well," Sam continued, "when I first set eyes on George, I threw up my hands in despair as if to say, 'Greta—why? Why are you trying to destroy the show? Is it because you're not the star?' "

Sam paused theatrically, the only way he does anything, and added: "Greta was the actress who'd recommended Steady to me, you see. She's one of the leads in this year's production, but last year I gave it to somebody else. She was annoyed, to put it mildly. But she wasn't suited for the heroine's role, which called for simpering and swooning. Greta neither simpers nor swoons with conviction, I'm afraid. Her simper, especially—"

"What are you babbling on about, Sam?"

I turned to see who'd spoken the words I was thinking. A young woman was looming over our table, hands on hips and glaring down at Sam. I'd seen her come in with a crowd of other kids a few moments earlier.

"Ah, Greta," Sam said without missing a beat, "you'll be delighted to know we've been talking about you."

He turned to me. "Peggy O'Neill," he said, "meet Greta Markham, who plays Florence, the spoiled but fundamentally good-hearted rich girl in our play this summer. It's a real stretch for her."

They held claws up to each other's face.

She didn't look like the lead in a romantic melodrama and I could see that she'd be hard-pressed to simper or swoon convincingly. She was an inch or two taller than I and I'm five-nine. You could say we both had red hair, but you wouldn't say mine was dyed a bright cherry red and cut short—probably with dull kitchen scissors. She had a nicely shaped head, large, strikingly dark eyes, and a wide mouth painted a fire-engine red that jarred horribly—to my eyes, anyway—with the color of her hair, which was probably her intention.

She was wearing an oversized black leather jacket that hung down to her knees, black tights, and hiking shoes. In her ears she had a variety of earrings, with one stuck through an eyebrow for good measure.

A tall, neatly dressed young man was standing behind her. Now he stepped up and draped a long arm around her shoulders like a pet snake. They made a shocking contrast.

She turned to him and said, "Get me a double skim cap, Rick, will you? I've got business to take care of here," and then, without waiting for his response, turned to Sam and me. Annoyance rippled across Rick's face as he turned on his heel and went to join the others at the counter.

"Peggy and I were just discussing poor Steady," Sam explained to Greta. "Peggy's the campus cop who fished the poor man out of the river."

"Another cop did that," I corrected him, "but I was there."

"I was sorry to hear about his drowning," she said. "I've known the guy a long time." She looked at me curiously. "You're a campus cop? Are you here on business? Steady didn't just fall overboard by himself or something? Or is this a social occasion I'm interrupting?"

"There are no social occasions for Peggy O'Neill," Sam replied. "Not when there's a corpse upwind of her. She never lets anybody die in peace if she can help it," he added ruefully, as well he should.

I asked her if she'd spoken much with George recently.

She shook her head. "Not recently. But the last couple of weeks he'd join us over here sometimes for coffee. He was quitting drinking, you know."

Another young man came over and joined us. This one was tall, with unruly hair and jug-handle ears.

"Steady claimed he was quitting drinking for us," he said. "I know enough about alcoholism to know that's not a very encouraging sign. If you're going to quit, it has to be for yourself, not somebody else."

"Oh, he was only joking, Paul," Greta said. "He only meant the play would flop without him at the piano."

"This is Paul Boone," Sam said to me, "our hero in the melodrama and Greta's dance partner in the oleos. They make beautiful music together—on stage," he added.

Greta's boyfriend Rick, who'd just returned with her coffee, glared down at Sam, as if Sam had meant something by that, then draped his free arm across her shoulders again.

Sam reached up and picked a necklace off Greta's chest and examined it with raised eyebrows, turning it this way and that. It was made of stones and wood, the wood with vaguely Native American–like patterns burned into it.

"What is this, Greta?" he asked. "Some kind of fetish you wear to ward off hostile reviews? It's heavy too—keeps you grounded, no doubt."

"A fan gave it to me," she said, taking it from him and looking down at it with a smile.

"Her mother," Rick said with a grin. He looked like a fraternity man, altogether too sleek for Greta.

"That's not funny!" she flared at him.

"Sorry!" Slightly red in the face, he looked at his watch and said, "Don't you have a biology class in a few minutes? You're going to have to hurry to make it."

"So I'll be late," she said huffily. "So big deal." Back to Sam, she said, "For my ballad after the first act, can you take it down a third? Steady played it for me in D. You can transpose, can't you?"

"Of course I can," Sam said with an offended sniff.

"And unless you pick up the tempo a little in the dance numbers, Steady's prediction that we'd flop without him will probably come true," she went on.

"Yes, Greta," Sam said meekly.

"Ciao," she said to me as she turned and walked away, with Rick half a step behind. I noticed that Paul seemed to consider following them, then shrugged and found another table.

When they were out of earshot, Sam shook his head and sighed. "Greta's in disguise. She's running away from herself, but since she doesn't know who she is, she doesn't know which direction to go. With luck, she'll take a wrong turn and come face-to-face with herself someday, and like what she sees."

I didn't reply for a minute, just watched until Greta disappeared out the door.

"What's she got on you?" I asked, turning back to Sam with a smile.

"Got . . . ?"

" 'Yes, Greta,' " I said, imitating the meek way he'd behaved toward her. Sam isn't naturally meek.

"Oh, that—she's got talent. You know I'll take anything from somebody with talent. She's especially good at comedy, but now that you don't have to look like Liz Taylor or Katharine Hepburn to get serious roles, she could star in drama too—on stage, at least. With a break or two she could go a long way."

"It would be nice to have a future like that," I said.

"I wish she thought so," Sam said, "but her parents are pressuring her to abandon the footlights for the dentist's chair. That rather dreary chap you saw with her is a dental student and Greta's supposed to become a dentist herself, marry him, and together they'll create a dental dynasty. Somehow I don't see it as a musical, do you, Peggy?"

"She didn't seem particularly fond of him."

"I hope you're right. But she'll probably marry him anyway, to please her mother. I'm doing all I can to break them up. I've banned dental students from rehearsals, for example, and am trying to fan the flames of passion between her and Paul Boone. Maybe some of Paul's determination to succeed as an actor will rub off on Greta."

I got back to business. "You were telling me how Greta put you on to Steadman George when you needed a pianist last year," I said.

"Yes. She'd heard him play at various venues around town and gave him a strong recommendation. I hired him after one audition, despite his somewhat dissolute appearance. He was a genius of sorts, Peggy, and very soon he and his piano playing became an integral part of the show. By the end of the summer, he had a following of his own— people who came just to see and hear him. So naturally I hired him for this year's production too."

"How'd he happen to be living on the Showboat?"

"Before I took over the summer Showboat productions," he said, "it was the custom that the director lived on the boat in the summers himself—to keep an eye on it, you know."

Sam looked down at himself with obvious pleasure. "But do I look like the sort of man to live on a paddle wheel boat? Of course not. So last year I hired a student to live on it."

He shuddered at some memory. "The boat was lucky to survive. So this year, I thought I could kill two birds with one stone: get a night watchman and get George out of the seedy little apartment he was living in and away from its various allures. My scheme worked," he added, "until last night."

He glanced at his watch, got up with a noisy sigh. "I have work to do before show time," he said, "trying to transpose one of Greta's songs and speed up the dances a little."

As we walked to the door, I asked him where the apartment was that George had lived in before he moved onto the Showboat.

"It's above that Italian restaurant just around the corner on Central," he said, "the one with a piece of the true cross over the jukebox and a giant color photograph of the Pope."

"The Via Appia," I said. "I eat there often."

"I'm not surprised."

Outside, I asked him how things were going with him

and Christian. Their relationship poses a big problem, since Christian is also the U football team's star quarterback and he wants to play professional football after he graduates next June. The professional scouts flock to his every game. It goes without saying that he's deep in the closet, where he plans to stay until he wins the Super Bowl, at which point he plans to come out and take Sam with him to Disney World.

Sam shrugged, stuffed his hands in his pockets. "Terrific," he said morosely, "a match made in heaven and played out in a fishbowl! We can't live together, of course, so Christian has to sneak over to my place if he wants to spend the night or just sit around holding hands and talking; sundry cheerleaders and other women on campus lust after him and wonder why he doesn't return the favor—but everything's just terrific, Peggy. Thanks for asking."

I gave him a hug, said I was sorry to hear that.

"If he'd just give up his idiotic football dream and go into theater," Sam said, "he could be a star."

"What'll you do if he gets a big contract with a pro team," I asked, "and has to move away from here?"

"Drop everything and go with him, of course. Wouldn't you?"

I told him I didn't want to talk about it.

Sixteen

It was a little after five when I rode my bike back to Central and down to the Via Appia, a couple of blocks from the Boardinghouse. I chained my bike to a lamppost, then stood at the bottom of the narrow flight of stairs between the restaurant and the Laundromat next door to it, staring up into the darkness where Steadman George had lived before moving onto the Showboat.

I asked myself what I thought I was doing, trying to turn a perfectly straightforward death into a mystery. What was odd about Steadman George falling off the wagon? He'd been a heavy drinker all his life and he wasn't, as far as I knew, in AA or getting any other support in his efforts to quit drinking. As Paul Boone had mentioned, he was trying to hook other people—me among them—into his efforts to quit, and that's never a good sign.

If I could find him, the man who'd been with George during his last hours could clear everything up for me in a minute, including explaining to me how he'd happened to wash his own glass and put it away before leaving the boat, if that's what he'd, in fact, done.

I walked up the creaking stairs to the second floor. The poorly lit hall smelled of insect spray and the herbed and spiced tomato sauce for which the Via Appia was roundly scorned by the cognoscenti and loved by me. Loud rock music was rattling the walls beside the first door I came to. I knocked and over the din heard a young man's voice call out, "*Entrez vous,* Haynes!"

I opened the door a crack and hollered into the wave of sound that washed over me, "It's not Haynes."

"Better than Haynes—*une fille!*"

It was a student lying on a sagging bed, holding a can of beer in one hand, a French textbook in the other. A CD player with wires leading to big speakers sat on the floor next to him. He gave me a look, immediately saw that he'd been mistaken about me, and said something that he probably meant to be, "*Alors, une vielle dame!* If you're here to save my soul, *madame,* forget it," he added. "I've already sold it to the Devil for a passing grade in intermediate *français.*"

"He's not keeping his part of the bargain," I shouted back. "For starters, he should've told you that French isn't pronounced the way it looks to the American eye."

"Never?"

"Never."

"Maybe the teacher covered that, one of the days I missed. So what can I do for you?"

"I'm looking for somebody who knew a man named Steadman George. He used to live up here somewhere."

He took a swallow of beer and wiped the foam off his upper lip with the back of his hand before answering. "You're the second person who's asked me that question today," he shouted. "I can only tell you what I told him, which is that I don't know anyone who would know anyone named Steadman George. However, down the hall somewhere there's an old trog who looks like he might know half a dozen Steadman Georges. I'm only here for summer school, and my friends all have names like Buzz and Cody and Wildguy. Except for Haynes, of course, who's in accounting."

"Thanks," I said, and backed out, glad to be closing the door behind me. I recognized the band as one that was making megabucks on songs of suicidal despair that shattered eardrums. I've never thought youth was wasted on the young; what other age group would have the stomach for it?

Nobody answered at the next two doors, but the one at the end of the hall opened after I'd knocked awhile and a man of about seventy stood in it glaring at me.

"Yes?" he asked, looking me up and down.

"I'm looking for somebody who knew Steadman George when he lived here."

He was barefoot, wearing baggy dark trousers with dangling suspenders and a sleeveless cotton undershirt. There was shaving cream on his face and he smelled of aftershave lotion.

"Another reporter? You're all just a pack of vultures! You wouldn't give poor old Steady the time of day when he was alive, but now he's dead, you're all lining up for a piece of him. Which piece you after?"

"I don't know yet," I said with a smile. "What piece tastes best, you think?"

"You want a nice pickled taste, try his liver!" he retorted. "What paper you with? The guy who was here this morning was from the *Tribune*—Dave Brown, his name was, although it should've been Gray since he was gray all over. If I hadn't already heard about Steady on the radio, him showing up at my door with the news of Steady's demise might've given me a fatal seizure."

"I'm a cop," I said, offering him my shield. He took it, groped for the glasses that were on top of his head, then scrutinized it.

As he handed it back, he looked me up and down over the top of the glasses. "Peggy O'Neill, huh? My late wife's name was Meg—short for Margaret, but she didn't like bein' called that, so I only did it when I was mad at her. My name's Woodrow—but everybody calls me Woody. You're plainclothes, huh? Carryin'?"

"Carrying?" I repeated. "Oh. No, not now."

"Good, 'cause I don't like guns. I oughtta frisk you, just to make sure you're tellin' the truth. Your eyes're set a little too close together for you to be completely trustworthy, missy, but your pointy nose spells basic human decency. You want to come in? I was just getting ready to go out for a bite to eat, but they'll hold my table."

"Thanks," I said, as he stood back to let me in and then shut the door. Even with a couple of apartments between us, I could hear the bass thudding of the summer student's stereo nihilism.

The room was small and dark, with an old braided rug on the floor in an apple green that matched the wallpaper.

Woody went over and sat on the bed and gestured to a straight-backed chair for me next to a table beneath a window.

"Murder," he said, drawing the word out ominously.

"What?"

"Old Steady got himself murdered, did he? Not surprised."

"Why not?"

"He'd been into a little bit of everything in his time—to hear him talk, anyway. Slowed up a lot the last couple of years, though. Age catches up with us all—as you'll find out soon enough, young lady," he added with grim satisfaction. "Take me, for example. Who'd of dreamed I'd come to this? I thought Steady fell off the boat and drowned. An accident."

"That's what it looks like," I said.

"Figures," Woody said without missing a beat. "I visited him a couple of times on that old tub and I warned him it was dangerous, but he wouldn't listen. So what's your interest? You think maybe somebody pushed him overboard?" He got up off the bed. "You don't mind if I get dressed while we talk, do you? I got a heavy date for after dinner."

"No, go right ahead," I said. "You've got a little shaving cream in your left ear. You said he'd been into a little bit of everything. Meaning what?"

"Nothing, probably." He began putting on a pair of battered black shoes that were polished to a high gloss. "To hear him talk, he had money in bank accounts in the Bahamas, he could find you a hit man or an untraceable gun in less than an hour, if you could pay the price or if he liked you—you name it. Most of it was probably bunk, but who knows? Some of what he said must've been true."

As Woody rambled on, I studied him, wondering if he could be the man I'd seen with George on the Showboat, but it was impossible to be sure one way or the other. He was tall enough, but seemed frailer and I didn't think he had as much hair. The hair of the man on the boat, as I recalled it, had seemed long and, in the light of the cabin, a kind of steel gray.

"You say you visited him on the Showboat sometimes?"

I asked, and watched Woody's face to see his reaction.

"A couple of times," he replied. "But we never fought," he added quickly. "We were friends."

"Were you there last night?"

His face fell into sad lines. "I woulda been, if he'd've had me, but he was too busy—too busy gettin' drunk and dyin'."

"What do you mean, you would've been there?" I asked.

"I mean I gave him a call right after the play—he was always askin' his friends to come and visit him on the boat. But last night he said he was busy. He was workin' on a project, he said—that's the word he used, 'project'—and needed to be alone. He sounded pretty excited, said he was gonna make enough money off his project to get a band together and cut a demo tape. Steady never made a record, you know. It's too bad, 'cause he was as good as a lot of musicians who do."

"Did he say anything about having company?"

Woody shook his head. "Like I said, he said he wanted to be alone to work on his project."

Maybe he'd worked on a project, but it hadn't been alone.

"Somebody was with him around midnight last night," I said. "Somebody who probably likes Wild Turkey."

"It wasn't me," Woody said. "I'm a beer man myself. Anyway, Steady was tryin' to go off the sauce. You tellin' me he was drunk?"

"Yes."

"That's too bad," he said, struggling into a white dress shirt that needed pressing. "I thought he was serious about quitting, on account of his liver. He said to me one day last week, he said, 'Woody, I'm too young to be lyin' there starin' up at the dark side of the lawn.' I told him he oughtta check out AA or something, instead of trying to quit on his own, but he said death was motivation enough. He said he still had a lot of music in him."

Woody began knotting a powder-gray tie with a pattern that looked like 1950s TV sets all over it, his long gnarled fingers working awkwardly.

"How long were you friends?" I asked, going over and

adjusting his threadbare collar so it covered the tie in back.

"My wife used to do that," he said, shaking his head. "Where'd the time go? You married?"

"No."

He looked me up and down. "You should be. What're you gonna have for memories when you get my age, Peggy O'Neill?"

He raised a protective hand, as if I were going to hit him. "I'm old," he went on quickly. "Just pretend I didn't say that. How long did I know Steady? Just since I retired from the U and moved into this dump—four, five years ago. Seems longer, somehow. I was a sanitation engineer, y'know. I was a janitor when I started out, but I got promoted, first to custodian, then to sanitation engineer.

"I didn't always live here, either, of course," he went on. "Owned my own home—my castle. I just moved here after Meg died. Why not? Who needs a castle, when your queen's dead? Besides, it keeps me young, stomping down the hall at the start of every semester to pound on the kids' doors and make 'em tone down that noise they call music.

"Anyways, after I moved in here, Steady and I struck up an acquaintance and we started going to the Getaway together—you know the place?"

I nodded.

"It was his hangout, y'see, and he used to play there in years past. He still did when the regular pianist was sick or something, although he hasn't been in the place since he quit drinking. Too much temptation, he said. After he moved onto the Showboat, he invited me to come visit him and I did sometimes."

He sighed, then picked up a dark blazer. I got up and held it for him as he slipped into it.

"Thanks," he said, giving me a grin of old, crooked teeth. "You wouldn't marry me, would you—let me make an honest woman of you? Or would I have to fight some other feller for the honor?"

"Too many to count," I said. "I'd like to find the guy who was with Steadman last night," I went on.

"You would, huh? Why? Why're you so interested in Steady, young lady?"

"I want to be sure he died the way the medical examiner

thinks he did," I answered. "The police aren't going to try to make something a murder that looks as much like an accident as this does. They've got too many obvious murders to deal with for that."

"Especially when it's a guy like Steady, right? Who doesn't make waves in high places when he falls into the river."

"Right," I said, though I wasn't sure about the image.

Woody nodded. "I'm with you, Peggy. What can I do to help?"

"You can give me the names of people who knew him. I'd like to talk to some of them."

"That's easy. I'm gonna tell you the same thing I told that reporter who was here this morning: talk to Vicki and the Waiters at the Getaway. They've known Steady a lot longer'n I have. Vicki has, anyway. They go way back."

"Vicki and the waiters at the Getaway?"

He chuckled. "Yeah—Waiters with a capital w. And it's not a singin' group, either. They're out-of-work musicians who sit around and wait for gigs. It's their idea of a joke. You know, 'They also serve who only sit and wait.' "

"It's 'stand and wait.' " I said.

"Not the way Vicki and the Waiters do it," he said. "They all played with Steady, one time or another. Vicki used to be a singer, and I sorta gathered there'd been something between her and Steady a long time ago, but she always shut him up when he tried to bring it up. Steady liked 'em young, y'see, and Vicki's no longer what you'd call young, exactly. Actually, I don't think he liked 'em at all anymore, he was just trying to keep up appearances."

Woody crossed the room to the door and I followed him out into the hall. As we walked past the student's room with the blaring rock music, Woody banged on the kid's door. "*Entrez vous, s'il vous plaît!*" the student called, but we'd started down the stairs by then.

Outside, I asked Woody if he thought I could find the Waiters and Vicki at the Getaway that night.

"Can you find the Pope in Italy? They're there most nights." He grinned slyly. "But they're a closedmouthed lot. They wouldn't tell you nothing unless they trusted you—especially if they knew you was a cop. If you want,

I could probably find the time to come with you. They'd be more likely to talk freely if they knew you were a friend of a friend.''

"Sounds good," I said. "When?" I was getting ready to drop from lack of sleep, but it was too early to go to bed yet.

"Lemme check my calendar," Woody said, "see if I'm free tonight." He groped in his jacket pocket, came out empty. "I left it in my other coat," he said, "but I'm available."

"I thought you had a date."

"I do now." He grinned again, the faded eyes under the gray shrubbery sparkling. "I'll meet you right here at nine on the button. We'll go dutch, of course."

"Nah," I said, "I can write it off as a business expense."

"Well, in that case . . ."

I unchained my bike from the parking meter and walked with Woody around the corner in the direction of the University. I asked him where he was going for dinner.

He pointed down the street. "See those golden arches? Just under them. The maître d' always saves me a choice table. It's nice to eat where they know your tastes and treat you like a human being. Besides, I work there some afternoons—not to supplement my Social Security and retirement income, or anything like that—I do it to stay young.''

Seventeen

It was almost noon and not many people had come to the fair yet, so there was time for Swallow and Bernie to wander around and check out other booths. Bernie knew some of the other concessionaires from fairs in the Southwest, but not as many as Swallow, who seemed to know everybody. There were artists and craftspeople of all kinds: potters, painters and photographers, woodworkers, silver and goldsmiths and glassblowers. A lot of jewelry makers too; most of their work was more stylish than Bernie's, she had to admit, but nobody had a selection of beads, findings, and feathers that could hold a candle to hers—Swallow had been right about that. There were also a few psychics besides Swallow: astrologers and tarot readers, palm readers, and even a man who diagnosed physical ailments just by sensing the heat your body gave off with his hands. He looked like a used-car salesman or television evangelist to Bernie and talked like one too: fast and oozy.

Bernie neither believed nor disbelieved in any of the New Age stuff. She knew a lot of people who did believe, though, people she respected, like Swallow. She knew that their beliefs were no stranger than what the organized religions preached. The only difference she could see was that the New Age people didn't use their beliefs to set one group of people above and against another, and she'd never met a pyschic who threatened nonbelievers with eternal damnation. That didn't make it true, necessarily. Just better.

She thought briefly of the minister at home, a man she'd been afraid of. She thought of the Reverend Mason—Pastor Ted—a man she should have been afraid of.

A woman wearing cotton pants, a sweatshirt, and a sweatband, all three in violently colorful tie-dye patterns, came up to them when they'd returned to their booths.

"Who's your friend?" she asked Swallow.

Swallow introduced her to Bernie. Roxie, a tie-dye artist, was taller than Bernie and as thin as a rail, with gray hair that looked as though it had been spun by a spider on speed, and fiery light blue eyes.

"I like your jewelry," she told Bernie gruffly. "Before the fair's over I'm going to buy something you've made. Or we could trade. You like tie-dye?"

Bernie didn't, actually, but she was too polite to say so, so she said yes.

"No, you don't," Roxie said, "you're just being polite. Screw it. I'll pay, although I could probably design something that'd be right for you. Serious, like the colors of your aura when it's not so muddy."

"Roxie does aural readings too," Swallow explained to Bernie.

"Muddy?" Fred Foster, who'd come over to visit, repeated.

Roxie looked him up and down as though about to say something about his aura too, then turned back to Bernie. "When life's going well for you, dearie, your aura's a shapely thing of great beauty—shades of blue, some indigo—but at the moment it's muddy. There's too much going on in your head and it's kind of bottom-heavy too. Looks like a pear."

"My head does?" Bernie asked.

"Your aura." As she walked away, Roxy called back over her shoulder, "I'll clear and balance your chakras in exchange for a pair of earrings!"

"You don't need your chakras cleared, whatever that means," Fred said to Bernie, "you just need to give up your nomadic ways and settle down."

"He's got something there," Swallow said.

When Fred had gone back to his own booth, Swallow went on, "You still haven't decided what to do about your daughter, have you?"

Bernie nodded. She *was* feeling oppressed and her thoughts were confused, so no wonder her aura looked muddled! She thought about Greta constantly, didn't know what she was going to do, thought about Linda Markham and her pleas to Bernie not to upset the idyllic life they were all living now. But why would it upset Mrs. Markham's and Greta's life anyway?

She wondered if she'd made a mistake coming back to Minnesota. She felt as though she were being watched, felt that she should be hiding. Why? Was some higher power telling her she was wrong for having come back?

Eighteen

Woody, wearing a white linen suit, was waiting for me at the curb when I pulled up at nine on the button, as he'd put it.

"Before you say anything," he said, getting into my car, "I want to tell you I know the suit's a little yellow in places, and frayed at the cuffs too. But the Getaway's dark, so it won't show. There's no dress code anyway. Spiffy car. New?"

"Almost. You look pretty spiffy yourself."

"But not so new," he replied.

The Getaway is located about half a mile downstream from the New Campus, at the end of a street that stops just before it falls into the river. It had begun life as a bar for the workers in the factories that, together with ratty student housing, make up the neighborhood. Later it became a good place to hear jazz, attracting a highbrow crowd that drove the workers away. Now the clientele is a mixture of students, faculty, and just about anybody else looking for a dark, not-too-noisy place to drink and carry on.

Woody held the door for me and we stepped inside. "Stay close to me," he whispered out of the corner of his mouth. "They know me here."

A bar ran the length of the front of the room with a grimy mural depicting how the river had looked a hundred years ago. In the back was a small dance floor with an upright piano next to it and a small raised stage behind that. A middle-aged woman with an enormous blond beehive hairdo was at the piano, a cigarette smoldering in an ashtray on its top, playing softly.

"Many's the night I've sat here listenin' to old Steady playin' that piano," Woody said, shaking his head sadly. "He'd still come in sometimes, you know, when he had the night off from the Showboat and play if they'd let him. Or he did until he stopped drinkin'. He'd put a glass up on the piano and before the night was over it'd be full of money—greenbacks."

I followed him as he made his way to a table in a corner in back. He paused behind a woman seated at it, put his hand on her shoulder.

She glanced up at him and smiled and gave him a cheek to peck. "Pull up a stool, honey," she said in a husky voice. "Who's your friend?"

"Vicki, Xerxes, Floyd, I'd like to introduce you to Peggy O'Neill," Woody said. "Peggy and I are just friends," he added.

"Yeah, I bet," Vicki said. "How come you don't dress up like that for us? Ain't we 'just friends' too?"

He had the grace to blush.

"Any friend of Woody's," Xerxes said to me.

Vicki was about forty-five, her hair a brassy henna, cheekbones like nobs, lips a smear of red that matched her nails. Floyd was a tall, thin man wearing dark glasses in radiant blue frames, and Xerxes was short and fat with a small white mustache under his pug nose. Floyd was a bassist and Xerxes a drummer, or vice versa.

"You're just in time, Woody," Vicki said as she moved over to make room for us at the table. "We're holding a wake for old Steady."

"Actually," Xerxes said, "the wake's for the money he owed us."

They all laughed. "Don't suppose he mentioned us in his will," Floyd said morosely.

"There was a reporter here a little while ago," Vicki told Woody. "You just missed him. He told us he was a feature writer for the *Trib* and doin' a piece on Steady. He said you sicced him on us. Thanks a million!"

"Not," growled Floyd.

"Is he still here?" I asked.

"He was a few minutes ago," Floyd said. "At the bar."

"I'd like to talk to him," I said. "Could you point him

out to me?'' I thought it would be interesting to see what kind of piece he was writing on George.

They all looked around the room. ''That's him,'' Vicki said, ''coming out of the men's room.''

I looked where Vicki was pointing. A tall gray-haired man was making his way through the crowd to the front door.

''Yeah,'' Woody said, ''that's the guy who talked to me this morning. Said his name was Brown but it should've been Gray.''

''I'll be right back,'' I said, and got up and went after him.

He was walking up the street away from the bar when I got outside.

''Excuse me,'' I called after him. He paused and turned and watched me approach.

He was tall—over six feet, I guessed—with long legs and arms. Although the streetlight was behind him, I thought his eyes were close-set and his mouth wide and thin in a bony face.

''I understand you're a feature writer for the *Tribune*,'' I said, ''doing a story on Steadman George.''

''That's right,'' he answered. ''You knew him?'' His voice was curiously light and toneless.

''A little. I thought I knew all the feature writers on the paper,'' I added. ''You must be new.''

''What's your interest in George?'' he asked, ignoring the implied question.

''It's personal, I guess. I'm the campus cop who found his body and, as I said, I knew him a little. I'm not entirely happy with the way he died.''

He gave a short laugh. ''Probably not as unhappy about it as he was! He drowned, didn't he? It was an accident—wasn't it?''

''That's what the police think—so far, at least,'' I said. ''But you don't?''

''I haven't made up my mind yet.''

''Why?''

''He was drunk when he died, but I thought he was still okay with trying to quit drinking, the last time I saw him. There was somebody with him around the time he must've drowned. I'd like to talk to whoever it was, find out what happened."

He stared at me a moment, as if expecting more, then shrugged and started to turn away.

"What's your angle going to be?" I asked him.

"Angle?"

"For the article you're writing."

"Oh." He shrugged. "George's musical life, what it was like to be a jazz musician around here twenty years ago—that kind of thing."

"Have you talked to many people who knew him?"

"Not yet. I've only just started, you know." He glanced at his watch. "Good night."

He turned to walk away. As he did, the streetlight behind him threw his head in profile—the profile of the man I'd seen in George's cabin: the same long nose and prominent chin, the same gray hair.

I watched him walk down the street. There were cars parked on both sides of it. About a quarter of the way to the end of the block he glanced back, then stopped and turned, stood in the middle of the sidewalk, his hands still in his pockets, as if waiting for me.

I walked down the street toward him, since there were plenty of people out and about.

When I got within a few feet of him, he said quietly, "If you're going my way, we can walk together."

"How far are you going?" I asked.

"Back to the U," he replied. "My car's parked over there."

He could've been telling the truth, I supposed, although if he really was a journalist who'd come to the Getaway tonight to interview Vicki and the Waiters, it didn't make any sense to park so far away. More likely his car was one of these on the street next to us and he didn't want me to see it and get the license number.

"You were the man on the Showboat last night with Steadman George," I said.

His face froze. "You're wrong."

"What's your name?"

"Dave Brown. What's yours?"

Why not tell him, I thought, since I'd already told him

I was a campus cop? I'm not in the phone book anyway.

"Peggy O'Neill," I said, and added, "Maybe you'd let me see some ID, just to satisfy my curiosity."

"I'm not in the business of satisfying your curiosity, Peggy O'Neill," he replied, as if tasting my name. Then he said, "Good night again," and turned and walked away, not hurrying.

Nineteen

I waited just inside the bar for a few minutes, peering out through the grimy window in the door to see if he would return for his car, but he didn't. Either I'd been wrong and he'd walked from the U as he'd said, or he was a very cautious man. I went back and joined Woody and his friends.

"You catch him?" Woody asked.

"Yes, but he wasn't very informative," I said, slumping into my chair.

A waitress hovered meaningfully and I ordered a Coke. I knew I'd have to pay three dollars for it, it would be flat, and there wouldn't be enough ice.

"Woody tells us you're a cop at the U," Floyd said, looking me over curiously, "and you found Steady's body. That right?"

"That's right," I said.

"Somethin' suspicious about Steady's death?" Vicki asked.

"The police don't think so," I said.

"The cops are right, for once," Xerxes pronounced authoritatively. "He was mixing drugs and booze and fell overboard and drowned. Steady killed Steady."

Maybe he was right, but it's possible to drown people without leaving marks, especially if they're too drunk to know what's happening. I'd just talked to someone I thought was capable of that.

I told them that I was pretty sure I'd seen the man who called himself Dave Brown on the Showboat with George around the time he must have drowned.

"Gettin' a head start on his article, huh?" Xerxes asked, raising an eyebrow.

"If he is a journalist," I answered.

"I sorta wondered about him myself when he was sittin' there talkin' to us," Vicki said. "He didn't know who Mc-Coy Tyner was and he thought Coleman Hawkins played piano. So why would he be writing about somebody in the jazz business?"

"He gave me the willies," Xerxes said. "He might've been a crime reporter once—or a war correspondent—and the experience burned him up inside—turned him to stone. He's seen things humans aren't supposed to see and now nothing really concerns him much anymore."

"Xerxes is a poet," Floyd said to me. "A *published* poet."

"The question is," Xerxes went on, waving aside with a plump hand any adulation I might be tempted to give him, "who is this guy and what does he want? Could old Steady have been involved in something dangerous, and this guy, this so-called journalist, is a hit man?"

Woody spoke up, telling them what he'd told me, that when he'd wanted to visit George last night George had said he was too busy. He was working on a project that was going to make him some money.

Vicki and the Waiters laughed.

"Steady was always working on some project that was gonna make him a lot of money," Vicki said. "Then he was gonna get a band together and cut a demo."

"And we were all gonna be on it with him," Floyd said mournfully.

"Were these projects of his usually outside the law?" I asked.

"Mostly they were just pipe dreams," Vicki said evasively. "'Moonspin,' he called 'em."

"Old Steady wouldn't hurt a fly," Xerxes added, "but he'd probably try to sell ones that were already dead to a blind baker as raisins."

"Maybe that's what he tried to do with this project," Floyd said. "Except the baker wasn't as blind as Steady thought."

"Or the flies as dead," Vicki said gloomily.

"So what did this so-called journalist ask you about?"
I said.

"Bernie," Floyd said, then tilted back his head and drained his glass.

"What!" I almost jumped out of my chair, and splashed Coke all over me.

"What do you mean, what?" Floyd asked.

"Who's Bernie?" I demanded.

Floyd looked at me as though I were about to attack him. "Beats me," he said. "I never heard of her."

The others all said the same thing.

"Did I just imagine it," I said, struggling to speak calmly, "or did you, Floyd, say 'Bernie'?"

"Yeah, I did. This so-called journalist, he told us Bernie was a gal Steady'd known back in the seventies. He wanted to interview her because they'd been lovers, he said, so he thought she'd be able to tell him a lot about Steady's life back then. None of us could recall her, though."

"I've known a couple of Bernies in my time," Vicki said, "both male and female, but none of 'em was connected with Steady that I can remember. I think somebody must've given the guy a bum steer."

"Of course," Xerxes mused, pursing fat lips beneath his little mustache, "this Bernie could've been a one-night stand. But that would hardly have qualified her as an expert on Steady in the seventies."

"It was kind of insulting," Floyd put in. "We all knew Steady in the seventies—except Woody, of course—and we could've told the guy a lot about what was goin' on in music here then, but he seemed to lose interest in us the moment we told him we didn't know any Bernies connected to Steady."

"Then he asked us if we could give him the names of any of Steady's other old pals," Vicki said.

"Did you?"

"Nah," she answered. "By that time, we'd decided we didn't like him so we made like little clams. He went away pissed off, probably thinkin' we could've told him more if we'd wanted to."

As Woody poured himself another glass of beer from the pitcher, he shot me a glance and said, "So who's Bernie,

Peggy, and why are you and this creepy Mr. Brown so interested in her? Don't deny it," he added before I could say anything. "You want me to go get some more napkins so you can dry yourself off?"

I didn't want to tell these people the story Steadman George had told me about Bernie and her child. I liked them, but I doubted Bernie would want her story told to strangers in a bar.

"She's just somebody George knew," I said, "who came back into town recently and got in touch with him."

"A real mystery woman, huh?" Xerxes said, giving me a skeptical look. "Apparently Peggy can make like a clam too, when she wants."

"She's playin' her cards close to her chest, the way a good cop does," Woody told him sternly. "She gives out information only on a 'need to know' basis. Right, Peggy?"

"Right," I said.

Vicki was destroying a circle of condensation from her glass with a long, garishly colored fingernail. Now she looked up at me with an odd smile.

"Funny," she said. "An old friend of Steady's called me up the other afternoon out of the blue. She said somebody she hadn't heard from in a long time had shown up at her door, wanting to know where she could get hold of Steady. She didn't say who she was or why she wanted him, though. I told her he was livin' on the Showboat and gave her his number." She glanced up at me. "You suppose that could've been Bernie?"

"When was this?" I asked.

"Monday night."

It was sometime after midnight that night that George had told me Bernie's story.

I asked Vicki if she'd give me the woman's name.

"I'm not sure I can," she said. "But first, Peggy, before I try, prove to us that you're who and what you say you are. Woody's already dropped one ringer on us tonight," she added dryly.

Woody hung his head.

I dug my shield out of my purse and handed it to her. She studied it a moment with the others peering over to see it too, then nodded and gave it back.

"Her name's Sue Ann," she said. "Used to be Maslowski or something like that twenty years ago, but she got married and took her husband's name. Kept it too after the divorce, according to Steady, on account of it had more class. I can't remember what it is, though. She's head buyer for that hoity-toity women's clothing store, Raggs."

"Naylor," Floyd said.

"Yeah, that's right," Vicki said. "Naylor. Sue Ann Naylor."

"Steady talked about Sue Ann a lot," Floyd explained to me with a melancholy smile. "She was the great love of his life."

"Crap!" Vicki snapped, and ordered another pitcher of beer.

"We could've told our friend the journalist about her," Xerxes said, "but we didn't." He grinned fiendishly.

Although I was close to dropping from lack of sleep, I forced myself to stay another hour or so for Woody's sake. My attention wandered and, at one point, I saw somebody I recognized come in. The short-cropped cherry-red hair, which stood out even in the garish smoky light of the bar, was unmistakable: it was Greta Markham, the Showboat actress who'd introduced Steadman George to Sam.

She stopped just inside the door and looked all around until she spotted whomever it was she was meeting, then made her way quickly over to him. As she got there, the actor Sam had introduced to me as Paul Boone slid out of a booth and gave her a hug. She averted her mouth just in time to catch a kiss on the cheek, which I didn't think had been his intention.

They sat across from each other in the booth, elbows on the table, heads in their hands, faces close together across the table. Then his lips moved and a moment later they both burst out laughing.

I wondered where the sleek young frat man was I'd seen her with at the Boardinghouse that afternoon, the future dentist Greta's parents, according to Sam, wanted her to marry. There was nothing sleek about Boone at all, with his lanky frame, bony face, and tousled hair. Sam had said he and Greta made beautiful music together on stage. I wondered what they were doing here together. They both had very mobile faces and I enjoyed watching them, although I couldn't hear a word.

Woody leaned over to me and whispered, "I'm ready to leave whenever you are."

"Okay," I said.

"How 'bout one chorus of 'Peggy O'Neil' before we go?" Xerxes announced. "I'll see if Wanda knows it. If not, we'll do it a cappella."

Before I could stop him, he was out of his chair and waddling over to the pianist. He whispered in her ear, then dropped a bill in the bowl on top of the piano and came back to our table.

I sat there, my sparkliest smile on my face, and listened as Woody and the Waiters sang the song my father had named me after. I thought Vicki was faking it.

My father had been a charming drunk who must have been a lot like Steadman George, I thought, except he didn't have musical ability to waste so he wasted his family instead and then himself.

As Woody and I were leaving the bar, Greta spotted me and called out, "Hey! It's Sam's friend, the cop."

I went over and said hello, surprised that she recognized me.

"Haven't seen you here before," she said. "Is it on account of Steady? He was a regular here."

"Yes," I said. "I was talking to some of his old pals."

I noticed she was still wearing traces of makeup from the night's performance. It didn't clash with anything else she had on, including the necklace Sam had remarked on that, apparently, a fan had given her, or her mother—I wasn't sure which, from the conversation in the Boardinghouse.

"I'm gonna miss Steady," she said, her face darkening. "I've known the guy a long time. He and my dad go back a long ways together, both having been in showbiz. I know you're only supposed to speak well of the dead, but it really pissed me off the way Steady wasted his talent. God gives you something like that, you should take care of it."

"Yeah," Paul Boone added, staring hard at her. "There

oughtta be a special place in hell for people who waste their talent.''

Greta's face turned red and she glared at him. ''Oh, shut up!'' she said.

I waved good-bye, happy to let Woody drag me out of there.

He protested all the way, but I insisted on accompanying him up to his little apartment. Dave Brown—if that was his name—had spooked me a little, and I wanted to be sure he hadn't come to talk to Woody some more.

Then I went home and slept for the first time in about thirty-five hours.

FRIDAY

Twenty

When Stan opened his door to his brother Friday morning, he was startled to see how pale he looked. There were also dark rings around his eyes and his hair was uncombed.

"Two visits in three days," Stan said. "I'm honored, brother." Ted had never set foot in Stan's apartment before Wednesday when he'd come begging for help—you'd think he was ashamed of him or something. Now that Stan thought about it, he was almost as well-kept a secret in his brother's life as Bernie! That would change, though. A lot of things would change, once he'd taken care of Bernie.

"Did you talk to—to Mr. George?" Ted asked, almost whispering, as he shut the door behind him.

" '*Mr.* George,' " Stan said. "How'd you know George was his last name, Ted?"

He felt like tormenting his brother a little. He'd failed to get anything out of the barflies at the Getaway last night, although he suspected they had information that could help him, and he had to take his frustration out on somebody. Ted would have to do, for now.

"There was an article in this morning's paper about a man—a musician—named Steadman George," Ted replied, sitting down on the edge of Stan's sofa. "He fell off the University's Showboat sometime Wednesday night or yesterday morning. The police think he drowned. Apparently he'd been drinking heavily. Was it the same man?"

His eyes searched his brother's face anxiously. The fact that he hadn't heard from George since his phone call on Wednesday was also cause for alarm. He'd said he was going to call yesterday with instructions for getting the money. Ted had waited in fear, unable to do anything, his heart pounding every time Marcie transferred a call to him.

"Yes, Ted," Stan said, handing his brother a cup of coffee, "the man who tried to blackmail you was named Steadman George and he lived on the University's Showboat."

"Did you—did you talk to him before he—before he drowned?"

Stan nodded. "He wasn't very helpful, though. As the newspaper said, he'd been drinking, and he was high on marijuana too." He laughed. "He even offered me some! However, I was able to find out that he lied to you when he told you Bernie didn't know where her daughter was."

"How? How'd you find that out?" Ted asked, staring at his brother in horror.

Stan gazed thoughtfully at his brother a moment before answering, even thought briefly of telling him the truth. "I didn't torture it out of him, Ted, if that's what you're thinking," he said.

He wondered what Ted would do if he told him what he'd done. Would his conscience allow him to live with it, or would he turn his brother in? Stan wouldn't bet money either way.

"Then . . . how? He just told you?"

Stan shook his head. "I saw them together—your child and her mother."

"Bernie and her daughter?" Ted yelped.

"That's another way of putting it," Stan said. "Your daughter's an actress, Ted."

He described the scene he'd witnessed between Bernie and Greta. There was something both terrible and funny in seeing his brother—the beloved pastor, the host of a popular Christian television program and the up-and-coming politician—sit there listening, his mouth open, pale and sweating with fear.

"Bernie just draped a necklace over the girl's head and turned and ran," Stan went on. "The girl obviously had no idea who she was, and Bernie didn't tell her. It was a very emotional scene, Ted. Too bad you weren't there to see it. Afterwards, your daughter laughed about it with her friends."

"Do you know her name?"

"Why? You want to meet her?"

"No!" Ted said quickly. Then, more softly, "No."

"No," Stan said, "I don't know her name."

He didn't know why he lied about it. It was just that, if push came to shove and he had to kill the girl too, he didn't want Ted seeing her name in the paper. Her death might be too much of a coincidence for even Ted to swallow, and that much knowledge wouldn't be good for a man who believed in concepts like good and evil.

He shook his head in mock admiration. "What a lucky man you are, brother! Two wonderful sons and now—a daughter! And look at me: unmarried and childless. Some people have all the luck."

"Stop it, Stan," Ted whispered, "please. That's enough."

He swallowed some of the coffee Stan had given him, winced at the bitterness of it. "I've got a sermon to write for Sunday," he cried, "letters to answer, an interview, and I've got to prepare for my cable program too. But how can I, with this hanging over my head?"

He got up and began pacing back and forth across the room. Stan stared out the window, waited.

"Maybe I should admit publicly what I did," Ted went on, "without mentioning the woman's name, of course. Then announce my resignation from the church. Wouldn't that be better than taking the risk of being exposed for a past indiscretion and tainting everything I've spent my life working for?"

"Sure," Stan said.

Ted spun around. "You mean that?"

"Better to step down than be hurled down."

"That's not what I meant!"

"Don't tell *me* what you meant!" Stan said, springing up. "We grew up together, Ted, remember? I know you. And anyway, what are you doing asking *me* for advice? Am I the pastor now?" He went over and put his face in his brother's and said, "What do *you* want to do, Ted?"

Ted backed away, up against the wall. He didn't recognize his brother; his face was as unreadable as a hard stone surface.

"I don't know," he whispered. "I don't know. What do you think Bernie's going to do? Is she going to tell the girl?"

He saw the disgust wash over his brother's face—his brother, who'd never created anything in his life, so how could he know how it felt to be faced with seeing everything he'd created destroyed for an indiscretion he'd committed twenty years ago!

He pulled himself together, went back to the couch, and sat down, forced himself to drink some more of the bitter coffee.

"What I mean," he said, "is that it would be irresponsible of me to subject myself and my family to the scorn of the media, lose any chance I have to make a difference in this state—and even lose my church and livelihood—if I don't have to. Don't you agree?"

"Yes, Ted, I do," Stan said, finding it hard to suppress a smile. "Before you do anything so drastic, I still want to talk to this woman and try to get a sense of who she is and what she wants. If I decide she's unreliable, or that she's going to tell her kid about you, well, then you can call in the media, get up in front of your congregation, and confess."

Ted shuddered and went cold at the thought.

"And she is a mother, after all," Stan went on. "Who knows? Maybe she shares your beliefs—about abortion, anyway. If she'd got an abortion the way you wanted her to—"

"I didn't want her to!" Mason flared. "I—"

"—where would her daughter be now? Or, if she isn't particularly Christian, maybe she'd accept money. She did once, didn't she?"

Ted took a deep breath, forced himself to look up and meet his brother's eyes. "All right," he said, nodding. "I won't do anything until you find out more about the woman."

"There's just one problem."

"What's that?"

"I don't know where to find her. Mr. George didn't seem to know, or wouldn't tell me."

"Then . . . ?"

"I'm going to have to look for her. I need to know everything you know about her. What's her last name, for starters?"

Ted shook his head. "I don't remember. Maybe I never did know. Patricia hired her. I just called her Bernie. That's all I know."

"Find out her last name. Ask Patricia."

"I can't do that."

"Why not?"

"What'll I give her as an excuse? She suspected something had happened between us then. This'll just bring it all back again."

"It *is* all back again."

Stan went over to his brother, stood looking down at him. "Talk to her, Ted," he said. "Tonight at dinner, over candles and wine. Mr. George called Bernie a runaway. Patricia wouldn't have hired her to take care of Matt without knowing something of her background. Ask her. You've always been good at making up convincing stories—that's why you're where you are."

Ted nodded and got to his feet slowly, like an automaton. He went to the door, opened it, and looked out as if expecting to see television cameras and reporters. He hesitated a moment and then came back into the room.

"Stan?" he whispered.

"Yes, Ted?"

"You didn't—I mean, George—Mr. George—" He couldn't finish it.

Stan couldn't contain his anger at his brother any longer. He stepped up to him. "What if it wasn't an accident, Ted?" he whispered. "What if I murdered him?"

His face and shirt drenched in sweat, Ted tried to say something, couldn't get the words out for a moment. Then: "Don't tease me, Stanley. This isn't a game."

"No, it's not, is it? It's your career, your life."

"What are you saying?"

Stan drew out the silence. "I mean Mr. George drowned, Ted," he said finally. "Was there anything in the paper that said otherwise?"

"No."

"Then?"

"All right, Stan. But promise me you won't hurt Bernie or her daughter. Promise me!"

"I promise, Ted," Stan said. His hands were clasped behind his back, fingers crossed. It was a habit he'd picked up as a child, when confronted like this by his older brother's moral squeamishness.

He didn't tell Ted about the woman he'd met—the campus cop who wasn't satisfied that George had drowned accidentally, and who thought she'd seen him on the boat. Knowing about her might tip the scales for Ted and send him straight to the media, where he'd confess his sins and beg for forgiveness—leaving Stan still out in the cold, or worse.

Twenty-one

Friday was hot, but there was a nice breeze off the river. The fair was jammed with people who'd kept Bernie busy, but around five there was a lull and she took the opportunity to sit down and rest her legs. She was considering whether she should close her booth early that night and go see the play again. It might help her make up her mind about what to do about Greta.

Sometimes when business was slow, she walked down to the river below the river road and gazed downstream to the Showboat. She imagined she could hear her daughter on stage singing and dancing to Steadman George's piano accompaniment.

Next to her, Swallow was in a deep discussion with Roxie, the tie-dye artist and psychic, about the correspondences between the tarot, the cabala, and the zodiac. Usually Bernie enjoyed eavesdropping on these kinds of arcane discussions, but not this afternoon. She couldn't concentrate, so she sat back in her chair and looked around at her surroundings, noticing them for the first time.

The Riverton Mall was surrounded by old abandoned flour mills, and she spent some time trying to make out the names and advertising slogans of some of the flour companies that were still visible on their sides in fading, peeling paint.

She caught sight of a blimp, its silver body glittering in the clear summer sky, and followed it with her eyes as it floated across the river to the fair. On its side it had the name of the Riverton Art Fair and the dates. It passed over a billboard on the roof of the building next to the mall.

Something about the billboard caught Bernie's eye. It featured the face of a man who looked oddly familiar to her. There was a sweet smile on his lips, and his eyes, warm and crinkling, seemed to gaze compassionately at her.

She read the message next to his face: PASTOR TED'S FIRESIDE HOUR, SUNDAY EVENINGS AT 7:30, CABLE CHANNEL 6.

It took a moment to register. Then she stood up with a muffled scream, the blood draining out of her face, and the chair crashed to the pavement with a loud clatter behind her.

"Bernie! Bernie, what's the matter?"

Swallow's voice reached her from a great distance, but she couldn't answer, she could only stare up in horror and disbelief into the eyes of the man on the billboard. It seemed like only a moment ago that he was staring into her eyes just like that and asking her if she was sure the baby was really his.

"It's that man," Roxie's voice rasped. She'd followed Bernie's gaze and seen the billboard. "Pastor Ted. He has that effect on me too!"

With an effort Bernie tore her eyes away from Ted's. "Who . . ." Her throat was dry; her tongue felt thick in her mouth. "Who is he?"

"A dangerous man," Roxie replied, "that's who."

"Why?" Bernie asked, stooping down to pick up the chair and also to get away from Ted's eyes—and Swallow's too.

"Why!" Roxie listed her reasons on long fingers. "He preaches prisons, punishment, and prayer as the answer to all our problems. He thinks that just because we've got serious problems now, the past was some kind of golden age. He's anti-choice and anti-poverty-programs and anti-health-care for the poor. He thinks AIDS is God's punishment for homosexuality. He claims he's a passionate defender of the family, but doesn't trust families to brain-wash their kids for him, so he wants the state to do it by censoring books and putting prayer back in the schools. Is that enough 'whys' for you, Bernie?" She stood in front of Bernie like some kind of kaleidoscope gone amok in her bright tie-dyed costume.

"He sounds like a crackpot," Swallow said, still staring at Bernie.

"Of course he's a crackpot," Roxie raged. "But haven't you noticed? Crackpots are the flavor of the month—honey-tongued crackpots in nice suits who can convince you that hate is love! He's in politics now—he'll probably be the next governor!"

She shook a finger at the billboard. "Just look at that smile, the smile of a man who loves babies! Of course, if you pay attention to his *words* instead of the sound of his voice, you realize he also believes that while every child has a right to life, only rich kids have a right to good health care and good schools!"

Mercifully, a customer who'd been hovering on the edges of the little group of women waiting for Roxie to run down took the opportunity to ask Bernie the price of some of her beads.

She pulled herself together and went quickly over to the customer, glad to have something to occupy her mind for a while besides Ted Mason.

She thought the day would never end. Everywhere she turned, she could feel Mason's eyes on her, as though following her around. She wished it would rain so she could cover her booth and hide inside, but the sky stayed cloudless. She longed for the night, but when it finally came, a floodlight came on above the billboard that made Mason's face seem to smile even more brightly down upon her.

Fred invited her to his booth for dinner and she accepted eagerly because Mason's eyes couldn't find her there. Fred got sandwiches, fruit, and coffee from the food vendors and they ate at one of his tables. He'd closed his tent door to keep them from being bothered by fairgoers and they ate in near-darkness. It reminded Bernie of her childhood: she and her brother had made tents of old blankets and hid in them, and imagined they were safe from their father. They weren't, though.

She could hear the people walking by outside, some of them commenting on Fred's furniture and discussing whether they wanted to come back later when the owner was there.

"I've been spying on you," Fred said, smiling. "You don't look like you've been enjoying yourself today—like you've got too much on your mind. What's the matter, don't you like getting rich?"

She looked into his gentle, handsome face, wanted to tell him the truth, but she couldn't. Not yet, anyway. Maybe never. She had to think it through herself first. So she just told him she hadn't slept well the night before. "I'm not used to the humidity," she added. "I guess I've been away too long."

He looked at her a long time, as if knowing there was more to it than that. Then he smiled again and said, "You'd get used to it fast enough, if you lived here. You have to know how to ease your way through humidity instead of trying to push your way through. It's an art."

As promised, after the fair had closed the night before, Fred's brother had taken them to see the building Fred was considering buying for his furniture business. Even Bernie could see that it was perfect—a place that could be a combination workshop and salesroom, with a big apartment upstairs. "It's a good location and the price is right too," Fred said enthusiastically. "And I've got enough money put away to live on until I build up a clientele."

"I think you should take it," Bernie said, "if that's what you want." Part of her mind was on Ted Mason and the past and part of it was on the future and the possibility she wouldn't see Fred again.

"Did you happen to notice," he said slyly, "that the showroom's big enough so you could have part of it for your beads and jewelry?"

She looked at him, startled. "What?"

"It is, you know. Beads, your homemade jewelry, and furniture—what could be a more perfect combination? You're a wonderful jewelry maker, you know, Bernie. If you weren't always on the road, you'd have more time to do it. And if you needed more space, or if I did, we could get the little store next door. It's up for rent too."

She laughed, but the idea scared her—not of settling down, but of what else Fred seemed to be hinting at. They were just friends, but she'd known for a long time that he'd wanted it to be more than that, he just hadn't known how to say it, or didn't have the courage to say it. They only saw each other four or five weeks a year, at most. They really didn't know each other very well.

"It'll be strictly a business arrangement," he went on, as if reading her mind. "We'd get a lawyer to draw up a contract and everything." He waited for her to say something. "Well, what you do think?"

"I don't know, Fred. I'll have to think about it."

"Will you?" he said, giving her a penetrating look. "Or are you just saying that, and you'll be out of here before the sun rises Monday morning?"

"I'll think about it," she said. "I promise."

She stood up quickly and thanked him for dinner and ducked out of his tent into the warm summer night. She went back to her booth, careful to keep her eyes on the ground.

Twenty-two

I slept late Friday morning. The first thing I did after I'd taken a long shower and while the coffee was brewing was call the *Tribune* and ask Max Weinstock, a feature writer I know through Gary, if anybody named Dave Brown worked there.

"Nope. Why?"

"It's a long story." I described the man I'd encountered the night before.

"Rings no bells," she said, "and nobody's doing a story on Steadman George either, although it's a good idea. I think I'll suggest it to my editor. You going to tell me what this is all about, Peggy?"

"Maybe someday," I said.

"Heard from Gary?"

"He called yesterday."

"You think he's going to leave us and move up to Pelican Lake?"

"Loon Lake. Yes."

"Lucky guy! I hear the fishing's great up there. You a fisherman, Peggy?"

"No," I said, and could imagine the thoughtful look that must have flitted across her face at hearing that. Max, a wholesome outdoorsy woman given to jeans and flannel shirts, had been hustling Gary for months, and now was her big chance: a jug of wine, a mess of nightcrawlers—and thou beside me singing in the wilderness. The image was mind-boggling, considering what Gary sounds like singing.

That reminded me I'd promised Gary I'd drive up to

Loon Lake and spend the weekend with him. Well, it didn't look like that was going to happen, so I called the number where he was staying to tell him so. He wasn't in—he and Kermit, the owner of the newspaper, were out on the lake fishing—but I left a message for him with Kermit's wife, who told me how much she and her husband liked Gary and how disappointed she was that I wasn't coming up. Gary'd told them so much about me.

Next I called someone I know in Homicide downtown, to ask if anybody had come forward who admitted having been with Steadman George the night he'd died. Nobody had. That didn't surprise me in the least.

Finally I looked up Sue Ann Naylor's number in the phone book, on the off chance she was home, but her answering machine told me to leave a message. I hung up and called the main office for Raggs, the locally owned upscale clothing store chain she worked for, according to Vicki, and asked the receptionist if I could speak with their head buyer, Sue Ann Naylor.

She came back on the phone a minute later to say she was sorry, Mrs. Naylor was in a meeting.

"When do you think the meeting'll be over?"

"God only knows!" she said. "It's a matter of haute couture, quality, and the bottom line! Afterwards, though, they'll all go to lunch. Why don't you try back around, say, two? Maybe they'll be back by then."

I thought of telling her I was a campus cop and demanding to talk to Mrs. Naylor immediately. But a bright summer morning, a good night's sleep, and a couple of cups of coffee had almost convinced me I was making something out of nothing. After all, I couldn't be sure the man I'd talked to outside the Getaway had really been the man I'd seen on the Showboat with George. I'd only caught a glimpse of him in George's cabin, and I hadn't been paying close attention either. And I had no solid evidence that George's death was anything other than what it seemed to be.

Dave Brown, with or without quotation marks around his name, could have been a freelance writer who told people he worked for the *Tribune* to impress them. There were innocent explanations for everything I found suspicious.

More important, I had no solid evidence to take to the homicide police.

But I still wanted to meet Bernie, find out who she was and get her story.

I spent the day working in my own backyard—or rather, Mrs. Hammer's, my landlady's. Since it was July, most of the flowers were in riotous bloom, but so were the weeds. I grow mostly daylilies in my part of the garden, on account of they require no care, but Mrs. Hammer is partial to sedum, which I think are more trouble than they're worth.

Paula Henderson called around one. "When're you expecting Gary back from Horsefly Lake?" Paula is no fonder of raw nature than I am.

"Sunday sometime, I think," I said. "Why?"

"Well, you're always complaining that we never do things together anymore, so how about, if he gets home in time, we all go to the Riverton Art Fair together? Sunday's the last day. Or if he doesn't get home in time, you come alone?"

"Okay," I said. "Gary and I usually go, but this year our schedules got a little screwed up."

"To put it mildly," Paula said. "We don't usually go, but Lawrence's pottery teacher has a booth."

For a year or so, Lawrence had been trying to write true crime stories and had amassed an impressive pile of rejection slips. A few months earlier, he'd given that up and switched to pottery. I have one of his coffee mugs, which I use as a doorjamb.

We agreed that as soon as I heard from Gary, I'd give them a call.

At two I called Sue Ann Naylor again and this time I got lucky.

I told her who I was and that I was a University cop.

"You're a what?" she interrupted me, before I could go on.

I explained what a campus cop was and that I'd found Steadman George's body, and went on to tell her I was interested in talking to a woman George had known named Bernie.

"Bernie! Why come to me?"

"A friend of yours thought you might know her."

"And which friend might that be?"

"Vicki Layne."

She laughed. "Figures," she said obscurely. "Yeah, I know Bernie. But what's the deal? Didn't Steadman just get drunk and fall off the Showboat like it said in the paper?"

"The police think that's what happened," I answered, "but I'm not so sure." Before she could ask me why, I asked her if she knew where I could get in touch with Bernie now.

"Haven't the foggiest," she said.

My heart sank. "But you did talk to her on Monday?"

"Yeah, but she just said she was in town to—" She broke off. "On business," she continued. "She didn't tell me where she was staying and I didn't ask."

I was pretty sure I knew what the business was that Sue Ann was discreet enough not to tell me.

"Listen," I said, "could I have twenty minutes, half an hour of your time today? I'm not sure, but I think Bernie's in trouble and right now you're the only lead I have to her."

"You say this isn't a part of some official investigation?" she asked skeptically.

"No, it's not."

"Then—oh, to hell with it! Sure, c'mon over, but be quick about it. I've got a couple of vendors bringin' in winter suits at four. Winter suits in a heat wave, for chrissakes, I'm sweating just thinking about it! Think you can get here before that?"

I knew I could.

Half an hour later I was walking across one of the parking lots of a sprawling industrial park a few miles outside of town that in its grim featurelessness reminded me of the New Campus of the University. I'd seen photographs of penitentiaries with more charm.

The building where Raggs had its offices was a low cement structure with painted-over windows. The offices were on the second floor and Sue Ann's was at the end of the hall, with a sign on it saying COME IN. I did.

"You're the campus cop, right?" she greeted me, looking up from a computer screen on a table next to her desk.

Apparently I didn't look like somebody in the garment industry to her.

"Right."

"Welcome to haute couture," she said. "Clear off a chair and make yourself comfortable."

I took a pile of fabric and color samples off the chair, stacked them on a radiator, and sat down.

Her office wasn't how I'd imagined the office of the head buyer for a clothing store as upscale as Raggs stores would look. It was small, dusty, and cluttered with papers, magazines, and catalogues, with color reproductions of fashion designs that looked torn out of magazines taped on the walls.

Sue Ann Naylor looked younger, in that purposeful way people who work hard at it do, than she probably was, if she'd been Steadman George's lover in the mid-'70s. She was about five-three, with short, curly dark hair, gray eyes, and cheeks and a chin that looked carved out of marble. She was wearing a trendy-looking linen suit that probably cost my clothing budget for the year.

She glanced at her watch and then at me. "So. Start at the beginning, why don't you?"

I quickly told her the things that were bothering me about Steadman George's death: the man I'd seen in the cabin of the Showboat with him, the one glass when I thought there should have been two, and the fact that I hadn't been able to find where he could have bought the Wild Turkey. I added that everyone I'd talked to had thought he was still on the wagon, right up to the night he died.

"But he did drown, right?" she asked when I'd finished. "I mean, you're not leaving out something, like a knife in his back or a hole in his head?"

"Apparently he drowned," I said. "No marks on the body."

"And the cops—the real cops, I mean—think it was an accident?"

"Yes."

"So it's just you, trying to make it murder."

"It's just me, trying to make sure it wasn't."

"Why?"

I told her how I'd spent a couple of my breaks with

George on the Showboat late at night, listening to his stories. "I didn't know him very well," I added, "and I didn't like him a lot. But he kind of got under my skin."

She laughed. "He knew how to do that," she said dryly. "He was a bastard from the word go, but he could charm your pants off. Not yours," she added, giving me a cool glance, "at least, not now. But twenty years ago, I wouldn't've bet against it!"

I smiled and didn't say anything to that.

"How about Bernie?" she went on "She get under your skin too, Peggy?"

"No, but I'm worried about her. The guy I'm pretty sure I saw in George's cabin is going around pretending to be a journalist and trying to find her."

"Oh, yeah? Why?"

"He claims she was somebody who knew George in the seventies and she'd be able to tell him a lot about his life back then. Is that true?"

"No, it's bullshit," she said. "Bernie only met Steadman a couple of times. She knows less about him than you do. But couldn't this guy be on the up-and-up—somebody just gave him a bum tip about Bernie?"

"I thought of that," I said. "But who would've done it? If George was telling me the truth, Bernie'd only just come back to town after being away a long time. And you say they hardly knew each other at all."

She nodded, tapping a blue pencil against her teeth. "Yeah, it doesn't make sense, does it? So what's the real reason this character's looking for her?"

"I'd like to find her and ask her that," I said. "Or at least make sure she knows he's out there looking for her."

"Well, I can't help you," she said. "All Bernie told me was she's in town to . . ." She stopped, gave me a thoughtful look. "So, Steadman told you about Bernie coming back to town, huh? Did he tell you what she'd come back for?"

"Yes," I said.

She waited for more.

"He tried to play it very coy," I went on, playing it coy myself—two could play the discretion game—"and pretended the story he was telling me was just that, a story.

But I didn't believe it. The only thing he didn't quite give away was whether the child was a boy or a girl. If I had to guess, though, I'd say it was a girl.''

Sue Ann smiled. "Why?"

"Because we agreed, for the sake of the story, to call the child 'her.' If it had been a boy, he would've slipped up and said 'him,' but he didn't. He wasn't really a very good liar."

"Wasn't he?" Sue Ann said with a melancholy smile. "He used to be, a long time ago. But you're right, Bernie's kid's a girl."

"Bernie asked your help in finding George?"

"Right, because he'd been the go-between between her and the people who bought her baby. I don't remember their names. Barker, Walker—something like that. They were in show business. That's how Steadman knew them. They're probably long gone by now—and the kid too."

"He told me he knew where the girl was," I said.

She shrugged. "Maybe he did. When he called me the next night—Tuesday—he said he and Bernie were getting together after the show that night. He'd even left a ticket for her so she could see the play. He wouldn't have set her up like that if he didn't have something for her."

"But he didn't tell you where the daughter is," I said.

"No—I didn't ask either. He probably wouldn't't've told me anyway. Steadman was a man who liked his secrets."

"And that was the last time you talked to him, Tuesday?"

"Yeah," Sue Ann said. "He called to find out what I knew about Bernie—he probably wanted to know if I thought she had any money. I tried to convince him she didn't—which is probably true—so he wouldn't try to hold her up."

She sighed, shook her head. "He told me he was off the sauce too. He was very proud of himself for having gone a couple of weeks without it. He invited me to come visit him on the boat some night when I didn't have anything better to do, but I told him I couldn't imagine a night like that."

She smiled sadly. "Those were the last words he ever heard from me," she added.

"What's Bernie's last name?" I asked.

"It was Knapp when I knew her and maybe it still is." She spelled it. "Bernadette Knapp, a runaway from—where? I dunno. A farm. And what was she running from? She wouldn't talk about it. When she told me she was pregnant, I asked her if she had family that could help her out. She just scowled and said no. She was only sixteen—sweet sixteen," she added. She looked at me. "You have kids, Peggy?"

"No."

"I've got a daughter. Nothing like Bernie at that age, though. Jenny's with her dad and wife *numero duo* or *tres* in France at the moment."

She brought out a cigarette and lighter. "You mind?" she asked me. When I said I didn't—a lie, but I wanted to keep her relaxed and talking—she lit up. "Not supposed to smoke in here," she said, exhaling, "but who's gonna know?

"Bernie was so thin," she went on. "And tall and gawky like a scarecrow—all hands and feet and eyes and mouth. She wore a mood ring," she added, giving me a look that indicated she thought that explained a lot. Since I'd worn a mood ring too when I was a kid, it did explain something.

I asked her how she'd happened to know Bernie in the first place.

"Back in the seventies, Raggs was a used clothing chain called Rags to Britches. I managed one of the stores, the one near the U. One of my part-time salespeople was a student, Geoff, spelled g, e, o, f, f. Bernie was his girlfriend—they both came from the same little town someplace and when Bernie ran away from home, she looked him up. Geoff has a warm, crooked smile that conceals a cold, crooked heart, something a naive kid like Bernie would be a sucker for.

"He brought her in one day and told me she needed a job. I didn't know she was a runaway—didn't ask either. She worked out fine. There wasn't much selling involved in those days. The clothes were on racks and maybe a step up from Goodwill, and the customers—kids, mostly—just pawed through it all until they found something they liked."

She tapped ash from her cigarette into an ashtray.

"Geoff's probably the father of her kid," she said flatly. "She denied it when I asked her, but I didn't believe her. She wasn't the type to sleep around, and they broke up right around that time too, I remember."

"Geoff what?"

"Seaton. A rat. He's a commodities trader now. I see him sometimes at the club. He's doing all right for himself. He's come on to me a few times, but the chemistry's not there."

I asked her what he looked like.

"He's a balding little guy with close-set eyes and a big nose. He's also a health nut. He works out and wants you to know it—compensation, I guess."

Well, he wasn't the man who was looking for Bernie, anyway.

"And so you convinced her to sell the baby instead of get an abortion," I said.

"Uh-uh, that was Steadman's doing. I'd told her to contact Planned Parenthood. He and I were living together at the time and I mentioned Bernie's problem to him. He said he knew some people who were looking for a black-market baby on account of none of the adoption agencies thought they were fit enough. So I introduced Bernie to Steadman and here we are."

Here we were.

"What did Bernie do after she had the baby?"

"Vanished. Poof—just like that! Until she showed up on my door Monday, I never saw her again. But she left enough of an impression that I never forgot her."

"Did she have any friends back then she might've got in touch with since she came back?"

"She hung out with a few other lost souls and runaways like herself," Sue Ann replied. "I'd see 'em sometimes when they'd come into the store, but I don't remember any of their names. You could call Geoff, of course. He might know, since she called him to get my number. He must be in the phone book."

She punched out her cigarette. "I remember she also babysat for the wife of a chaplain at the U a couple of days a week. She might've talked to him about being pregnant—

I mean, that's what chaplains are for, right? The trouble is, I don't know his name, if I ever did.''

And chaplains don't stay long anyway, I thought, so whoever it was, was probably long gone by now.

The door opened behind me and a couple of men started pushing in a rack of canvas garment bags.

"I'm not quite through here, guys," Sue Ann told them. "Wait outside a minute."

They left the rack inside the door and disappeared.

"You interested in what's new for winter?" she asked me, getting up and coming around her desk.

"No," I replied as I got up too.

"I don't suppose you are," she said, looking me up and down.

"Did she tell you what she's been doing since she disappeared?"

Sue Ann laughed, smoked a moment. "She lives in a trailer she tows behind a big old yellow school bus, and she drives all over the Southwest selling beads on Indian reservations—at powwows and things like that. I always thought 'powwow' was a word you only heard in old westerns, but Bernie told me they're real, sort of big clan gatherings.

"It must be a funny kind of life," she went on, "but I guess it suits her, and she seemed content. So what does she do to screw it up? Comes back to look for the kid she left behind!"

I asked her if Bernie had given any indication of how long she planned to stay in town.

"She said if she couldn't find out what happened to her kid by Sunday, she probably wasn't meant to. She couldn't afford to stay away from her 'powwows' any longer than that, she said. So by now she could be anywhere. If Steadman told her where her daughter is, she might be back on the road looking for her someplace else. If he didn't, I suppose she's back among the Indians."

Right, Bernie could be anywhere, might even have done the same disappearing act she'd done twenty years ago. A part of me hoped she had disappeared before the man who was looking for her found her. Another part of me hoped she was still in town because I wanted to find her and learn the details of the story, Steadman George's story, that I'd been searching for for two days now.

As I headed for the door, I thanked her for her time, although I wanted to wring her neck for having shown so little curiosity about Bernie Knapp's life. "I didn't ask" could have been Sue Ann's mantra.

I asked her if she thought Bernie might get in touch with her again.

"I doubt it—we didn't have that much to talk about." She laughed suddenly. "You want to know what sums Bernie up in a nutshell?"

"Sure. What?"

"This." She reached inside her jacket and pulled out a necklace she'd been wearing under it.

I looked at it, then gave her a questioning look.

"Bernie gave it to me," she explained. "To the me I was twenty years ago."

I smiled and turned away—and then spun back. "Let me see that!"

I studied the necklace a moment, then glanced up at Sue Ann, who was looking at me with raised eyebrows and a quizzical smile.

"She made this?" I asked.

"Uh-huh. She makes jewelry on the side when she's got time, she told me. I assume it's a clue."

"Yes," I said, wondering what I was going to do now.

"But you're not going to tell me what you think it means, are you?"

"Not now," I replied. "Thanks, Sue Ann." I was genuinely grateful to her, in spite of her lack of interest in Bernie's life story.

"I don't know why I wear the damned thing," she said as she tucked the necklace back under her jacket. "It's too clunky for me, but Bernie's got a nice eye for mixing texture and color, don't you think? And she must carve the designs on the wooden spacers herself. I guess I just like the feel of it, and knowing it's there."

Twenty-three

Ted Mason smiled at his wife across the dinner table. She'd been beautiful when he'd first met her: tall, blond, with the largest china-blue eyes he'd ever seen. And her father had been the president of the church college he'd attended, but that—and the doors he could open for Ted—hadn't been a factor in his falling in love with Patricia, he was sure of that!

Unfortunately, she hadn't aged well. With the years, the blue had faded from her eyes and now their largeness only made them look hollow—an effect emphasized by the cheekbones that had once been so striking. It was a gaunt, lined face now that reminded him of a tired horse.

When they were young, she'd postponed her own career—she'd earned a degree in family social work and wanted to be a therapist—to help him establish his. She'd taken care of the children, kept the home, and done all the things expected of a pastor's wife.

At first, they'd agreed that once the boys were in school she could begin her practice. But then Ted became a successful writer and speaker, his political involvement took him away from home more and more frequently, and they had to entertain on an ever larger scale. So she continued to postpone her career for his, until she discovered, too late, that while he constantly met new challenges that kept him young and intellectually alive, the duties of the wife who stands behind her man are always the same—and so is the view.

"What're you smiling at?" she asked him.

"Nothing," he said quickly. "I mean, I was just reminiscing about when we were young."

"You were? Why?"

It had been many years since she'd seen Ted in a sentimental mood.

"Do I need a reason?" he asked with a laugh.

"No, I don't suppose you do," she said, and speared a forkful of food.

"I guess I was thinking about the past because some woman called me today at the church to ask me if we still stayed in touch with a babysitter we once had—Bernie something. I said the name rang a faint bell, but that was all. Do you remember her, Patricia?"

She paused with the fork halfway to her mouth. "Of course I do. It was the year I was getting my M.A."

"Do you remember her last name?"

"Not offhand," she said. "This woman who called you doesn't know Bernie's last name? How odd." Her big eyes bored into Ted's. Among her less attractive traits, Ted had always thought, was a mind like a steel trap.

He'd never been good at lying to Patricia and could feel a trickle of cold sweat run down his side. "She said they'd worked together years ago. Bernie mentioned to her that she'd babysat for us. She said Bernie had made a strong impression on her, and she'd like to know what's become of her."

"I would too," Patricia said. "It surprised me when she left us so abruptly and without any explanation. I'd thought she'd seemed unusually responsible, for someone her age." She gave Ted a frosty little smile and added, "For a time I even wondered if she might be buried in the basement, but there were no signs of freshly turned soil." The home near campus they'd had when Ted was chaplain was old and run-down and its basement had a dirt floor.

He laughed, pretending to think she was joking.

She recognized his laugh as the one he used in his speeches when telling a rehearsed joke. Ted, she realized with a jolt, no longer had any other kind of laugh.

"Bernie's probably married now anyway," she said, "and has a different last name."

"Yes, of course."

They ate in silence for a few minutes and then he said, "We paid her using checks, didn't we?"

She waited a beat, then looked up at him and asked, "Who?"

"Bernie." He knew she was tormenting him.

"I suppose so," she said. "And I suppose we still have the canceled checks in the basement. We've never thrown away anything of importance, Ted, have we?"

What did she mean by that? His eyelids fluttered and he looked quickly down at his plate again. "I thought I'd do the woman this favor, if I can."

"You probably can," his wife said. "Just wear old clothes. The basement's pretty dusty."

He was on his hands and knees on the basement floor, in a pool of harsh light cast by the naked bulb dangling from a cord above his head. Two old wooden file drawers were open beside him, and he was going through old tax records filed in large manila envelopes by year. He found what he was looking for, the checks he'd made out to Bernie for babysitting: Bernadette Knapp. An ugly name. He wondered if he'd ever known it.

He continued through the checks, pausing briefly at each one, noting her neat schoolgirl signature on their backs. He stopped at the last one, the one he'd made out to her the day she'd told him she was pregnant—the last day she'd babysat for them. He tried to read in his signature the terror he remembered having felt at that moment, for it was the most horrifying day of his life—until he received the call from Steadman George on Wednesday, anyway.

He could clearly recall how she'd looked at him at the time—as if waiting for something. But what did she expect of him? What could she expect of him? That he'd leave his wife for her?

No, of course not. To be fair to Bernie, she'd never indicated she wanted anything of the sort.

He'd blurted out, "Are you sure it's mine?" and immediately realized that was a mistake, because whether it was or wasn't, she could ruin him by insisting it was.

"Yes," she said, her voice quivering. "I'm sure."

And even though he hadn't asked, she'd told him about

how she'd had her period since breaking up with her boy-friend—and anyway, her boyfriend had always used a con-dom, she said. He could hear the accusation in her voice when she said that, or thought he could.

He didn't know if she was telling the truth or not. There'd be time for lawyers and blood tests later, if worst came to worst.

His heart in his throat, he'd asked her what she was go-ing to do.

She'd looked at him a long time after he'd said that, as if measuring him with her large dark eyes. And then she'd said, softly, "I'm going to get an abortion."

"You are?" he'd asked stupidly.

That wasn't his finest moment, he knew that, and when-ever he remembered it, he still flinched with embarrass-ment.

She'd smiled. He could still see that smile. Sometimes it seemed scornful, almost demonic; at other times compas-sionate, as if she'd meant it to comfort him.

Did she know how opposed he was to abortion? *Roe versus Wade* had just been made the law of the land and he was already active in the movement to get it repealed. There was a lot of literature about it around the church and his home too, and she must have seen it.

He'd tried to talk her out of it, hadn't he? Asked her if she was sure it was the right thing to do, told her about adoption agencies. She'd listened to him, watching him un-blinkingly as he spoke. What was she expecting him to do? What could he do?

He'd been young and just getting started, with a two-year-old son and another child on the way! Patricia would almost certainly have divorced him. At best she would never have trusted him again—and how can a marriage survive without trust?

He didn't want to argue with Bernie, for fear it would upset her. She was so young—who could know what she might do if he made her angry? He couldn't tell her that having an abortion was a sin, could he, after what he'd done—*they'd* done?

Then she'd told him she didn't want to try to get an abortion at one of the free clinics someplace, she wanted it to be in a real hospital and she expected him to pay for it. That's all she was asking of him, she said. He promised to get the money for her if she'd wait a few days. And he did.

Apparently she hadn't gotten the abortion! Why? And why hadn't she tried to get more money out of him back then? Maybe she didn't think of it—maybe Stan was right and that's what she was back to do now, with the help of that man George. If that was the way it was, she'd be calling him herself soon. Or maybe, with George dead, she'd given up and disappeared again.

Oh, if he could only count on that!

He rummaged through the checks until he came to the one for the afternoon they'd made love. He stared at it, his hand trembling, remembering. It had happened less than an hour before he'd written that check and he must still have had the smell of her on his hands when he wrote it.

She'd been unhappy all that week, moping, answering him in monosyllables, until finally he'd asked her what was bothering her. Sniffling, she'd told him how she'd caught her boyfriend with another girl. So he'd sat down beside her and put his arm around her and tried to comfort her.

It was as though a dam had burst in her, and she told him the whole wretched story of her life: how her brother hadn't wanted to go into the Army and fight in Vietnam and so he'd committed suicide rather than face his father's wrath. And then her mother had died—Bernie had believed it was from a broken heart—and so she'd run away from home, to get away from her father, whom she blamed for everything.

It started as his attempt to comfort her—it really had! After a while, he kissed her on the forehead and whispered, "You have such beautiful eyes!" And that was true. Her eyes—big, filled with pain—*were* beautiful, and so he kissed them too. She was beautiful in her youth and innocence, although in fact she wasn't pretty at all.

He couldn't remember how it went from that to sex, just that she didn't resist, didn't protest. God, how he'd needed it! It had been over a month since Patricia had let him touch her.

Afterward, of course, he was appalled at what he'd done,

and frightened too—and remorseful, genuinely remorseful! He'd apologized profusely.

She'd just smiled placidly and told him it was all right. It didn't mean anything, she'd said, it was just something that happened.

It hadn't meant anything to her, "it was just something that happened"! And God knows this couldn't have been the first time it had "just happened"! It would be a miracle if it was, with her kind of morality! He was lucky he didn't get a disease from her.

For a long time afterward, he'd lived in fear that one day she would show up at his door with a baby on her arm. But the summer passed and fall turned to winter, spring came, and nothing happened. A year passed and the fear began to fade, and after a few more years he could forget Bernie entirely for years at a time.

He'd gotten away with it.

Now he didn't know what to think. Why had she come back? Had God set him up for a bigger fall than the one he would have taken had Bernie destroyed him two decades ago?

"Oh, God, give me a sign!" he whispered, putting his hands to his face.

"Bernadette Knapp."

He let out a scream, looked up, terrified. Patricia was standing in the darkness at the bottom of the stairs.

"You scared me," he said breathlessly. He knew it was impossible to come down those stairs noiselessly without trying. "I know," he added. "I found the checks. You don't remember where she came from, do you?"

She shook her head. "No, but you could ask Arnie Sorensen, if he's still alive."

"Arnie Sorensen?"

"The handyman who worked at the church back then. Don't you remember?"

Then he did, a tall, quiet man who didn't like Ted for some reason and made no bones about it.

"You think he'd know anything about her?"

"Of course he would," she said. "He was the one who recommended her to me in the first place—they came from the same town—Pine City. He's probably dead now, though," she added. "He was in his sixties then."

He scrambled to his feet, went over to her. "Who would know?" he asked.

She didn't reply for a minute, just stared into his face with her great pale eyes. "Is this something that's going to blow up in our faces?" she asked quietly.

"No, Patricia, I swear! It's nothing. I promised I'd make every effort to get her last name, that's all." He laughed. "It's kind of fun, being a detective for a little while."

He put his arms around her the way he used to years ago, and pulled her close. "Indulge me," he said softly.

"I'll try to find out for you," she said, and pulled away from him. "Come to bed now," she added, as she turned and went up the stairs. "Tomorrow's Saturday and you have a busy day."

He watched her go, noted how broad she'd become in the seat, fought the anger he felt at her for putting on weight and at himself for noticing, as he went back to put away the files.

Twenty-four

Bernie couldn't sleep. She stared up at the low ceiling of her trailer and thought. Gideon was snoring lightly in his bed on the floor next to her.

She could still see Ted Mason's eyes gazing mildly down at her from the billboard—a far cry from the way they'd stared at her when she'd told him she was pregnant.

It was after she'd seen Geoff Seaton with another girl and confronted him about it and he'd laughed at her and called her a romantic fool.

Looking back on it now, she realized she should have seen it coming. Patricia Mason had hired her to babysit Matt because she was pregnant with their second child and trying to finish up her coursework at the U. Mason was too busy with his writing and church work to babysit. But as the weeks passed he began spending more and more time with her, when Matt was asleep, instead of in his study or at the campus church.

He wanted to know all about her life, about what girls her age think about things like sex and marriage and God.

She didn't mind answering. She was flattered too, that he was interested in what she had to say about life. She hadn't even finished high school.

Soon after she'd realized it was all over between her and Geoff, Mason had asked her why she was so downcast, and she'd broken down and told him the whole story. And once she'd started, she couldn't stop. She even told him about her brother's suicide and how her mother had died soon afterward of a broken heart and how she'd run away from home after that.

He'd seemed genuinely concerned for her. He'd put an arm around her and kissed her on the forehead and then he'd told her she had beautiful eyes and kissed them too.

Geoff was right, she was a romantic fool! She'd thought Mason was just being fatherly, although *her* father had never so much as given her a hug, ever, but the next thing she knew, she was on her back on the couch and Mason— he wanted everybody to call him Ted back then—was on top of her, pulling down her jeans.

She'd been too surprised to resist. She wasn't sure she wanted to resist—she wasn't even sure she should!

It had been so confusing. She was angry at Geoff, felt betrayed and abandoned—that was one thing. But Mason was so desperate, so *needy*—that was another. Lying in the hot trailer, listening to Gideon snore, she could still hear Mason's sobbing. And she remembered thinking: it can't be wrong, if he's doing it!

Afterward, she'd seen in the horror on his face and the fear in his voice how wrong it had been after all.

He'd been so terrified that she'd done the only thing she could think of to do: told him it was okay. Over and over again, because he was so scared and because she realized that what he'd done gave her power over him.

That was the most terrible thing of all for her, when she saw in his face that she had power over him. She didn't *want* power over another person—the kind of power that can make people afraid of you! Her father had had that kind of power over her and her brother, and he used it to diminish them, shame them, and finally destroy Carl.

So she'd assured Mason that what happened didn't mean anything to her, and she'd continued to babysit Matt for a few more months. For a while, Mason had come in to ask her, awkwardly, how she was doing. They'd never had sex again, but later, years later when she was less naive, she suspected that if she'd shown any signs of willingness, he would have done it with her again. He'd also tried to get her to put into words what the experience had meant to her, but she'd just shook her head and smiled and told him she didn't want to talk about it.

She waited until she was sure she was pregnant before telling him, and she saw again the terror blossom on his face as he realized she could bring his entire life down around him like a church in an earthquake. But she'd only told him because she wanted to hear what advice he might have.

Instead, he'd asked her if she was sure the child was his! Of course she was. She and Geoff hadn't had sex for weeks—not since he starting seeing that other girl and putting her off with lies—and she'd had her period after that. Besides, Geoff always used condoms. Mason hadn't.

She'd told him she was going to get an abortion and expected him to pay for it—she'd used her power over him for that, anyway. She expected him to object, but he didn't—not for long. He'd offered to make discreet inquiries about homes for unwed mothers, where she could live until she had the baby and then put it up for adoption, but she'd heard other girls talk about places like that. She couldn't stand the thought of spending months in one of them. Besides, they would have wanted to know where she came from and might have tried to contact her father.

Mason had found out how much an abortion cost at a good clinic and given her the money one evening at the campus church. As he'd handed her the money in the envelope, he'd looked like a common criminal.

She'd told Sue Ann she was pregnant, since she was so much older and might be a support for her when she went in to get the abortion. Sue Ann introduced her to Steadman George, who'd persuaded her to have the baby instead and sell it.

Luckily she'd been strong and healthy, and the pregnancy wasn't unusually difficult, but it had been hard, being alone in a big city, just seventeen, and pregnant. Sue Ann had been sympathetic, of course, but she couldn't be there for her much of the time. They didn't have anything in common, really. Sue Ann was a lot older and had her own life to live.

She considered returning the money for the abortion to Mason. She'd even gone to his church one Sunday to do it and sat through the service. Something about the sight of him standing at the altar in his clean white gown with the blue shawl, preaching God's love, made her mad. She'd wanted to stand up and holler something at him—''You hypocrite!''—something like that, anyway.

But what good would it have done? And who would have believed her story anyway?

Besides, she'd liked Mason's wife and little Matt, and she wouldn't have hurt them for anything. So she waited until the congregation stood to sing a hymn and then snuck out and never saw him again.

And now he was famous, preaching against abortion and homosexuality and welfare programs for the needy—and he might even become governor of the state, if she could believe Roxie. Bernie had gay friends and friends who'd had abortions too, and she knew families on welfare through no fault of their own.

Mason was an even worse hypocrite than she'd thought! Could she stop him if she did what she'd refused to do two decades ago—get up and tell the world what he'd done to her?

Could she use the power she had over him now?

SATURDAY

Twenty-five

I sat in my apartment Saturday morning, drinking coffee and wondering what to do next. There was no question in my mind that Bernie Knapp had made both Sue Ann's and Greta Markham's necklaces. The stones by themselves wouldn't have told me they'd come from the same hand, but the bleached-wood spacers between the stones, with Native American–like designs burned into them, did. But I wouldn't have noticed those similarities if Greta's boyfriend hadn't sneered, "Her mother," at the Boardinghouse when Sam had asked her where she'd gotten the necklace, and if Greta hadn't snapped at him on account of it.

Did that mean she knew Bernie was her mother?

And at the Getaway the other night, Greta had said Steadman George had known her father a long time, they were both in show business. Maybe if I hadn't been so tired, and the room so noisy and smoky, I would have picked up on that.

The question was, how was I going to find out if Greta knew about Bernie and knew where she was now? Could I just go up to Greta and ask her what she knew about the woman who'd given her the necklace? I'd do that if I had to, but I decided to try to talk to Geoff Seaton first, Bernie's boyfriend from the time she got pregnant, and see if he knew where Bernie was. She'd contacted him when she first arrived in town to get Sue Ann's address and might have told him where she was staying.

Sue Ann thought he was the father of Bernie's child, since they'd been going together at the time she got pregnant and, Sue Ann thought, Bernie wasn't the type to play around. I wondered if Seaton knew about the child.

I'd driven by Seaton's place last night after leaving Sue Ann, but he didn't answer his doorbell and the house was dark, so he probably hadn't come home from work yet. I'd also tried to call him later, but got his answering machine, where a voice, speaking against a background of cool jazz, expressed the hope that I'd leave a message, or not. Whatever.

Well, last night had been Friday night and Sue Ann had implied that he was unmarried and a swinger, so that wasn't surprising.

It was also possible, of course, that Seaton, Bernie, and their daughter—whoever she was—were together someplace right now, getting reacquainted, putting a new spin on the term "family values." And the man I thought was looking for Bernie was just a bill collector or a repo man wanting to repossess her bus or trailer.

The phone rang. It was Gary.

"Got your message," he said with what I imagined was forced cheerfulness. "Sorry you're not coming up."

"Me too," I said, not entirely truthfully. "I got busy."

"With what?"

"Chasing corpses, Ginny would call it."

"What does that mean?"

"It's a long story. You sure you want to hear it?"

"Steadman George again?"

"That's how it started, yes. But now I seem to have fallen into another story that's interesting too, a story about a woman who sold her baby twenty-some years ago."

"There's a connection between these two stories?"

"Yes. A man I saw with George just before he died."

"Who?"

"He called himself Dave Brown and tried to pass himself off as a feature writer on the *Tribune* to some people I've talked to. He's looking for Bernie. Ever heard of a Dave Brown?"

"Lots of 'em, but none who work for the *Trib*. But that doesn't have to mean anything sinister. He could be freelance and claiming a connection with the paper just to get them to talk to him. It's been known to happen. Bernie could be a viable lead, or he could just think she is. False leads happen too, Peggy.''

I wasn't going to argue with him. If he'd been outside the Getaway with me last night, he would have agreed with me that Mr. Brown was no journalist. Whether he would have agreed that Brown was also a scary man, I wasn't sure.

"Do you think there's any danger involved for you?" he asked, as if reading my mind.

"Not if it's all in my head," I said.

After a thoughtful, medium-length pause, he said, "Guess what?"

"What?"

"There's an opening on the Loon Lake police force. I talked to the chief about it—everybody knows everybody else up here, you know—and told him about you. He hinted strongly that if you applied you'd be a shoo-in for the job."

"Why's that?" I asked. It didn't surprise me that I was eligible for the position, since campus cops get the same training as any other state-licensed peace officer.

"Because everybody in town is rooting for me to buy the newspaper," he replied. "They're afraid Kermit'll just fold it if I don't. So I kind of made it clear that I might not buy it unless . . ." He let the sentence dangle.

I stared out the window in my living room, from where I can see a corner of Lake Eleanor. That's all the lake I need, and it's right smack in the middle of the city.

"I'm flattered, Gary," I said. "But please don't make that a condition for buying the paper."

"No, I won't," he said, sounding a little hurt.

I told him that Paula had called to invite us to join her and Lawrence at the Riverton Art Fair tomorrow evening, if he got back in time.

"It's all the same crap, year after year," he grumbled. "But sure, why not? We haven't seen Paula and Lawrence in a while. You can buy me a brat and a beer."

And on that unenthusiastic note, we hung up.

Twenty-six

"Well?" Stan said as he came into Ted's office early Saturday morning and closed the door behind him. He'd never been in there before, but Ted wanted it that way. Nobody else would be there that early, and he didn't want Stan coming to his home. Patricia was suspicious enough without that. "What did Patricia tell you?"

Ted started to say, "Couldn't you have called?" but thought better of it. Instead he said, "I spent the night wrestling with this, Stan, and I'm having second thoughts about trying to find her."

"Why's that, brother?" Stan asked as he came across the room and sat on the corner of his brother's big, shiny desk. He noted that Ted was pale and his eyes looked bruised. His normally perfectly arranged hair was rumpled too, as if he'd forgotten to comb it that morning. Not a good sign.

"She hasn't made any attempt to contact me," Ted replied. "And even if she does want money, she might not ask for much. She didn't the last time, after all."

"She didn't want much money from you last time," Stan said acidly, "because you didn't have much to give her back then. And you didn't have as much to lose either, if she'd told. She's older now, and no doubt sadder and wiser. She also knows you can afford to pay more now and have a lot more to lose if you don't."

"Maybe," Ted tried once more, "when she heard about George's death, she got cold feet and went away. Or maybe George was acting purely on his own and she doesn't know anything about his attempt to blackmail me."

"But she knows who her daughter is," Stan countered. "Do you really think she's not going to tell her who you are?"

"You think the girl would want money too?"

"I have no idea," Stan said. "She might want something else, though."

"What?"

"She's an actress, remember—and a woman. You really think she could keep her mouth shut about you, once she learned that Pastor Ted—the great advocate of 'family values'—is her father and paid her mother to get an abortion? Besides, she'd know it would both help her career and advance her pro-abortion, feminist cause if she stood up, pointed at you, and said, 'That pious hypocrite is my father!' What woman could resist that? For that matter," he added, "what man could? You should see her, Ted. She's got a head of chopped hair painted red, jewelry stuck all over her face—and a bumper sticker on her car that says, 'Keep your laws off my body.' "

Ted squeezed his eyes shut. He remembered that George had taunted him with the bumper sticker too. "How do you know Bernie hasn't already told her?" he asked.

"I don't know for sure," Stan replied, "but it didn't look like it to me. Mr. George told you Bernie was going to think about it before making up her mind what to do and that she's only going to be in town through tomorrow. So she's gotta make up her mind soon, doesn't she?"

"Maybe she'll decide not to tell her," Ted said.

"Shall we sit around and do nothing and wait and see, or do you still want me to try to talk to her first?"

To avoid his brother's angry face, Ted got up and went to the window that looked out on the church's garden. He placed his hands on the window frame and leaned his forehead against the cool glass. The morning sun threw his shadow in the shape of a cross on the shiny floor behind him. It was just habit; he knew the effect was wasted on his brother, although it sometimes worked on journalists for the religious press.

Without turning around to face his brother, he said, "Her maiden name was Knapp." He spelled it. "She could be married by now, of course."

"What else, Ted? What else did you find out about her?"

"She was recommended to Patricia by the church custodian back then, a man named Arnie Sorensen. He and Bernie both came from Pine City. It's about a hundred miles north of here."

"Is Sorensen still alive?"

"I don't know. He moved back up there after he retired. One of Pat's friends from the University church says he's in a rest home. I've got the address." Ted turned to his brother, started to reach into his shirt pocket, hesitated.

"You're just going to talk to Bernie, aren't you, Stan?" he asked.

"What do you think I'm gonna do, Ted—kill her?"

Ted shuddered involuntarily at the word. "No," he said quickly, trying to laugh and failing dismally, "of course not. Maybe, if you think it would do any good, you could arrange a meeting between us, someplace private where Bernie and I can talk. Yes," he said, his voice deepening with conviction, "that's what I want you to do, Stan."

"All right, Ted," Stan said, then took the piece of paper his brother handed him and left the church before he could change his mind again.

As he drove north to Pine City, rage at having to pretend with his brother burned inside Stan. He didn't know how Ted could go along with the pretense that he hadn't killed George and wouldn't kill Bernie. But he knew it was better to talk to Ted as though they were two civilized people discussing inviting a woman to tea and sounding her out on her ideas about what to serve at the next ice-cream social.

Was it worth it? He'd got away with one murder, he had no doubts about that. The perfect murder wasn't that hard to commit—people did it every day. Killing Bernie might be a little harder, though. He'd have to wait and see. It would depend on where he found her and who she'd be with.

And then there was this woman who was looking for Bernie too, this campus cop who'd told him she'd seen him with George the night he'd killed him.

He hadn't told Ted about her. He knew that, if he did, it might be enough to scare Ted into telling Stan to forget the whole thing. Stan wasn't interested in forgetting the whole thing. He had too much invested in ensuring that his brother could live the rest of his life worry-free—with Stan at his right hand.

Twenty-seven

I decided to go over to Geoff Seaton's house unannounced and, if he was home, see if he would talk to me. Since Bernie had called him on Monday to get Sue Ann's address, he might know where she was now, or remember the names of people who'd known her twenty years ago who might. It was a hot humid day and I dressed for it and for visiting a successful commodities trader: sandals, pale yellow pants, and a green sleeveless cotton blouse.

He lived on a lake north of Lake Eleanor, about a mile—and half a million dollars—from me, so I biked over. His house was a sprawling white split-level with a plate-glass window that took up the entire front wall, and from the street looked like a display window for an interior decorator.

Last night when I'd come by, the driveway had been empty, but now there was a fire-engine-red sports car parked in it, its top down to reveal soft, expensive leather covering the seats and dashboard.

Sue Ann Naylor had been right when she'd told me Seaton enjoyed displaying his body. He met me at the door barefoot and in a skimpy swimsuit.

"Well, hello," he sang, running his eyes over me slowly. "What're you selling, encyclopedias or religion? The Mormons were here last Saturday around this time, but I shooed 'em away. Am I gonna shoo you away too?"

He was a short, balding man in his early forties with the body of someone who works out regularly at an expensive club. His bright brown eyes were set too close together on either side of a large nose, and I'd owned a doll as a child that had lashes like his.

"I hope not," I said pleasantly. "I'm looking for a woman named Bernie Knapp. Sue Ann Naylor told me you might be able to help me find her."

"Find Bernie!" he said, looking puzzled. "Why? Is she lost?"

I smiled to show him I appreciated his wit. "I don't think so," I said. "It's just that I don't know where she is."

He laughed. "C'mon in, sweetheart. Leave your sandals in the entry, though—I just had the carpet cleaned." Without waiting to hear from me, he turned and padded across the living room to open sliding glass doors in the back wall.

The living room had all the warmth and personality of a motel room in Las Vegas as seen on TV, and the less said about it the better. I followed him out onto a patio with a large swimming pool that sparkled invitingly in the afternoon sunlight. A high cedar fence protected it from neighbor eyes and kids.

He indicated a pair of lounge chairs side by side under an awning, but I passed on that and took a plastic chair next to a glass-topped table with an umbrella.

"If you want to swim," he said casually as he flopped down in one of the chairs I'd rejected, "I've got a couple women's swimsuits around someplace would probably fit you. Or you can skinny-dip if you want. Some gals do, some don't."

"Thanks," I said, "but I can't stay long."

"That so? Just come to get something and then you're outta here, huh?" He flicked me a smile. "Okay. What's your interest in Bernie?" He folded his hands across his flat belly as though prepared to hear an interesting story.

I'd given the answer to that question some thought on the way over. I couldn't tell him the truth because, whether he was the father of Bernie's daughter or not, it wasn't any of his business until Bernie made it so, if she hadn't already.

"I think she might be in danger," I said. "I'd like to talk to her about it, warn her. Do you know where I can get hold of her?"

He just smiled at my question. "Danger, huh?" he said. "What kind of danger?"

I told him about the death of Steadman George and the man I'd seen with George the night he died who was looking for Bernie. All the while I was talking, I had the feeling Seaton was amused by something. It gave me the creeps, since it wasn't a particularly funny story.

When I'd finished, he pointed to the thermos on the table next to me. "Pour me some of that juice, will ya? Have some yourself. It's carrot. Good for ya. Helps prevent cancer."

I poured juice into two glasses—I like carrot juice—and got up and took his over to him. He took it with one hand, grabbed my wrist with the other. "Sit down here next to me, why don't you? It's friendlier that way, and you won't have to shout."

"Thanks, no," I said, and tried to free myself. He had a strong grip.

I grabbed the arm of his chair with my other hand to keep from being pulled down onto his lap and said quietly, "Let go." Green eyes in a pale face under red hair can be extremely cold, even on a hot afternoon. I know; I've practiced in front of a mirror.

"Sure," he said finally, and let go. He didn't look upset. As a commodities trader, he was probably accustomed to taking the occasional loss.

"So what was Bernie's connection with the old piano player on the Showboat?" he asked, still looking amused.

I gave him by best apologetic smile. "I'm sorry," I said, "that's not my story to tell. It's Bernie's."

"Not even to the proud father?" he asked.

It took me a moment to realize what he meant. Then I thought: Damn Sue Ann!

He saw the look on my face and laughed. "Bernie's calling me on Monday outta the blue," he said, "asking for Sue Ann's phone number, really brought the seventies back home, you know? So when I saw Sue Ann last night at the club, I invited her out for a drink and to talk over old times. We all worked together, you know—me, Sue Ann, and Bernie—at a store called Rags to Britches. I got Bernie the job there," he added. "I guess you know that."

He stared down into his carrot juice. "Anyway, we ended up having dinner too, and made a real night of it. Sue Ann's a few years older than me, of course, but she keeps herself in great shape. Anyway, before the night was over, she told me all about your visit and how you wanted to know about that dead pianist Steadman George and my old pal Bernie. She also told me what Bernie's in town for—to look for her kid. Mine too, I guess."

"You're sure about that?"

"It has to be mine," he said. "Bernie wasn't the type to mess around. The only other possibility is that she jumped into the sack with another guy right after we broke up, and she wouldn't've done that. If you'd known Bernie, you'd know she wasn't the type. But I did wonder about it at the time. I mean, I was careful. I've always been careful—the original 'Mr. Precaution.' "

He shrugged and gave me a "What can you do?" look. "Well, anyway, now that everything's out in the open, suppose you tell me why you think somebody's out to get Bernie. Sue Ann was a little vague about that."

"I don't know," I answered. "I just know somebody's looking for her who I'm sure was with Steadman George the night he drowned—and I'm not convinced George's drowning was an accident."

"According to Sue Ann, the guy you think you saw on the boat's writing an article about George," Seaton said. "Wouldn't that explain why he was with him that night?"

"That's an odd time to be interviewing anybody," I said. "And it's too much of a coincidence for me. Besides, so far he hasn't informed the police he was there that night. Have you ever heard of a journalist who'd deny being the last person to talk to a man right before he died—especially if he was the subject of an article you were doing?"

"There were drugs involved, right? Have you ever heard of anybody who'd want to get involved in something like that when there're drugs involved?"

"I realize there's an innocent explanation for each thing I find suspicious," I said, "but not for all of them together."

"And what's the reason anybody'd want to harm Bernie?"

"I don't know," I said.

He shook his head in disbelief. "You don't know Bernie either. Nobody'd want to hurt her—nobody."

He thought for a minute, sipping carrot juice and staring out across his pool. "Since talking to Sue Ann last night," he went on, "I've been thinking maybe I oughtta go see Bernie myself, tell her I know why she's here and get her story."

"You know where she is?"

"Sure. At least, I know where she said she'd be until tomorrow night." He grinned. "But I'm not telling you, sweetheart. You say Bernie's story isn't yours to tell. Well, her whereabouts aren't mine to tell either, to somebody I don't know from Adam. Bernie has the right to decide for herself if she wants to talk to you."

A nice time for Geoff Seaton to start behaving nobly toward Bernie, I thought—realizing I could probably get her whereabouts from him quickly and easily if I was willing to swap sex for it. He was a commodities trader, after all.

"Would you tell her about me and that I think she's in danger? And ask her to call me?"

"Frankly, lady," he said with a grin, "I don't usually reward puritanical behavior in a woman, but I'm gonna make an exception for you. Bernie always did bring out the best in me. Too bad there wasn't much of it. Just leave your phone number on my desk—it's in my study to the right of the front door—as you leave. And close the front door behind you."

"When are you going to see her?" I asked as I got up.

"I got a ticket to the ball game this afternoon, but Bernie's not far from there," he said. He scratched his chin and smiled dreamily. "I'll stop by and see her after the game—maybe spring for a hot dog and a beer like we're still sweethearts or something, and sort of ease into whether I'm a father or not. I got a party to go to later tonight. Maybe, if Bernie's story is interesting enough, I'll skip it. A guy doesn't learn he's got a daughter every day, you know."

As I passed him on my way back to the living room, he sprang up. I tensed, thinking he was hoping to get his pound of flesh, but he just grinned, flopped down on the deck, and began doing one-handed push-ups.

I found his study, which consisted only of a white desk and chair, a desktop computer with a screensaver of naked women gyrating lazily across the large monitor like fish, a fax machine, and a telephone. I wrote down my name and phone number on the pad next to the phone and turned to leave.

He was leaning against the doorframe, watching me: compact and muscular, the smile of a man who thinks he's irresistible playing on his lips. Again I realized I could probably trade Bernie's whereabouts for sex. Would I have done it to save the life of a woman I didn't know if I was certain she was in danger? Or would I have tried to overpower him and then torture it out of him?

Probably the latter, but I didn't know Bernie was in real danger and I don't spend a lot of time on hypothetical questions, so I just walked toward Seaton, keeping as pleasant an expression on my face as I could without encouraging him to think I'd changed my mind about his sexual allure.

"You've got a ball game to go to," I reminded him.

"It doesn't start for an hour," he replied, but stepped aside.

"It's funny," he said, as if he didn't want me to leave. "I didn't know she was pregnant when we broke up. I really didn't. I still saw her around sometimes for a while after that, but she wouldn't talk to me. But then she just dropped out of sight.

"Then one day, six, seven months later, I happened to glance across the street and there she was, big as life. Bigger, in fact—she was pregnant. I thought, Oh, shit—I'm too young to be a father. And then I thought, She'll try to make me marry her or pay her child support or something!

"I couldn't sleep that night thinking about it, or for a lot of nights after that either, waiting for her to show up at the door. I even thought of running away, leaving no forwarding address, but luckily for me, I didn't. I hung in there and never saw her again, or heard anything from her until Monday when she called."

He blew a bemused laugh down through his nose. "It's funny," he went on with a wistful smile, "I never wanted kids, but now that it looks like I've got one, I'd sort of like to meet her—check her out. Of course, Bernie probably hasn't found her. A lot can happen to a kid in twenty years, y'know. But maybe, if Bernie hasn't found her, I could help. I could afford a private detective or something.'' He chuckled. ''It'd be something we could do together, like parents. . . .''

I thanked him as graciously as I could and got out of there before I threw up.

Twenty-eight

Stan didn't have to spend much time in Pine City, just an hour up, thirty minutes to find the right rest home, thirty minutes with Arnie Sorensen, and back to town again.

"Bernie Knapp?" The old man said, his blind eyes searching the darkness where the voice was coming from. "Sure I remember Bernie. Why're you interested in her?"

He was standing in the middle of the room, leaning on a cane. He was well into his eighties, but he was in good shape for all that: tall—almost as tall as Stan—a full head of white hair, and a heavily lined face.

"I'm a writer," Stan told him, "doing an article on a jazz musician named Steadman George—a pianist. Ever hear of him?"

Sorensen scratched his jaw noisily with his free hand. "Name sounds familiar, but I can't place it. Just how does Bernie fit in with this feller?"

"She knew him pretty well in the seventies. I'd like to talk to her about him, get some firsthand impressions of the music scene back then."

The old man crossed his room to a chair, felt to make sure it was where it was supposed to be—visitors moved things sometimes for no good reason—and sat down.

"Funny," he said, resting his chin on the nob of the cane, "I never knew Bernie hung around with musicians. Didn't seem the type. Too young and too . . . what's the word I'm looking for? Otherworldly, I guess you'd say. Least she was when I knew her. But I dunno. It seems there was somethin' else about her. . . ."

He frowned, tried to remember.

"You knew her when she lived here in Pine City too, didn't you?"

"Here? Nah—I never met Bernie till she ran away— went down to the city and started babysitting for the chaplain's wife at the U. I knew her mom and dad, though, before she was born. Everybody knew the Knapp family. God must've had it in for them folks."

"What do you mean by that?"

The old man tried to pierce the darkness, to see his questioner. "Who're you interested in, Mr. Brown, some piano player or Bernie Knapp?" he demanded suspiciously.

"It sounds as though she'd make a good human-interest story too," Stan said smoothly. "I'm always interested in those."

Sorensen considered a moment, like an animal sniffing the air. He nodded finally, said, "Yeah, I guess Bernie'd make a pretty good human-interest story, at that. Her dad was a terror—a bully. Everybody in town was afraid of him. His wife was a mousy thing who kept three things: the house, quiet, and out of her husband's way. Bernie's brother, Carl, didn't want to go to Vietnam. All the menfolk in that family had fought in one war or another, so he was supposed to too. Instead, he hanged himself in the barn— couldn't stand his daddy's bullying, his uncles' scorn. The mother died a couple years later and that was the last straw for Bernie. She dropped out of school and took the first bus she could down to the city."

"So she probably wouldn't be here now," Stan said.

"Here? Hell, no! Why would she come back to Pine City? Nothin' left for her here. Dad's dead, anyway, even if she did want to kiss and make up."

He frowned, thinking. The only sounds were the traffic going by in the street outside his window. "Somethin' funny about Bernie, I seem to recall. What was it, now?"

"Funny?"

The old man nodded. "She up and left the chaplain's without giving any notice. Left the chaplain's wife in a hell of a bind, you'll excuse my French. She was takin' courses at the University, which was why she needed a babysitter in the first place. And the chaplain was too busy doin'

God's work to bother with his family," he added sarcastically.

"I felt sorta responsible," he went on, "since I'd recommended Bernie to 'em in the first place." He shook his head. "But she seemed like a nice kid to me."

Stan knew a version of this story and struggled to keep the impatience off his face, before remembering it wouldn't make any difference.

"I think my grandson knocked her up," Sorensen said finally.

"Your *grandson*!"

Sorensen peered in the direction the words had come from, nodded, then got up and began pacing the room, rapping things with his cane. Stan kept away from him.

"I never asked him about it, of course, but that's what I think happened. You see, I saw Bernie again six, seven months after she left the chaplain's. She come to the church one Sunday, and she was in the family way—and that's puttin' it mildly! She sat way in back, looking miserable—as who wouldn't if they was big with child and just a child themself? I thought maybe she'd come up afterwards and say something to the chaplain but she didn't, halfway through the service she just up and slunk out of the church."

"But what's your grandson got to do with it?" Stan demanded impatiently.

"They was goin' together, Geoff and Bernie," Sorensen replied just as impatiently, as though the entire world must know that. "They'd known each other here when they was kids, before Geoff moved down to the city to go to the University. She got in touch with him down there when she ran away from home. Geoff happened to mention to me that she was looking for a part-time job, and I told him the Masons was looking for a babysitter. Or was it the other way around?" He shrugged. "Don't suppose it matters."

"And you think this Geoff—your grandson—might be the father of Bernie's kid?"

"Who else? You think it could've been the chaplain?" He chuckled at his little attempt at a joke. "I never liked that man—he was too slick, somehow—but he had a wife and kid and another on the way. He wouldn't get involved with a young girl like Bernie, would he?''

"Maybe your grandson knows where I can find Bernie," Stan said. "What's his name?"

"Seaton. Geoff Seaton. He's a stockbroker, lives in a fancy house by one of the lakes, just sits in front of one of them computers and taps on some keys and bingo! he's made a million dollars or lost a million—he don't care, either way. I don't know how people can live like that.''

Stan had heard enough. He left quickly, barely remembering to thank Sorensen for his help. The old man stood in the sunlight in the middle of the room and stared after him with his milky eyes.

"If you see Geoff," he hollered after him, "you tell him I'm still alive—that'll be news to him. And tell him if he don't come visit me someday I'll cut him out of my will.'' He chuckled sardonically. "That oughtta bring him running!"

Twenty-nine

After leaving Geoff Seaton, I killed a couple of hours on Lake Eleanor, keeping one ear cocked to the noises of the ball game coming out of various radios in the sand around me, just in case the game was called or a blowout that Seaton might be tempted to leave early—especially if he really wanted to get in touch with Bernie and officially become a father. I wanted to be home in case Bernie called.

When the game ended at a little after five, I strolled home, hoping to find a message from Bernie on my answering machine. There wasn't one.

I sat down with a book and tried to read, but found it hard to concentrate, imagining that Bernie and Seaton were sitting around somewhere together—maybe with their daughter—and had forgotten all about me or agreed that I was a nutcase who could wait.

By seven, I couldn't take it any longer and called Seaton and got his answering machine. "It's Peggy O'Neill," I told the damned thing. "Please call me."

I called him again at eight-thirty with the same result and then gave up.

The uncertainty began to get on my nerves. Had he decided not to talk to her and was off partying with friends somewhere? Was he with her now and they were getting reacquainted and Bernie figured I could wait? Or possibly he'd been unable to find her? Or she knew all about who was looking for her and didn't want to talk to me about it for reasons of her own?

After all, I had no idea what kind of person she was or what she'd been up to the past two decades. The man I thought was pursuing her could be somebody she knew and wanted to avoid for reasons having nothing to do with murder or her child. For all I knew, he could be a bill collector.

Except I didn't believe it. Or rather, I wanted to know for sure before dropping it and getting back to my everyday life—whatever that was now.

By nine I'd decided I couldn't just sit around and wait any longer for Seaton or Bernie to call. After all, she was supposed to be in town only through tomorrow. So I decided to try to find her through Greta Markham and the necklace.

I knew the play on the Showboat started at eight and lasted about two hours, so I got there at a quarter to ten and stood on the shore next to the boat and skipped stones on the river until it was over. I could hear the actors' voices occasionally, when one of them shouted, the audience's laughter and cheers and boos, and Sam Allen's piano playing.

At a few minutes after ten, the actors dashed off the boat and lined up on shore, talking animatedly among themselves and ready to greet members of the audience as they poured down the gangplank.

I got to Greta before the crowd did. I barely recognized her in her costume and makeup. She looked as different from the way I'd seen her before as a young Victorian lady looks from a '90s punk rocker.

She was surprised to see me, since I hadn't come from the boat. "Well, hello!" she said. "What're you doing here? Still trying to make Steady's death a murder?"

"Something like that," I replied. "And I'd like to talk to you about it."

"Me? Why?" She smiled at a member of the audience who came up and told her how much he'd enjoyed the play.

"Can we talk about it after you've changed?" I asked.

"Thank you," she said, giving another member of the audience a dazzling smile. To me she said, "I don't know. I'm going out with some friends. What's it about?"

"That necklace one of your fans gave you," I said. "Or was it your mother?"

Her eyes widened in surprise. "What about it?"

"Do you know who gave it to you?"

She shook her head. "No—but I'd like to! Do you know?"

"Let's talk about it," I said, feeling the hostile gazes of the people whose way to her I was blocking.

She gave me a searching look. I returned one of my own. "All right," she said finally. "I'll meet you here in half an hour."

Sam, at the end of the line of actors, spotted me over the heads of some of his admirers, so I went down and said hello.

"You saw the play?" he asked.

"No, I'm here to talk to Greta."

"About George's death or this Oscar Wildean woman who sold her baby?"

Both, actually, I thought, but I just told Sam I wanted to talk to her about her recollections of George. "She told me he was a friend of her father's," I added.

"Well, just don't arrest her," Sam said. "Her understudy's fine for the play but she can't sing or dance worth a damn."

She came off the boat with some of the other actors, said something to them, and came quickly over to me. She was dressed in a white T-shirt, black tights, and hiking shoes. Only the oversized black leather jacket was missing from the costume she'd been wearing the first time I'd seen her. She was wearing the necklace I was sure Bernie had given her.

"Is this gonna take a while?" she demanded.

"I don't know," I said. "It could."

She nodded, went back and spoke to her friends for a minute. I recognized the man she'd been with at the Getaway the night I'd been there with Woody and Steadman George's other friends. Rick, her boyfriend, was nowhere to be seen.

When she came back, I suggested we walk down the river a way and sit on the shore—I knew a nice spot, I said, under an old river willow.

"Weirder and weirder," she said, but followed me. When we were settled on the bank, she looked around and said, "A nice spot, huh? Couldn't be far from where you found poor Steady, could it?'' She gave a mock shudder.

I pointed to the necklace and asked her to tell me how she'd gotten it.

She looked at me curiously. ''What is it, some kind of sacred relic? That strange woman who gave it to me was being pursued by little brown men wearing big turbans who'd do anything to get it back and as they closed in on her, she couldn't think of anything to do except throw it over my head and run?''

''Is that what happened?'' I asked.

''Sort of.'' She swallowed hard. ''This is so weird, you know—you wanting to know about it. Right after the play—it was the night Steady drowned—she came up to me and before I knew it, she'd draped the necklace over my head and said, 'I made this for you,' and hurried off. I tried to give it back, told her I couldn't accept it, but the look on her face was so—so *desolate,* I changed my mind. I just hollered, 'Thank you,' after her. I don't know if she even heard me.''

''That guy you're going with—Rick—joked at the Boardinghouse the other day that she was your mother,'' I said.

She laughed uneasily. ''Rick's a jerk. He heard some of the other actors teasing me about it. They thought she looked like me.'' She added softly: ''And to me she looked like somebody I'd known all my life.''

''You've been wearing the necklace ever since,'' I pointed out. ''Why's that?''

She smiled down at it, shrugged. ''I don't—'' She stopped abruptly and looked up at me, her eyes wide. ''What are you getting at, Peggy? You know something you're not telling me. What is it? C'mon, give!''

''Steadman George told me an interesting story a couple of days before he died,'' I said.

''Steady had lots of interesting stories,'' she said impatiently. ''Get to the point, will you?''

''It was about a woman—a girl, actually. She was seventeen—sixteen when she got pregnant twenty years ago. Her name's Bernie. She was going to get an abortion, but George persuaded her to have the baby instead and sell it to some people he knew.''

"True story?" Greta asked. As she did, she scrambled to her feet, as if getting ready to run.

"True story," I replied. "Now, for some reason, she's decided she wants to find her daughter again. She contacted a woman she'd known back then—somebody who knew where she could find Steadman George. She gave her a necklace that's a close match to yours. Same style, same kind of stones, and the same decorations on the wooden pieces."

"You're sure?" she asked, almost whispering.

I nodded.

She continued to stare at me for a moment and then her eyes jumped to the bushes and trees behind me, as if searching for something, an explanation for what I'd told her that didn't involve her, perhaps. Then she groped behind her for the willow tree and stood next to it, an arm around it, almost hugging it.

I wondered if I'd made a terrible mistake, telling her the story, but wondered what else I could have done, short of abandoning my search for Bernie.

She shook her head. "No—no, it's gotta be a mistake, Peggy," she said, her voice pleading, "I can't be her kid. There's no way—I can't be!"

Before I could say anything, she went on, more urgently, the words tumbling over one another. "But I've gotta find her—I've gotta ask her why she thinks I'm her daughter! I mean, it's crazy! Steady could've told her it was me as a joke—he had a nasty sense of humor sometimes, you know—but you didn't know him, Peggy, so you can't know that about him, can you? But he did. Or she could be one of those poor crazy women who've lost their kids and go around accosting people they think look like them." She stopped suddenly and waited for me to say something.

"Isn't that right?" she demanded, when I didn't.

"Yes," I said.

"But you don't think so, do you?" She laughed wildly. "No—of course you don't! Of course you don't." She looked around some more, as if for help. "Do you know where she is?"

"No," I replied. "I was hoping you did."

"I haven't seen her since she gave me this," she answered, holding up the necklace, staring down at it as though it were that sacred relic she'd joked about.

Her expression brightened a little. "Maybe she realized she'd made a mistake and her daughter's somebody else! I mean, I've seen my birth certificate, Peggy. A bunch of us decided to have our horoscopes done when we were in high school and we needed to know the exact time and place we were born. I don't believe in that crap, but I went along with it as a joke. So Mom got me a copy of mine. If I was bought and sold, there wouldn't be one, would there?"

I told her how Steadman George said he'd arranged it.

"Oh," she said softly then, her face falling. She didn't say anything for a minute when I'd finished, just turned her back to me and stared out at the dark river, her body silhouetted against the starry sky. When she turned back again to me, her eyes were glittering with tears.

"So she might actually have had me—her kid, I mean—in her arms for a while," she said, more quietly now, "and then traded her for thirty pieces of silver. Right?"

I nodded.

"Well, she was just a poor kid herself, I guess," she went on, "so it must've been a pretty scary time for her, and the money she got for—for her kid—probably meant a lot to her, a lot more than a baby could've meant."

Suddenly she glared down at me. I could see the tracks the tears had made on her face, as well as some of the greasepaint she'd missed in the dressing room. "Dragging a person down to a river in the middle of the night and telling her she's adopted without any real proof isn't very nice, is it?" she demanded hoarsely.

"No," I agreed, "it's not. But I couldn't think of anything else to do to try to find Bernie. I'm worried about her."

"Worried?" There was sudden concern in her voice. "Why?"

I explained it as best I could—my curiosity about how George had gotten drunk and drowned and about the man I'd seen on the boat with him who I later learned was looking for Bernie.

She thought about that a minute. "This Bernie's probably lived a kind of hand-to-mouth existence since she sold her baby," she said with unconvincing indifference—especially for such a good actress, according to Sam. "Maybe this guy you think is out to get her is just somebody she owes money to—or maybe he's an ex-boyfriend or even a husband who's stalking her." She paused a moment. "He could even be the—the kid's father. Or the father of some other kid she sold."

"Yes," I agreed, "she could be any of those things."

I saw no reason to tell Greta about Geoff Seaton. If he was her father, she'd probably be better off not knowing. "But I want to talk to her," I added, "to find out which—and to make sure she knows that somebody's looking for her."

Greta continued to glare at me another minute, her face pouty and tear-streaked. Then her shoulders slumped and she came over and sat down next to me. "I want to talk to her too," she said.

We were silent for a while, the only noise the lapping of the river on the shore in front of us. Then Greta turned to me. "Steady drowned Wednesday night, didn't he?"

"Or sometime after midnight Thursday morning. Why?"

"Because I talked to Mom Wednesday afternoon on the phone and she sounded upset—edgy. I asked her if there was anything wrong, but she said no. I didn't believe her, but I didn't nag her about it either, just figured if it was anything serious, I'd hear about it soon enough."

She waited for me to say something. When I didn't, she asked: "Do you think this Bernie could've got in touch with Mom?"

"I don't know," I said. "Has she said anything to you about George's death?"

"I called her to tell her about it Thursday afternoon. She wanted to know all the details—was it an accident, did the police suspect foul play? That kind of stuff. I remember thinking at the time it was odd, her making a big deal out of it, because she'd never liked Steady."

She looked at me. "But it doesn't have to mean anything, Peggy—I could be imagining things. And so could you."

"Yes," I said, "I know. We could both be imagining things."

She rested her chin on a knee, wrinkled her brow in thought. "But I can't just call Mom and ask her about it. I mean, if you're right and she's not my mom—my biological mom—it must've been important to her to keep it from me all these years. I can't just pry it out of her over the phone, can I?"

"No, you can't," I agreed, although I wished she'd do it anyway, since it was possible her mother would know where Bernie was now.

"What I have to do is go out there," she said, "take mom's favorite coffee cake—I think I've got some in the freezer—and sit with her in the backyard and lead her up to it gently."

"When?" I asked, trying to keep the eagerness out of my voice.

"Tomorrow, after she and Loren—my stepdad—get back from church and Loren goes off to play golf. Maybe I'll even surprise them and go to church with them."

I had to admit that that was the most I could expect, given the lateness of the hour.

Neither of us apparently wanted to get up and return to the Showboat and the parking lot, so we stayed there a little while longer. We should have had marshmallows, and a bonfire.

"I loved my dad," she said softly after a few minutes, as though speaking to the river. "And I love my mom too, of course. But if you're right about me and Bernie, it would explain some things that've puzzled me all my life."

"Such as?" I asked, amazed at how calmly she was considering the matter now, after the initial shock had passed.

She smiled. "Oh, like, I remember as a kid my aunts would be sitting around discussing who-all the cousins took after. They'd squint at me and cock their heads and say, 'Well, Greta has Uncle Dave's eyes, I think,' but they sounded doubtful and I couldn't see any resemblance. I was big and gawky and stuck out among my cousins like the swan among the other ducklings.

"I always liked that story as a kid and I dreamt about the day when I'd finally start looking like the swan I really was—until it finally struck me that I was a duck among swans, not the other way around!"

"There's nothing wrong with being a duck," I said.

"I know that now!" she said with an impatient shrug. "But there is until you grow out of thinking you're supposed to be a swan."

She held her hands out in front of her, looked from the one to the other. "You should see my mom's hands. They're beautiful. She helped pay the bills as a hand model when I was growing up, you know—until Dad died and she married Loren. With my hands, I could probably get a job modeling Corn Husker's Lotion!"

"According to Sam you're very talented," I said, "and it would be a shame if you went into dentistry instead of show business."

"Oh, Sam—he's such a romantic! The thing is, my mom and stepdad want me to go to dental school and become a partner with Loren and then take over the practice when he retires. I mean, it's something a lot of people would jump at—good dental practices don't just grow on trees, you know!"

"Neither do good actors."

"You sound like Paul."

"The guy you were with at the Getaway the other night?"

"Yeah. He's a romantic too." She laughed suddenly. "Paul keeps telling me that if I give up showbiz and go into dentistry, I'd be betraying my dad. Well, I guess that wouldn't be a factor anymore, would it—if by some chance you're right and he's not my dad."

She frowned. "But he'd be my dad anyway," she went on, giving me a stern look as though expecting me to contradict her, "no matter who my biological father was. Whatever talent I have, it comes from him."

I asked her how long her father had been dead.

"He died when I was eleven. He was a lot of fun when he was home, but he wasn't home nearly enough, he was always out in the sticks somewhere—wherever he could get a part in a play. Mom wanted him to get out of theater and get a regular job. I don't blame her for that, but acting was all he ever wanted to do. We used to talk about how someday we'd act in plays together."

She smiled at the memory. "It used to freak Mom out

when we'd talk like that. When Dad was in a play in town, I'd beg to be allowed to go. Mom didn't want me to, but he managed to talk her into it. God, how I loved to watch him act! I'd forget it was just a play sometimes. Once he died on stage and I cried, even though I knew he'd get up when the curtain went down and we'd go out for ice cream. I've been waiting for the curtain to go down and him to get up ever since. I dreamed of someday acting opposite him in a play, as his wife or lover. I still do. Is that incest, I wonder?

"Sometimes, after the play, he'd take me with him to the bar where the actors hung out and Steady would be there, playing the piano alone or with a group. He'd come over and somebody would buy him a drink. That's how I got to know him. He'd sometimes bounce me on his knee and call me 'Steadman's little girl.' He had bad breath— booze and cigarettes."

A thought seemed to strike her. "Somebody—me or some other kid—probably owes her life to old Steady, doesn't she? I mean, if it hadn't been for him, Bernie would've got an abortion. Right?"

"Apparently so."

She thought about it a minute. "You believe in abortion?"

I told her I believed in a woman's absolute right to her own body.

"That's not quite the same thing, is it?" she said with a smile. "But I know what you mean. I wonder where I'd be now if my mom—whoever she is—had got one. It's kind of like that question I sometimes ask myself when I'm down. You know, who would I be if my parents had married somebody else? Would I be two people, each with only half of me? And would maybe the one half meet and fall in love with the other half? What would the result of that be? Me?"

"Or what if our parents had decided to wait until the next egg to fertilize," I asked, "or the next night to fertilize it?"

I'm also given to asking the heavy questions when I'm down. I don't know anybody who asks them when they're up.

She glanced at her watch. "It's late," she said reluctantly. "I guess I gotta go. My friends are probably wondering where I am."

We got up and walked back to the Showboat and the parking lot, not saying much. Once I tripped over a tree root, and wished I had the flashlight I carry when I'm on patrol.

Before letting her get into her car, I checked the backseat to make sure it was empty, the legacy of a bad scare I'd had a few months earlier, then stood and watched her drive off.

She wasn't convinced she was Bernie's daughter, I knew, but I also knew she was more than capable of handling it if she was.

When I got home, I checked my answering machine for messages from Geoff Seaton or Bernie. There were none.

Thirty

Saturday was one of the busiest days Bernie had ever had, since she'd never been part of a fair in a city as big as this one. Swallow had been right that the kind of things she had to sell would be popular. She'd sold almost all of her turquoise chips, hairpipe—both the bone and horn—feathers, and pheasant hides. She was grateful for the crowds and the noise and the customers—they kept her eyes off the billboard with Ted Mason's face smiling down at her.

Fred seemed to neglect his own business a lot that day, hanging around her. That was a diversion too, although she'd felt she had to pretend to be happier than she really was around him, which was something of a strain.

Around two, Swallow was doing a tarot reading for an elderly man who was concerned about his wife's health and wanted to know what to do about it. The doctors had tried everything, he'd told her, but she was still suffering from anxiety and stomach problems.

Out of the corner of her eye, Bernie saw Swallow studying the cards, then heard her ask him if he and his wife had been thinking about taking a vacation—perhaps to Europe somewhere—southern Europe.

"Italy!" the man—who'd made it clear when the reading started that he was very skeptical of the tarot—exclaimed in surprise. "We've been talking about it for years, but we've put it off. And now, with Marge not feeling well . . ."

Swallow looked up from the cards. "Now would be a good time to go," she told him.

His face clouded. "Does that mean . . . ?" He stopped,

laughed nervously. "Well, of course, it makes sense to go now, doesn't it, while we're both still able to enjoy it! Who knows what the future holds? No offense," he added.

After the man had paid and gone on his way, Swallow, with a twinkle in her eye, looked up at Bernie and said, "Fred's offer sounds like a good one to me. I hope you're gonna take it. As he says, it wouldn't have to be anything more than a business arrangement. And you wouldn't have to sell the bus and trailer, you know, you could park it out behind the store, all gassed up, and whenever you felt like it, just take off."

"Fred told you what we talked about last night?" Bernie said.

"Did he?" Swallow replied mysteriously, riffling a deck of cards with her plump hands.

"I have a lot of regular customers waiting for me," Bernie said. "I can't leave them in the lurch."

"Oh, silly me, I forgot! You're indispensable, aren't you? The only bead lady in the Southwest. How would those poor Indians make jewelry without Bernie's Bead Bus?"

She gave a loud and scornful laugh. "You're only indispensable to yourself, Bernie. But before you can ever live peacefully with yourself anywhere, you've got something you have to do here. Otherwise, you'll just keep wandering the planet, restless, rootless, till the end of your days."

In spite of herself, Bernie laughed. Swallow had always been given to extreme and poetic ways of putting things.

Swallow lowered her voice. "Have you decided what you're going to do about your daughter?"

Bernie shook her head.

"I didn't think so. We'll do a tarot reading tonight, back at the trailer park where it's quiet and we won't be disturbed. Tarot readings are especially powerful under oak trees, did you know that? You've got a customer."

Bernie turned to the man standing next to her, who was examining some crystals in a box. "Are you looking for anything in particular?" she asked him.

He looked at her, unsmiling. "Yes," he said, his voice curiously soft, "as a matter of fact, I am."

Swallow glanced up at him from her table. She didn't like the sound of his voice or the look in his eyes. His long narrow face and thick gray hair reminded her of wolves she'd seen. And he looked like he'd recently been in a fight: there was a deep scratch on one side of his face, with angry swelling around it. He also had an aura as black as pitch that you could almost reach out and touch—but who would dare?

"Tell me about these crystals," he went on to Bernie. "I understand some people think they have magical properties."

Bernie said, "Yes, some people do."

"But you don't? I notice you're not wearing any crystals yourself."

"I do sometimes," she answered. The way he was looking at her made her uncomfortable. His eyes reminded her of Ted Mason's on the billboard on the roof of the building behind him.

"Can you recommend one that's especially good for warding off evil?" he asked.

She shook her head. "I'm sorry, I can't."

"That's too bad," he said, and gave her a long look, then turned and walked away.

Thirty-one

Once he'd found Bernie, courtesy of Geoff Seaton, and even spoken to her, Stan wandered around the fair for a while, ate a couple of chili dogs, and drank a couple of beers, wondering at the kinds of crap people made to sell at places like this.

He figured Bernie wouldn't be leaving the fair until it closed for the night at ten—business was too good. He thought of going back to his own place, but rejected the idea. Ted might call, wanting to know what progress he'd made in finding Bernie, or even ordering Stan to stop looking for her. Stan wasn't about to do that. He'd invested too much in finding Bernie and disposing of her to quit now, and there was too much at stake anyway—for him as well as for Ted. All he had to do was kill Bernie and the connection to her daughter and Ted was severed for good.

He walked down to the river and strolled upstream to the waterfalls above Riverton Mall that had once powered the flour mills. He climbed to the bridge above the falls and leaned on the guardrail and watched the water going over them. On the surface it looked so calm and seemed to move so slowly—but try to get out of it, once you got close to the edge!

Stan smiled. Bernie was floating in a current like that, totally unaware of how close to the edge she was.

He considered trying to lure her onto the bridge and throwing her over. Nobody would be able to tell her death wasn't an accident, once the falls were finished with her. But there was too much traffic on the bridge for that.

He shrugged, drifted back downstream past the mall and

the fair, in the direction of the University and the Show-boat. Now that he'd found Bernie, it was just a matter of time before he'd have the opportunity to kill her. He'd just have to be patient. If he couldn't drown her in the river and make it look like an accident, the next best thing would be to kill her and take her body out into the woods someplace and bury it. He'd learned a long time ago, in Vietnam, that the secret of success lay in always being prepared for whatever the circumstances offered.

Take Steadman George, for example. He'd left no marks on him—nobody would ever be able to prove his death wasn't an accident.

Geoff Seaton hadn't been as easy. For one thing, he hadn't been able to catch him off his guard, and for another, Seaton had been in good physical shape. Stan touched the deep scratch on his face, a painful reminder of that.

He came to the Showboat. The matinee performance must have just ended because the actors were lined up on shore and the audience was coming off the boat. Where Steadman George had been standing the first time Stan had seen him, there was now a tall heavy man with a black beard who threw back his head and laughed at something a member of the audience was telling him.

Stan studied him a moment in disgust—he hated faggots. The other night, after ditching the campus cop out in front of the Getaway, he'd crossed the river to the Showboat and waited until the performance was over. Then he'd followed the actors and the faggot—who'd apparently taken over playing the piano from George—to a coffeehouse of some kind, where he'd nursed a cup of coffee and eavesdropped, to try to get an idea of what Greta Markham might know and what kind of person she was.

His eyes moved to Greta, smiling and chatting with members of the audience. From the costume she was wear-ing, you couldn't tell the kind of person she really was, but Stan had seen her in the coffeehouse, the way she really looked and acted—loud and brazen, like she thought she owned the world. She'd been wearing the necklace Bernie had draped over her head the night he'd killed George. One of the other actors had teased her about it and wondered why members of the audience didn't bring pretty gifts more often. Greta had just smiled.

Watching her and her friends talking and laughing, hugging and kissing, homosexuals and heterosexuals, black and white, Stan had felt a cold righteousness as he contemplated killing Greta's mother—and Greta too, if it came to that. She looked as capable of indiscriminate sex as Bernie, and as likely to dispose of her babies through abortion. Women like that debased life with their amorality and robbed it of all meaning.

The thought popped into his head that Greta was probably his niece. He brushed it aside angrily and went back to the fair, to keep an eye on Bernie.

Thirty-two

Bernie was glad when ten o'clock finally came and they could close up and go home. She and Swallow said goodnight to Fred and then walked through the mall to the parking ramp, where Swallow had parked her old car. As they were getting into the car, Swallow glanced back over her shoulder.

"There's that creepy guy," she said, "the one who was asking you about crystals earlier today."

"Where?" Bernie asked. She saw a man walking quickly away from them at the end of the aisle.

"He turned when I saw him," Swallow said. "I don't like it. I've seen him around the fair all evening, like he's keeping an eye on us."

"Well, he can't catch us now," Bernie said as they drove out of the Mall, their doors locked. You ran into some weird people at fairs—even scary ones, sometimes.

At the trailer park, they stood talking for a minute beside Swallow's tent, a few rows away from Bernie's trailer. Bernie said she'd make coffee and bring it over after she'd taken Gideon out for his nightly run, if Swallow was sure she wanted to do a reading after doing so many that day at the fair.

"Of course I'm sure," Swallow said. "I wouldn't offer if I wasn't, would I?"

Bernie walked back to the trailer park office to get Gideon. She exchanged a few words with the manager about the weather and then took Gideon for his run along the river. Then she made a cup of instant coffee and took it over to Swallow's tent. She didn't really believe in the tarot, but she knew she'd have trouble getting to sleep that night anyway, so she welcomed the chance of Swallow's company for a while longer. Whatever the truth of the cards, Swallow made her readings interesting.

She found Swallow already seated at the picnic table in front of her tent, four well-thumbed tarot decks lying in the soft glow of an old Coleman lantern.

"You know the drill," Swallow said, sipping from her cup of undrinkable herb tea. "You've heard me say it often enough to my clients. Choose the deck you feel most comfortable with. Play with 'em all first, if you want. Take your time. Think of a specific question while you're doing it, if you'd like to—but it's not necessary. And you don't have to tell me what the question is, if you do."

Bernie had once asked Swallow who she thought spoke through the cards and Swallow had replied, without hesitation, "God."

When Bernie had smiled at that, she'd gone on: "You think God's too busy and too far away to pay attention to a couple of people huddled over a deck of dog-eared cards, don't you?"

Bernie had shrugged evasively.

"Well, you're right—*that* God is, for sure!" She waved a dismissing hand at the sky. "I'm not speaking of *that* God, that divine CEO—'lord,' 'master,' 'thy kingdom come'—sitting all-powerfully on a throne high up in the sky somewhere and surrounded by stern-faced vice presidents, assistant vice presidents and assorted flunkies with halos, robes, and wings.

"Oh, no, Bernie, the God I'm talking about is the God in you and me and everyone else who's willing to listen. And when I sit with people at my little table and talk about what I see in the cards, I'm only helping them tune in to the voice of their inner God."

When Bernie had chosen a deck, Swallow took it from her and began laying out the cards.

Thirty-three

Stan followed Bernie and the squat psychic through the empty shopping mall and up the dead escalator to the parking ramp. They were nattering away a mile a minute, totally unaware of him following along behind. He could have been breathing down their necks and they wouldn't have noticed. He was disappointed that Bernie wasn't alone, but it didn't matter, it just delayed the inevitable a little longer.

When he saw Bernie and Swallow get into a car together, he went quickly down to his four-wheeler parked close to the exit, then waited until they drove out of the ramp and followed them as they took the river road out of town.

After about fifteen minutes the car's brake lights went on and it slowed and turned into a driveway. A sign next to it said it was the Riverview Campgrounds. Through the trees he could glimpse campers and trailers glittering in the moonlight, lights burning in some of their little windows.

He turned in after the car and followed it down the narrow road through the trees, trailers and campers parked on both sides. When the taillights came on again and the car stopped, Stan stopped too, doused his lights, got out, and went quickly down the road, staying in shadow, until he could see Bernie and the psychic get out of the car and stand talking together next to it.

He almost laughed: about twenty yards in front of him was a big old yellow school bus. On the side, in black lettering, were the words BERNIE'S BEAD BUS BEADS & FINDINGS.

He looked at his watch. It was only a little before eleven

and people were still awake in the campground. He could hear the voices and canned laughter of television programs coming from some of the trailers, a child's whining voice, an adult's annoyed reply. He'd noticed a bar a few miles back, and decided to kill time there while waiting for the trailer park, and Bernie, to get to sleep.

Thirty-four

Swallow had dealt the cards into what Bernie had heard her call "the ancient Celtic cross spread," a cross of six cards and, next to it, a vertical line of four. Bernie looked at the cards too as Swallow studied them. She'd chosen this deck because the pictures reminded her of the children's books her mother had owned as a child and passed on to her, with bright but slightly faded primary colors and simply drawn pictures. She'd left all of those things behind when she'd run away from home and, thinking of them now for the first time in years, wondered what her father had done with them. Tossed them in the trash, probably.

In spite of the fact that she didn't really believe in the tarot, her heart sank when she saw the tenth card, which she knew was the most important card, the final outcome of the reading. It depicted two destitute people, sick, hungry, and cold, one of them on crutches, passing a lighted window in a snowstorm. Not very encouraging! She wondered what Swallow would make of it when she got to it.

Swallow looked up and smiled, as though she knew what Bernie was thinking. "One card—even the last—isn't the whole story," she said, "any more than one chapter of a novel is the whole book."

She took a sip of her tea. "I always look first for a predominance of any one suit," she said. "You've got three pentacles and three swords, which makes it interesting, since pentacles symbolize love and swords strife."

There were two cards in the middle of the cross, one on top of the other. Swallow picked up the bottom card.

"A card in this position represents your biggest concerns

right now," she said. "The Four of Cups tells me you've been thinking a lot about your life lately and you're feeling that something's missing. It also tells me you're feeling out of touch with people close to you—family, or friends."

Before Bernie could say anything, she laughed, holding up a hand. "I know, Bernie, I know! It doesn't take a psychic to know that about you, but there's more to it than that. It also tells me that what you've got in the way of material things isn't enough for you anymore. See, the young man on the card doesn't show any pleasure in being offered another cup. He's got four already and they haven't made him happy."

She put that card down and picked up the other card in the middle of the cross. "Now this card," she went on, "represents the forces standing in your way." She pursed her lips a moment, then said: "The Knight of Wands is a good card, but not in this position in the spread. See how boldly he's charging into the future. That means that your impulsive nature isn't going to do you any good."

Bernie laughed. "I don't have an impulsive nature!"

"Maybe you don't think so, but you do. In the matter that's concerning you now, the card's telling you to watch out for impulsive behavior. Think before you act!"

She put that card down and picked up the card at the top of the cross. "This is one of my favorite cards," she said. "The Ace of Cups. And it's in a good position. It represents what's going to happen soon—or the best you can hope for. You can tell just by looking at it that it symbolizes peace and contentment. It also symbolizes eternal life, which is probably the same thing."

"There's something sort of passive about it," Bernie remarked doubtfully. "It's just the opposite of the Knight of Wands."

"That's right. It means you're probably not going to get what you want through direct, bold action, you're going to get it through love."

Bernie smiled, but didn't say anything.

Next Swallow picked up the card at the bottom of the cross, saying, "This card represents what you're standing on, Bernie."

"Standing on?" It wasn't a very pleasant-looking card—

in fact, it was quite miserable-looking. It showed a young woman sitting up in bed, her head in her hands as if she were weeping. Nine swords were suspended in the air behind her.

"It's what happened to you in the past," Swallow explained. "It symbolizes death, deception, disappointment, and despair. This is why you smile so rarely, Bernie—and why, when you do, it's so beautiful."

"And that's what I have to stand on?" Bernie asked, trying to make a joke out of it. "I'm nothing like that woman!" she protested angrily.

"You're being too literal for your own good!" Swallow snapped. "All the card means is that you have somebody like that inside you somewhere and she needs to be heard now."

Bernie didn't say anything to that.

The fifth card was on the left arm of the cross.

"The card here," Swallow said, "is about what's going on in your life now, but is ready to pass out of it. The Eight of Wands, upside down, is a good card to have passing away—let me tell you! It represents jealousy, hostility."

She looked up at Bernie. "You've been feeling some hostility, haven't you?"

In spite of herself, Bernie gave the question some thought. Yes, she had to admit to herself that she'd been feeling some jealousy—hostility, even—toward her daughter's mother—stepmother, that is.

"Doesn't everybody feel some hostility?" she asked Swallow sulkily.

Swallow smiled and let the card fall onto the table. "It doesn't matter anyway," she said. "It'll soon be gone from your life."

She frowned as she picked up the card on the right arm of the cross. "Frankly, the Swords aren't my favorite suit," she said, "and the King is my least favorite Sword. But at least it's not reversed—that's something. The card in this position represents what's coming up in your near future."

She brooded over it for a minute. "It's a person coming into your life," she said, "somebody in a position of authority." She looked up at Bernie. "Does that ring any bells?"

Bernie shook her head. There'd been times when she'd had to ask some pretty stern-looking people for credit—for bus and trailer repairs, especially—but not recently. All her bills were paid and she didn't owe anybody anything.

"Well," Swallow said, "if you do meet somebody like that—and I feel sure you're going to soon—be careful."

She let the card fall, glared at it. "Look at his face!" she said. "It's the embodiment of law over mercy."

Next she turned her attention to the four cards in a vertical line to the right of the cross. Her face lit up, as though she hadn't noticed the bottom card before. "I love the Tower!" she exclaimed as she picked it up.

Bernie couldn't see why, although Swallow had an odd take on most things in life. The card showed a tower being struck by lightning. It was on fire and two people, one of them wearing a crown, were plunging headfirst from it. Maybe Swallow liked it because she thought the person wearing the crown was the King of Swords.

"It stands for destruction," Swallow said. "But not all destruction is bad, you know! Especially if what's destroyed isn't worth saving. In this position, a card represents what you're worried about. You're worried about change, Bernie—the destruction of something to bring about something else." She smiled. "Maybe you're going to give up your bus and trailer and settle down."

Bernie gazed down at it, her brow furrowed. She wondered if it could represent what would happen if she tried to force her way into Greta's life—to herself or, worse, to Greta.

The next card was the Seven of Swords, upside down. It showed a figure carrying swords and sneaking away from what looked like a fair with colorful tents and waving pennants.

"The position of this card," Swallow said, "signifies the influence of your friends and family on your problem." She laughed. "She looks like you, Bernie."

"She looks like a thief," Bernie said.

"You're being too literal again! Anyway, the card's reversed, which tells me you're going to get what you wish for, but in some unexpected way."

It means I'm going to have to steal it, Bernie thought.

The next to last card was the Nine of Cups, which featured a self-satisfied-looking woman on a bench, her arms folded, a sated expression on her face, nine goblets on a wall behind her.

"Oh, Bernie!" Swallow exclaimed.

"What?"

"I didn't realize you were such a dreamer!"

"Me!"

"This card represents your hopes for the outcome—and you can't hope for better than this! Just look at her—doesn't she look just like the cat that ate the canary? She represents you—who you want to be!"

Bernie didn't think it looked like her at all. She wondered if that was what absolutely contented people look like inside. It wasn't what she looked like, anyway!

"You're not going to leave out the last card, are you?" she asked, cutting through Swallow's enthusiasm.

The picture on the Five of Pentacles told you everything you needed to know about that card, she thought. It was the opposite in every way of the Nine of Cups, a picture of unrelieved misery to Bernie's eye. A card like that could only predict something awful, and the position it was in, she knew, made it the most important card of all: it was what would come, the final result of the workings of all the other cards in the spread.

She was sure Swallow could make something positive out of it, since Swallow never ended a reading on a down note, but she was curious how she'd manage it.

Swallow didn't say anything for a minute.

"Too bad the woman on the Nine of Cups can't share with these people, isn't it?" Bernie couldn't resist saying with uncharacteristic sarcasm.

Swallow looked up and gave her one of her dazzling smiles.

"Oh, but when you take it in the context of everything that's gone before," she said, "it's not as bad as it looks. Most of the cards are favorable—or they would be if you'd let them. What this card means in this spread is that you're in danger of running away from your happiness, the happiness shown by the Nine of Cups."

"My life up to now has been happy enough for me!"

Bernie interrupted her. "It's been nothing like the lives of these poor people! You know that, Swallow. And where in this card do you see any happiness these people could be running from, anyway?"

"Don't you have eyes, Bernie?" Swallow asked, annoyed by Bernie's tone. "Look at the window behind them! It's glowing with light and warmth, but they don't see it because their faces are turned away! You're just as blind as they are. If they would just look to their left, they'd see the light and go inside and maybe they'd be permitted to share in the warmth and the light. But they're just like you—too stubborn or afraid to see what's right under their noses."

She sat back in her chair. "Here's what the reading tells me, Bernie," she said fiercely. "You've been thinking a lot about your life, about whether or not to change it. You're carrying around a lot of garbage—shame, sorrow, loss, and anger. You don't even realize yourself how much. You've put off doing anything about it for a long time and you want to do something about it now, but you're afraid of the consequences, both for yourself and others.

"You've spent too much of your life trying to please others. It's time to stop and begin being good to yourself instead. It won't hurt—you just think it will! And you think it would be selfish to go after what you want."

She paused, took a deep breath before continuing.

"You're going to encounter change, Bernie, whether you like it or not. That's what the Knight of Wands and the Tower are telling you. It's going to be scary, but in the long run it'll be for the best. And you've got to trust your friends and family, because you're going to need them."

Her face clouded. "But there are also people in your life working against you."

"Who? I don't know anybody like the King of Swords."

Swallow nodded, her expression darkening. "Maybe not," she said. "But I don't like him where he is. Watch out for him. He's a lot worse than the Five of Pentacles!"

For a few minutes neither of them said anything, just listened to the breeze rustling in the leaves in the oak tree above them and the soft hiss of the Coleman lantern. It was late and the trailer park was dark and silent now.

"Thanks, Swallow," Bernie said finally. She stretched, forced herself to yawn, even though she wasn't tired. "It's almost midnight—time to go to bed. We have to get up early tomorrow."

Swallow looked up at her unhappily. "Did you get your question answered?"

Bernie shrugged. "I don't know. I'll have to think about it," she added, because she didn't want to disappoint Swallow entirely.

Suddenly Swallow leaned across the table. "That man on the billboard," she said. "Pastor Ted. He's the father of your child, isn't he?"

Bernie nodded.

Swallow stared at her a moment, her small dark eyes glittering, her face suddenly cronelike in the white glow of the lantern. "Stay away from him," she said. "He's dangerous."

"Dangerous? Why?"

"Think what it would do to his career if it got out that you'd had his baby twenty years ago!"

Bernie had thought about that. She hadn't thought about what he might do to prevent it, though.

"There's no way he could know anything about it," she said. "He probably doesn't even remember me anymore."

"Good. Because you never want to threaten the power of the King of Swords!"

Thirty-five

Stan sat in a dark corner of the bar and nursed his beer, careful not to drink too much. All around him people were talking, shouting, and laughing, some were dancing to loud country music, but he didn't hear them. He had a remarkable ability to tune out distractions when he wanted to think his own thoughts. Occasionally someone would cast an incurious glance over at the somber, grayish man huddled in the corner with the angry gash on his face, but that didn't bother him. Nobody knew who he was and, when he'd done what he'd come to do, nobody would connect him with it either. There were other single men in the bar, huddled over glasses in the dark.

He sat and thought. He'd done a lot of thinking about what was wrong with the world and he'd finally come to the conclusion that, while women were at the heart of the problem, men were ultimately to blame for having given women power they were not equipped by nature to possess.

Women didn't think like men, Stan was certain of that. When they tried to, the result was always second-rate, since it didn't come natural to them. Thinking—the kind that created law and order—required reflection and detachment. Women were too close to nature for that. Their useful adult lives were bounded on the one side by the onset of their periods and on the other by menopause, with PMS, menstruation, and pregnancy filling the intervening years. They'd been designed to breed and feed, and not much else. Anybody with eyes could see that. Men—the hunters, the planners—were designed to think.

Call it God, as Ted did, or natural selection, as Darwin

did, the result was the same: women were designed to *be*, men were designed to *do*.

With the invention of civilization—invented by men to give both men and women security—came the home, which Stan saw as a kind of "moon" to civilization's "sun," in that the home couldn't exist without civilization. The women were allowed to run the home—under the guidance of the man, of course, who knew how it fit into the bigger picture of the civilization as a whole.

As long as the world was a dangerous place, with all kinds of enemies lurking out beyond the clearing men had carved from the wilderness, just waiting for their chance to conquer your village and carry off your wives and children, women were content with this arrangment. They needed men to fight for them, and bring them food. Being pregnant or nursing so much of the time, women couldn't do those things.

But that didn't mean women believed in the family, in civilization! And they certainly didn't believe in monogamy—another male invention designed to keep sexuality, both men's and women's, but especially women's, within bounds. Women don't care who the father of their children is—they're not bred to care, they're bred to breed. Women simply went along with monogamy because men had the power to force them to.

Like any inferior species, or anybody in an inferior position, women resented their subordination, and when civilization and technology finally made the world so safe that they no longer needed men to protect them and their children, when they no longer even needed to have children if they didn't want to, they suddenly announced that they were not only as good as men, they were better!

And just look at what that had done to the family! And it was getting worse all the time.

It was time for men to reassert themselves. One way that could happen, of course, would be if some kind of natural or human catastrophe destroyed civilization—that would bring women back to their senses and restore the natural order! Until that happened—and Stan was sure it would, sooner or later—the next best thing would be to reassert the will of God.

Stan didn't believe in God himself, but he was convinced that the belief in an angry God—a Father with a capital F—was necessary to restore men to their natural positions of authority. Not that Stan idealized men. Hell, no! He'd be the first to admit that they fell short of their ideals, as Ted had with Bernie twenty years ago. But at least men *had* ideals! And wasn't it proof of how high those ideals were that they were so hard to live up to?

Bernie had caught Ted at a weak moment—every man has weak moments, for chrissakes!—when his pregnant wife wouldn't let him touch her. She'd offered him the comfort of her body. That was only natural—what else does a woman have to offer? It was understandable but not, in this case, forgivable.

Did Bernie ever agonize over what she'd done? Not likely! She'd taken Ted's money to get an abortion and then turned around and sold her baby! How many more times had she done that? And how many abortions had she got?

Stan had killed babies in war. He'd killed mothers too. He knew that. He'd called down air strikes on Viet Cong villages and gone in afterward and seen the results. Not pretty! But Stan had killed babies to save civilization; women killed them to destroy it!

How would his primitive ancestors have reacted if, when they'd returned home from war, they'd found their women killing their babies so they could be free of their biological destinies?

They'd react exactly as Stan was reacting now.

He looked at the clock over the bar: twelve-thirty. The trailer park and Bernie would be asleep now: it was time to get to work. He got up from the booth and walked out of the bar into the night.

Thirty-six

Bernie couldn't sleep. She lay on her bed in the trailer, the faint breeze coming through the screens in the open windows not enough to relieve the heat and humidity, listening to the night noises outside. A lot of what Swallow had told her could easily have been intuition—Swallow had known Bernie a long time and, of course, Bernie had told her why she'd come back here too. And she'd seen how Bernie had reacted to the face of Ted Mason on the billboard.

Images of the tarot cards floated in and out of her mind like childhood toys. The Tower: Swallow had given it a positive interpretation, but Bernie wasn't convinced. No matter how you looked at it, it was clearly a scene of violence. And the girl sitting up in bed with her head in her hands, and the two beggars in the snow! Violence, sadness, and misery, everywhere you looked.

Who was to say Swallow's interpretation was the correct one? Why weren't Bernie's feelings about the cards truer?

She—Bernie—was the smug woman in the Nine of Cups who sat there with her hands crossed over her fat belly, oblivious to the harm she was causing! Or worse, she was the thief in the Seven of Swords, trying to steal away with something that didn't belong to her.

And the woman sobbing in the bed with the swords behind her: couldn't that be Linda Markham—or even Greta—if Bernie went to Greta and told her who she was?

Why would she want to suddenly show up in Greta's life? Greta seemed happy. Who knows what it might do to her if she found out the truth? That could easily be the meaning of the Tower.

Bernie had never thought of anybody but herself her entire life and now she wanted a share of a child she'd had no part in raising! She was only being selfish again, as she'd been when she told Ted Mason she wanted an abortion because she couldn't support a child, and then had turned around and had the child and sold it—and kept the money he'd given her!

And she'd sold her baby to people vouched for by a man like Steadman George! It wasn't any thanks to her that Greta had turned out so well—or survived at all, she added, remembering the story about the mother who'd murdered her adopted child.

What did she have to give Greta? What could she teach her? That life wasn't all fake fireplaces and glass-topped coffee tables and lawns that looked fake too? That sometimes life could be scary and uncertain, when you didn't know if your bus would make it over the mountain to the next town or if you'd make enough at the next powwow or fair or gem show to pay for the gas it took to get there?

And what would Greta make of people like Swallow—not to mention Roxie? An image of Greta as Florence in the Showboat melodrama came into her head. In spite of herself, she had to smile at the thought of Florence trying to think of something to say to Roxie.

Bernie lay sweating on her narrow bed—her air conditioner had broken the summer before and she didn't want to spend the money to repair it—and recalled the Markhams' home: without weather or personality, unreal, like homes she'd seen in movies that looked too good to be true.

"Careful, Bernie," she whispered. "You're building a hate-case against the Markhams again!"

At the memory of the fireplace bursting into flame when Linda Markham had pointed that device at it, she felt the ache in her lower leg where she'd cut it on the glass coffee table: it had become infected and she'd had to put some ointment on it and a bandage.

Fred Foster, now. He made *real* coffee tables. He made them out of wood the way they were supposed to be, with the grain, like flames running the length of the surfaces, showing, and burnished to a soft glow! Why did people want to conceal the grain of wood? Were they ashamed of it? Why pay good money for a coffee table you couldn't even see until you'd walked into it?

She knew that every time she crossed the Markhams' living room she'd bang her leg against that thing. In her mind's eye—Bernie had a strong visual imagination—she could see Greta turning her eyes away in pained embarrassment. "This is my mother? Who let her in?"

And another thing: If she told Greta about herself, she'd also have to tell her about her father—Ted Mason—"Pastor Ted."

And Pastor Ted, to Bernie, was the most embarrassing thing of all. She was sure that no daughter of hers would want a father like that, or could understand how her mother could have let him touch her!

She shook her head and squeezed her eyes shut again. She'd told Mrs. Markham that she would make up her mind what she was going to do by tonight. Was she lying awake too, as Bernie was, anxiously waiting for the phone to ring and to hear Bernie's decision?

Bernie had to do something about it, had to call her first thing tomorrow morning and tell her not to worry, that her secret was safe. She was going away again and this time she'd never come back.

She'd sold Greta twenty years ago; this time she was giving her up freely. She liked the way that sounded so much, she started to say it again—then realized she was trying to make herself better than she was, and clamped her mouth shut.

The decision made, she started to turn over on her side, the way she always slept, and failed to hear something scrape against the screen in the door or see the shadow appear in the window.

Thirty-seven

Stan turned onto a narrow dirt road and followed it down to the river, then backed his four-wheeler into the shrubbery where it couldn't be seen by anybody who might happen by, although that was unlikely at that hour of the night.

He hiked back to the road and walked down to the trailer park, past the trailers and RVs sleeping like great metallic seed pods under the trees. He wasn't too concerned about being heard, since most of the trailers growled or hummed with the noise of their air conditioners.

Even if some insomniac happened to be looking out one of the little trailer windows, it was doubtful he would see Stan slipping from shadow to shadow, avoiding the patches of moonlight that filtered through the trees. He'd been with the Special Forces in Vietnam, and getting into and out of a village unseen was a trick that, like riding a bike, you never lost the hang of—and a trailer park in Middle America wasn't exactly a Viet Cong village.

The yellow school bus was parked in the last row before the ground dropped away to the river. Seeing it like that, off in a corner by itself, Stan felt the same sense of confidence he'd felt when he'd taken care of the loose end called Steadman George. Now here was Bernie, off guard and nearly as isolated as George had been.

He approached cautiously, studied the bus for a moment from the shadow of a tree, considering the best way to get in without awakening Bernie. Finally he crept softly up to it and, on tiptoe, peered through one of the side windows.

It was empty, with only a few boxes and other odds and ends scattered in the aisle. He backed away, realizing it wasn't for living in, and then spotted the little trailer nestled in the shrubbery farther to his left.

He crept over to it, then smiled when he saw that the glass in the window in the door was open. The silence told him Bernie didn't have an air conditioner, so she needed her windows open to catch the summer breeze.

He tried the door, very gently. It was locked and he didn't have the tools he'd need to pick the lock. But that was no problem; he could cut through the screen with his knife, reach inside, and open the door.

If he could keep Bernie quiet, he'd force her to go with him down to the river and drown her there as he'd drowned Steadman George. Then he'd return and remove the damaged screen, close the window, and there'd be no sign of a break-in. Bernie had just gone for a walk by the river, fallen in somehow, and drowned.

With any luck, that campus cop, Peggy O'Neill, might never hear about it, since the trailer park was located out of town and the death wouldn't be investigated by the police who'd investigated George's and Seaton's deaths. People fall in rivers and drown all the time out in the country.

He drew his knife out of his windbreaker, then touched the point of the blade to the screen and pushed.

Something exploded against the door from inside so violently that he could feel it shake. He fell back, dropping the knife as a dog began barking and a woman's voice hollered, ''Who's out there! I'm letting out the dog!''

As a light went on in the trailer, Stan stumbled through the trees and shrubbery down to the river, cursing under his breath and praying Bernie wouldn't let the dog out. He plunged into the muddy water and splashed downstream, prepared to swim if he had to.

Thirty-eight

Gideon was too old to chase an intruder, although he didn't think so, so Bernie held him tightly by his collar and told him to hush, and in the silence heard the sounds of somebody crashing through the underbrush on the slope down to the river.

She shined the light through the window on the river side of the trailer and spotted the intruder as he disappeared in the trees that lined the shore. When she got outside, other trailer lights were coming on and Swallow was running toward her.

Swallow found the knife on the ground outside Bernie's door. She held it up so Bernie could see it.

"The King of Swords," she said, puffing noisily.

She wanted Bernie to call the police and report what had happened, but Bernie, still holding Gideon's collar, looked at the tear in her window screen and shook her head. Whoever had done this would be long gone by the time the police showed up.

She wasn't as concerned as Swallow about the attempted break-in: some men thought women who lived alone in trailers were easy prey, and whoever had tried to break into her trailer had probably chosen it because it was the most isolated in the park. She didn't keep Gideon only for company.

Besides, if Swallow was right and the would-be assailant really was the King of Swords, then she didn't have anything left to worry about on that score, thanks to Gideon. Gideon, of course, had been the Knight of Wands, although to look at him you wouldn't guess it.

SUNDAY

Thirty-nine

The Markhams were getting ready for church the next morning when the phone rang on the table by the bed. Loren Markham, in the bathroom shaving, said, "Would you get that, honey?"

Mrs. Markham, in her bra and panty hose, snatched it up and said hello. She was pale and there was a tremble in her voice. She'd been waiting for Bernie to call her all week long.

"Hello, Mrs. Markham. It's Bernie."

Mrs. Markham tried to say something but couldn't get the words out.

Bernie understood. She said quickly: "I've thought it over and I'm not going to tell Greta. I'm just going to go away again, and I'm not coming back. So your secret's safe--with me, at least. And I don't think Steadman George would tell anybody," she added. "He hasn't so far. I'll talk to him before I leave and tell him what I've decided, so he won't be wondering."

"Who is it?" Loren Markham said, coming out of the bathroom, drying his face.

Mrs. Markham waved him off. "Thank you," she said softly into the phone. "Thank you, Bernie." Bernie didn't know George was dead. Well, what difference did it make? And she couldn't tell her now anyway, with Loren standing right there.

Bernie heard Loren Markham's voice and understood that Mrs. Markham couldn't talk freely. She felt a little disappointed. She didn't want to break this connection with her daughter so abruptly.

"I'm sorry if I've caused you any pain," she said. "I didn't mean to, I really just came back to make sure my daugh—Greta was okay." She tried to laugh but couldn't quite bring it off.

"I wouldn't've stayed long anyway," she went on, forcing as much indifference into her voice as she could. "I'm kind of a restless spirit—here today, gone tomorrow—and I can't stand the humidity either—I've been away too long, I guess. I probably couldn't take the winters anymore either. So what would be the good of telling Greta about me, if I'm just going to leave again?"

She didn't know why she was babbling like this. She knew Mrs. Markham wasn't interested. She was only saying it for her own sake, she realized, hoping the words would make it true.

"Yes, I understand," Mrs. Markham breathed, trying to convey her gratitude through those words as her husband began dressing next to her, but at the same time wishing Bernie would finish saying what she had to say and hang up.

"Anyway," Bernie continued, "the fair closes tonight— the Riverton Art Fair, you know—and then I'll be heading out of town tomorrow. There's a powwow on the Navajo reservation at Yuma next week, you see, and my customers are expecting me, so I can't dawdle."

She didn't know why she told Mrs. Markham where the crafts fair was. Was it to give her a chance to tell Greta, if she wanted to?

"I understand," Mrs. Markham said again. Her husband was knotting his tie, watching her in the bedroom mirror. She forced herself to smile at him, roll her eyes.

"Listen, Bernie," she said, "I appreciate the call, I really do. But we're getting ready for church now and my husband's tapping his foot and staring at his watch. Please drive carefully, and thanks again for calling." She put as much feeling into the "thanks again" as she felt she could without arousing Loren's suspicion. Then she waited, holding her breath, for Bernie to say good-bye first.

When he heard her society voice, Loren lost interest in the conversation and concentrated on straightening his collar.

"Good-bye, Mrs. Markham," Bernie said. "Thanks for being a good mother to Greta. Give her a hug for me, will you?" she added, and hung up quickly, before she started crying.

"Who was that?" Loren asked.

"Bernice Evans," Mrs. Markham replied as she slipped into her dress. "You've met her, I think—a friend of Joan's. She was supposed to take Joan's place in our bridge game on Wednesday but has to cancel. Family emergency."

She turned her back on him so he could zip her up, then turned around and kissed him.

"Hey," he said, taking her into his arms and pulling her body against his. "That's nice. How about...?" He backed her up to the bed.

"We can't," she whispered, although, suddenly free of the terrible anxiety she'd been living with for almost a week, she wanted to. "I told you, Greta called last night. She's meeting us at the church."

"Why the hell does she have to go and get a dose of religion now?" he grumbled good-naturedly, and let her go.

Forty

Greta was waiting for them when they got to church.

"Hi, Mom! Hi, Loren!" she greeted them, with sunny smiles and big hugs. She'd never been able to call her step-father "Dad," even though she knew he'd like her to. She liked him all right—once she'd gotten past the wispy little mustache—but she'd loved her real dad. No matter what the truth was, Bob Walker was her real dad.

"This is a surprise, young lady," Loren boomed heartily. "To what do we owe this sudden burst of religious zeal?"

"Oh, nothing," she said, linking her arm in theirs as they walked into the church. "I just haven't seen you in a while and thought I'd spend a little quality time with the family. Isn't that what Pastor Ted's all about anyway?" she added with a grin.

"How kind of you!" he said. "And thanks for leaving all that jewelry you stick in your face home too. Too bad women don't have to wear hats anymore in church—it'd cover that god-awful hair of yours. Oh, well, we can't ask for everything, can we? Nice dress." He picked up the necklace Greta was wearing. "Doesn't quite go with the dress, though, does it? You into jewelry making now?"

"No," she replied, giving her mother a curious look. "What do you think of it, Mom?"

"It's very nice, dear," Mrs. Markham said, "but it's not you."

She scrutinized her daughter closely. Greta's calling the night before to announce she was coming to church had aroused Mrs. Markham's suspicions, although Bernie's call this morning had eased her mind somewhat. How could

232

Greta know anything, if Bernie hadn't told her? Could Steadman George have said something to her before he died?

The service began. Because they'd come in late, they'd had to find seats in back and so they could barely make out Pastor Ted at the altar in his white robe with the blue shawl, but the state-of-the-art loudspeakers built discreetly into the walls of the church brought his words to them as clear as if he were standing next to them.

Greta had always disliked the man. To her he was a capable actor who played his role well, but anybody who knew anything about acting knew it was only a role. She thought she could see the real man behind it, and he was as different from Pastor Ted as she was from Florence in the Showboat melodrama.

She couldn't help grudgingly admire his acting skill, but she despised the beliefs he professed. She'd made scornful comments about him to her mother and Loren, but they just waved her objections away. They'd been members of the church before Mason had become its pastor, and enjoyed the ritual and the music and the sound of Mason's voice.

His sermon this morning, "On Living in Truth," didn't seem as well-organized as they usually were, Greta thought, and Mason sounded like an actor who hadn't properly memorized his lines. His voice was raspy too, and he stammered, as though uncertain of what he was saying. Maybe he was coming down with something.

When the service was over, Loren hurried them out to their cars, anxious not to be late for his golf game.

"I brought Mom's favorite kind of coffee cake," Greta said. "I thought we could go home and have it with coffee."

They drove home and sat out on the glass-enclosed porch. The Markhams were touched by Greta's sudden daughterliness. It was so unlike her, in fact, that Mrs. Markham kept glancing nervously at her out of the corners of her eyes, wondering if there was anything behind it.

Loren gulped down a piece of cake and chased it with coffee, then kissed his wife and Greta, thanked Greta for the Sunday surprise, and went in to change into his golf clothes.

Greta made small talk with her mother until they heard his car drive off and then she said, "Mom, are you really my biological mother?"

Mrs. Markham was ready for it. She didn't know what had aroused Greta's suspicions, but she had Bernie's promise that she was leaving town and never coming back, so she had nothing to be afraid of. She was sure she could handle this. In a way, it would be like the scenes she played out for family and friends when, twenty-one years ago, she was pretending to be pregnant.

Her eyes widened and her mouth dropped. "What in the world makes you ask that?" she said, her coffee cup stopped just below her mouth.

"Are you, Mom?"

"Of course I am, Greta!"

"You didn't buy me from a woman named Bernie?"

"Where'd you get *that* idea?"

Greta studied her mother's face a moment uncertainly. Was it real or was it acting? She couldn't be sure.

"Did you?"

"No! Who put such a crazy notion into your pretty little head, Greta?"

Greta told her about Bernie and the necklace and what she'd learned from Peggy O'Neill, watching her mother closely all the while. "You see, Mom," she went on, "Peggy thinks Bernie's in danger, on account of there's a man after her who might've killed Steadman George. She wants to find her and warn her."

"Might've killed George!" Mrs. Markham almost spit. "Things like that only happen in movies, Greta! You told me yourself that the police—the real police, not some campus policewoman—say it was an accident, and that's good enough for me. It's no surprise to anyone who knew the man that he fell off the Showboat and drowned. He shouldn't have been allowed to live on the boat in the first place! This Peggy O'Neill sounds irresponsible to me, coming to you with a story like that, planting doubts in your mind about your poor father and me!"

That struck home to Greta—especially the part about her

father. Here in her mother's and Loren's well-groomed backyard, the stillness broken only by the quiet drone of gas-powered lawn mowers in the distance, the story Peggy O'Neill had told her the night before on the riverbank sounded like something you'd hear around a bonfire at summer camp.

"Okay, Mom," she said. She quickly ducked her head to the plate of coffee cake to avoid the hurt look her mother was giving her.

After a moment, she laughed and sighed dramatically. "It's too bad, though, in a way."

"What do you mean, dear?" her mother asked. "Why is it too bad?"

"Oh, I don't know. Doesn't every kid wish she was adopted sometimes, when she's growing up? I did, anyway. Of course, I always thought of myself as the ugly duckling, and I never felt I really belonged—in your family, anyway. Dad's, maybe—I look a little more like some of his people."

She laughed. "And then that woman Bernie showed up and draped this necklace over my head and gave me a horribly desperate smile. After Peggy told me she thought she was my mother, I thought back and imagined I recognized that smile as my own before Loren had my teeth fixed."

"You were never an ugly duckling, darling," Mrs. Markham said firmly. "You were always beautiful. I was *never* sorry I couldn't have more children, because I had you." She put her hands on one of Greta's.

Greta looked down at her mother's hand, noticed with a pang of annoyance that it was still beautiful even though she was fifty-two. "Thanks, Mom," she said, giving her mother a sudden grin.

"Anyway, the life this Bernie's led sounds dreadful to me. I've lived on the road too, you know, with your father—not knowing if we had enough gas to get to our next destination, not knowing what's waiting for us when we got there. Sometimes the theater would've folded or they decided Bob or I weren't right for the part—somebody else was who just happened to be one of the theater's advertiser's relatives. You can thank your lucky stars you weren't raised like that."

"Thanks, lucky stars," Greta said.

They changed the subject, talked of other things, and then Greta looked at her watch and jumped up. "Oh, my God—I'm gonna be late for the performance and Sam's gonna kill me! 'Bye, Mom."

The performance was at two—there was only the one on Sunday.

She bent and kissed her mother on the forehead and dashed across the lawn to the house, her mother following her. As she passed through the living room, she banged her leg against the glass top of the coffee table.

"Ouch," she said, kneeling, looking at the gash, which had started bleeding. "Damm it, Mom, why don't you put electrical tape on the edges of this booby trap—or helium balloons around it or something? Or better yet, get something less tacky! I gash myself on that goddamned thing every time I come over here!"

"Don't swear, dear," her mother said. "I'll get a Band-Aid. One of the flesh-colored ones so you won't even know it's there."

"Hurry, okay? I'm late."

She stood and looked down at her mother, kneeling at her feet, head bent as she put antiseptic ointment on the cut and then carefully smoothed a Band-Aid over it.

"If I was adopted," she said softly, "you'd tell me now if I asked, wouldn't you?"

Her mother winced, but continued to run her fingers over the Band-Aid on her daughter's leg, not daring to look up.

"Mom, you still down there?"

"Of course I'd tell you, dear," her mother said, scrambling to her feet and leading the way quickly to the door, since she didn't want Greta to see her face just then.

"You'd trust me with that knowledge, Mom?" Greta persisted, following her.

"Of *course* I would, darling!"

Greta gave her mother a long, searching look, then a quick kiss and a pat on the cheek. She hurried off to her car.

Forty-one

I usually enjoy spending Sundays alone when I have the chance, working in the garden or walking around a lake or reading, but not that Sunday. I sat out in the backyard in a lawn chair and skimmed the Sunday paper, a thermos of coffee and my cordless phone beside me. When I finished the paper and Greta still hadn't called, I started a letter to my mother in Los Angeles, but couldn't concentrate enough even to formulate the innocuous lies she expects of me.

Church was long over. Why hadn't Greta called to tell me how things had gone with her mother—and why hadn't Bernie called to find out what I was worried about?

Bernie had told both Sue Ann Naylor and Geoff Seaton that she'd only be in town through today. Well, maybe she'd found her daughter after talking to Steadman George and, mission accomplished, was now either happily getting acquainted with her somewhere and didn't have time for me or had vanished again as suddenly as she'd appeared.

There'd been nothing on the television news about a woman named Bernie being murdered, and nothing in the paper either. I'd looked.

I thought of the folk tale about stone soup, and wondered if that's what I'd been making for the past four days. Well, I'd spent time on less worthwhile projects than this, I thought—although I couldn't think of what they were off-hand.

Greta had told me she planned to talk to her mother right after church—I suppose she thought she'd get her in a religious mood when she'd be more likely to tell the truth—

and before she had to be back to the Showboat for the two o'clock matinee.

When I figured the play must have started and she still hadn't called, I told myself the conversation she'd had with her mother might have been so upsetting that she'd forgotten to call me afterward, or had lasted so long that she didn't have time to call me before the play began.

At three Paula called, asking if Gary was back yet. When I told her no, she said, "Well, Lawrence wants to go to the fair now—today's the last day and it's probably going to be jam-packed with people. You want to come with?"

"I'm sorry, Paula," I said. "I'm waiting for an important phone call."

"Huh! More important than us, is it? And you're always complaining we never do anything together anymore."

"I'm sorry," I said. "Stone soup takes a long time to make," I added, "and patience."

"I have no idea what you're talking about," she said, and after a few more pleasantries, we hung up.

Greta finally called at a little before five.

"Mom denies it," she said without any preliminaries.

"Oh," I replied, disappointed to see my entire scenario crumbling around me.

"I don't know what to think," she went on, sounding anguished.

"What do you mean?"

"I don't know! That woman—Bernie—she must've meant something by what she did, giving me that necklace and looking at me like that. And I'll swear on a stack of Bibles that I felt something pass between us when our eyes met. I don't know how to describe it—a kind of recognition, like we'd known each other in a previous life, like we were related. You think ties of blood are that strong, Peggy?"

"But your mother denied it," I said, instead of answering her question.

"Yeah, she did." She was silent for a minute. "And she was very convincing too. But I've got a kind of feeling about it. She was convincing, but thinking about it afterwards, I thought it might've been a convincing *performance*. I wasn't sure at the time. I mean, the story you told me about Bernie on the river just seemed so—so—oh, I don't know!"

Oscar Wildean, I thought, remembering what Sam had said about it.

"And anyway," she went on, "I had to get back for the play and didn't have time to talk to her any more about it. Maybe I'll go out there tomorrow, when Loren's at work, and try again."

I heard voices in the background. "I gotta go now, Peggy," she said. "Some of us are going over to the Boardinghouse for coffee."

She laughed suddenly. "I'm sorry I couldn't give you better news—better for you, anyway. Hell, maybe better for me too. I mean, wouldn't it be kind of fun to have two mothers—one a *Leave It to Beaver* kind of mom, the other a jewelry maker who lives in an old school bus? Well, we'll see. I have a feeling the play's not over yet."

I called Paula and Lawrence to see if they hadn't left for the fair yet, but they weren't home. I thought of going to the fair and looking for them, but realized that the chances of finding them in the crowd would be small.

Forty-two

All day Sunday Bernie brooded, in spite of the fact that it was another busy day. From time to time Swallow, between clients, glanced over at her, as if reproaching her for something. She could feel her eyes on her. They weren't as awful as Pastor Ted's, but they made her uncomfortable anyway.

Once, during a lull in business, Swallow couldn't contain herself anymore. She came over and stood in front of Bernie and said, "It's obvious what you have to do. You have to tell your daughter who you are. You have to do it as much for your own sake as for hers! Unless you do, you can't be happy anywhere now. You know that as well as I do, Bernie Knapp!"

Was that true? Bernie wondered. She was happy most of the time, living the life she did in her trailer, with her bus, her dog, her friends and customers. Or had been, until she'd gotten the notion to come back here and look for Greta. Would she never be happy again?

It was too late to do anything about it now. She'd given Mrs. Markham her word that she was leaving town without telling Greta anything. She would keep her word.

Eventually the pain of leaving Greta a second time would fade, just as it had the first time. And anyway, hadn't she gotten what she came for, to find out if her daughter was all right? She no longer had that to worry about—that was something, that was a lot! Why should she ask for more? She'd even gotten to see her on the stage, acting and singing and dancing. That was a memory she'd have forever!

She wished she'd thought to ask Mrs. Markham for a photograph of Greta, but it was too late for that now too.

She didn't know if coming back had been a mistake or not, but at least nobody had been hurt by it. Well, maybe Mrs. Markham—for a little while anyway. But on the phone she sounded as though she'd recovered, Bernie thought with a tinge of bitterness, once Bernie had assured her she'd go away and never return.

Somewhere from the direction of the Showboat she could hear bells striking seven, reminding her that the fair would be over soon and she'd be leaving town—maybe not even waiting until tomorrow, but just driving away in the night and stopping to sleep at the side of the road later, when she was safely over the state line.

What harm would it do, she asked herself, to go see the play one last time? It started at eight. If she left now, she'd have plenty of time to get down to the Showboat and get a good seat. She'd made enough money from the fair; she could afford to close early tonight.

She turned to Swallow and said, "I'm going down to the Showboat to see the play again. Keep an eye on my booth for me, will you? Just tell people I'm closed—I don't have much left to sell anyway. I'll be back by ten."

Swallow nodded, the hope that Bernie had decided to talk to her daughter showing on her face. "Take your time," she said.

As she made her way through the crowd and down the steps to the river, Bernie wondered if what she was doing was dumb. Wasn't she just torturing herself? But she had to see Greta one last time—she had to! Her biggest concern was if the evening performance might have started early because it was Sunday, or already be sold out. Sunday must be a big day on the Showboat too.

As she approached the path leading down to the boat, her eyes narrowed with concern: she couldn't see anybody on or around the boat! Had the play started already? No— the parking lot was empty too. With a crushing sense of disappointment, she realized there wasn't a performance Sunday night.

The sun was low in the sky and the boat, in shadow on the river with its lights out, looked abandoned, stripped of all its magic.

She stood at the gangplank and stared up at it, wondering

if Steadman George was in his cabin. She'd mentioned to Mrs. Markham that she might see him once more before leaving, to tell him her decision about Greta. She might as well do it, since she was here.

"Mr. George!" she called up to his cabin. "Mr. George!"

There was no answer.

She walked up the gangplank and stepped over the chain barring the way onto the boat, one long leg after the other. She passed the ticket window where she'd picked up her ticket the night she'd seen her daughter for the first time since giving her up—since selling her! She noticed that the schedule in the window listed only a matinee performance on Sundays. She'd missed it, missed her last chance to see her daughter!

Hesitantly, she started up the stairs to the upper deck, paused at the top, then went over and knocked on the door of George's cabin.

Still no answer. She peered in the window, saw through a crack in the drapes that the cabin was dark.

She started to turn, to go back down the stairs and leave the boat, but then she remembered the last time she'd stood here like this. George had brought her to his door and then looked both ways as if to be sure he wasn't being observed, and then he'd slid up the window next to the door, reached in, and opened the door from the inside. He'd told her he'd lost his key.

She stood irresolutely a moment, considering. He'd told her he could also enter the theater directly through the cabin.

She tried the window and it slid up. Guiltily, she looked all around, then reached in, opened the door, went inside.

"Mr. George?" she called, in case he might be sleeping. No answer.

She crossed the room quickly, pulled open the door in the back wall, and peered down the stairs, then went down them into the darkness. She left the door open for light, since she didn't know where the theater's light switches were.

At the bottom of the stairs she waited until her eyes got used to the dark, realized she was standing next to the upright piano below the stage. Curious to know what it felt like to be Greta and looking out at an audience, she climbed the steps and walked onto the stage, her work boots echoing loudly in the empty theater.

She stood in the middle of the stage in front of the curtain and peered out at the rows of empty seats, imagined every one of them filled and a spotlight on her. She took a few clumsy steps to the music she remembered Steadman George playing, but she'd never been a dancer, and she suddenly felt as ridiculous as she was sure she looked and she went quickly back to the steps and down into the theater again.

She walked up the aisle and took the middle seat about ten rows back from the stage—as a child she'd always liked to sit close up and in the middle in movie theaters.

On the curtain she could make out the painting of a showboat that looked just like this one. It was pulling into a small river town, its pennants flying, smoke billowing from its stacks, its paddlewheel churning up the water. People in nineteenth century costumes were running down to the dock to meet it. She stared at it a long time until she could see through it to the brightly lit stage where her daughter, in her role as the spoiled but good-hearted Florence, was exchanging witty banter with the hero.

Then she imagined she could hear piano music again and see George at the battered old upright, and she remembered how he'd looked with his straw boater tilted at an angle on his head, his hands flying over the keys as Greta and the other actors danced and sang.

She smiled at the vision and could feel the tears forming in her eyes and starting to run down her cheeks and she knew she needed to blow her nose, but she didn't have a Kleenex and didn't care. She hadn't cried, really cried, in a long time—not since she was packing to leave town after she'd watched the Walkers drive off with her baby—but she could now, because she was alone here and nobody could see her.

Movement in the open door next to the stage caught her eye. A man was standing in the shadows at the bottom of the stairs.

"Mr. George?" she called.

No answer.

"Mr. George?" she said again, more anxiously this time. "It's just Bernie," she added, getting up and wiping her eyes with the back of her hand. As the man moved out of the shadows and into the theater, she could see it wasn't Steadman George—he was too tall and thin.

Then she recognized him—the man from the fair yesterday whom Swallow had been worried about.

"Who are you?" she asked. "What do you want?"

Forty-three

All day Sunday, Linda Markham brooded. Why hadn't she told Greta the truth when she'd asked? What was she afraid of?

She and Bob had agreed not to tell anybody that she was adopted. Why should they? Out of fear of being caught, they'd pretended she was pregnant for nine months, carrying out the fiction with family and friends. How could they later admit it had all been a lie? Besides, it was no laughing matter to buy and sell a baby! She wasn't sure even now what problems she and Greta—and Bernie too—might have to face if what they'd done came to the ears of the authorities.

It didn't take long for Linda to come to believe that Greta was her own flesh and blood, just as Bob had.

Bob's death had put a seal on the lie, an unbreakable seal.

Surely Bob would have admired her performance when, feeling her daughter's eyes burning into the back of her head as she'd knelt at her feet, she'd reaffirmed the lie. That had been her finest moment as an actress. She smiled as she imagined she heard Bob's applause.

Then she saw Greta's face and heard her say, "You'd tell me if I was adopted. You'd trust me with that knowledge, Mom?"

She'd come so close to admitting the truth then. But why should she tell the truth now—bring the whole fiction down like a house of cards, betray Bob's memory—just when Steadman George was dead and Bernie was about to leave town, taking the secret with her? Besides, she'd have to tell

Loren the truth too. She couldn't even imagine how he'd react to discovering that Greta had been illegally adopted.

She'd pulled it off with Greta and was home free. Why make trouble for herself—for everyone—now?

So she should be celebrating! Why wasn't she? Why was there such a heavy weight pressing on her heart? What was it Greta had said about that campus policewoman? That she'd thought Bernie was in danger, somebody was out looking for her, who might have murdered Steadman George.

Nonsense! George drowned—that's what the police said. Drowned while drunk and possibly high on drugs. That was no surprise to anybody who knew him. And as for Bernie, who knows what kind of life she'd lived these past twenty years, and where she'd been? She should never have returned. She'd have to face the consequences of that, whatever they were, herself. If it was true that somebody was looking for her, it was probably just a collection agency.

Forty-four

Rick, Greta's boyfriend, walked into the Boardinghouse with a scowl on his face and marched over to the table where Greta was sitting with some of the other actors from the play. He looked at his watch, then down at her. Seeing Paul Boone sitting next to her didn't improve the expression on his face.

"You know where we're supposed to be in half an hour, Greta, don't you?" he asked in the nasal tone of voice he used when he was annoyed with her about something.

It took her a moment. Then she said, "Oh, damn! I totally forgot. I'm sorry, Rick." She'd had too much on her mind today. Tonight was Rick's mother's birthday dinner and she was expected to be there.

"Are you?" he queried. "Well, it takes half an hour to get out there, as you know, and you have to go home and change. I'm not going to take you out there looking like that. I'll call them and let them know we're going to be a little late."

She looked around helplessly. The others had their faces buried in their coffees. They didn't like Rick. She didn't either, actually, but she'd grown up with him, even let him take her to her senior prom in high school. Besides, he was Loren's partner's son, and she didn't know how to get rid of him without hurting Loren and creating tension between the two families.

Paul Boone turned to her, put his face close to hers, and said, "Well, if Rick can't take you out to see his mother looking like *that,* then maybe he can take you out there looking like *this.*"

He crossed his eyes and stuck out his tongue.

At first she didn't know how to react. Then she burst out laughing.

"Or like this," he said, and hunched up one shoulder and put a huge grimace on his face and turned it up to Rick.

Rick, taking the high road, shook his head sadly and said, "Not funny, Boone."

Greta was trying to keep from laughing again by drinking some coffee. When Rick said, "Not funny, Boone," she choked on her coffee, spraying it across the table. Paul began pounding her on the back.

" 'Not funny, Boone!' " she gasped. "But quite *humerus*! Get it—humerus! Funny Boone!"

"I don't understand how you can do this to me, Greta," Rick said. "And to Mother. Are you coming or not?"

She sobered up, thought a moment, and said, "No."

Rick nodded, gave the lot of them a withering look, turned on his heels, and stomped across the floor to the exit.

"Shit," Greta said. "That wasn't very nice, was it?"

"Another round of cappuccino, waiter, please," Paul said, to no one in particular, since the Boardinghouse didn't have waiters.

Forty-five

Paul dropped Greta off in front of her apartment building at a few minutes before seven. They sat in his car and talked for a while, a little sobered by what they'd done to Rick.

"If I ever have an abscessed tooth," Paul said, "I know one dentist I'll never go to."

"Since I'll probably be his partner," she said, "I'll make sure he doesn't hurt you."

"After what happened tonight, you'd be lucky to get a job mopping up the blood after his extractions," Paul said, with a certain satisfaction.

"Are you kidding? I could get Rick back in a snap, if I wanted. I've treated him badly before, but business partnerships are thicker than blood any day, you know."

"A match made in heaven," Paul said dryly. "But you don't want to get him back, Greta. You're too funny—at least, I thought so until that humerus joke—and you've got too much talent to waste it filling cavities. 'Say ah!' just isn't a line you can do much with, is it? You're an actress and a comedian. The world needs more of those right now than dentists."

"My mom hated showbiz," she said. "It got old for her real fast."

"That's because she wasn't any good at it. Don't glare at me like that, you've said so yourself! She was only in it on account of your dad."

"Maybe I don't have enough talent either."

"Oh, so it's going to be the old 'maybe-I-don't-have-what-it-takes' ploy that people use to avoid taking risks, huh? Well, we both know you do—you inherited it from your dad. The poor man's probably turning over in his grave right now at the thought of you becoming a dentist. Isn't it bad enough he's dead, without that?''

"Paul!"

He ignored her indignation. Quoting his lines from the play, he said, " 'You can sing and paint and play on the pianner, and in your own particular circle you're some pumpkins.' "

"Yeah—but what about outside my own particular circle? Would I still be 'some pumpkins' or just small potatoes?''

"Hey, somebody's got to be small potatoes, don't they? What's wrong with that, if you're happy? You'll never know unless you give it a try, will you? If you don't like it after, say, thirty years, you can quit. There'll probably still be a few teeth left to clean, fill, or pull.''

"My dad was small potatoes," she said, her expression darkening. "He was happy—but Mom and I weren't.''

"That's because he left you at home. The secret is, you all go together.''

"But what if I wanted kids?" she asked. "I hated being an only child, growing up. I promised myself a long time ago that if I ever had kids, I'd have at least half a dozen. How would I balance them with an acting career? I don't want to learn that my kid took her first step from the day-care provider!''

"Well, if I were the father—heaven forbid!—I'd want to spend as much time with the kids as my wife did. I'm the oldest of six myself, so I'm an expert at micromanaging two-legged mammals and for some reason, small creatures adore me. I can't imagine why.'' He crossed his eyes and wiggled his ears. "If you were on stage somewhere, I'd make 'em wait, or I'd come and get you when they're about to take their first steps.''

Greta laughed. "I thought all a guy wanted in a woman was someone who could milk cows, sit up butter—whatever that is—and make cheese," she said, quoting from the play again.

"That's what we've got supermarkets for now," he replied, "not women. Haven't you noticed? We live in the late twentieth century."

She didn't say anything to that, just sat there a moment. From the University, she could hear the clock in the bell tower striking seven.

Then he reached over and slowly, no fast moves, took hold of her shoulders and turned her to him and kissed her. It lasted awhile and then suddenly they both burst out laughing, splattering saliva in each other's face.

"You were peeking," they both said at once.

She disentangled herself a few minutes later and quickly opened the car door and slipped out. He wanted to follow her, but she said no. He wanted to know why not and she told him she didn't answer why-questions. She walked quickly over to her apartment house entrance, not looking back until she got there, for fear she'd change her mind.

Inside her apartment, she noticed the button on her cheap little answering machine winking at her. She made a face. It was probably Rick, calling to tell her what a bitch she was, or Rick's mother, calling to tell her how sorry she was that she was too sick to make it to her party and hoping she'd be well soon. Rick's mother was a thoughtful woman and Greta liked her.

She went to the bathroom. When she came out, the little red button was still blinking. With a sigh, she went over and pressed play, bracing herself.

It was her mother.

"That woman you were asking me about," she said. Her voice had a slight tremble in it. "Bernie. She's at the Riverton Mall—that big art fair they have there every summer. Apparently she's got a booth and sells beads and her home-made jewelry. She's leaving town early tomorrow and isn't coming back. I love you, Greta," she added, and hung up.

Greta thought of calling Peggy but decided she wanted to talk to Bernie alone first and hear her story. Peggy would just have to wait her turn.

The Riverton Mall was only a ten-minute drive from her apartment, but it took longer than she'd expected to find a place to park on account of the fair. The ramp was full, so she had to park a couple of blocks away. She could almost have saved time by walking.

She wove her way through the throngs of people that crowded the cobbled street made narrow by the booths and tents and food stands, looking for a booth with Bernie's name on it, or at least one that sold beads and the kind of jewelry she knew Bernie made.

She bumped into some people she knew who were eating hot dogs and drinking beer. They called to her to join them, but she waved them away and kept going. A tall, thin banjo player suddenly jumped in front of her, ducking and bobbing and not letting her pass until she dropped some change into his straw hat. Then he bowed and stepped aside.

She almost missed it among the jumble of booths and the crowds of people, but crystals hanging from long threads and glittering in the low evening sun caught her eye and drew her to them. A small hand-painted sign—BERNIE'S BEADS AND FINDINGS—hung from one of the horizontal pipes that held up the tent.

She felt suddenly shy as she looked around for the woman who'd given her the necklace. She didn't see her anywhere. She stood there uncertainly for a moment, then noticed a woman seated in front of a tent that advertised tarot readings. Her head was bent over cards laid out on a table and a woman was sitting opposite her, watching her expectantly.

Greta went over and stood uncertainly, not knowing what to do. She watched the psychic pick up a card and knew from its position that she was in for a long wait. A sign next to the tent said the readings lasted half an hour.

After a few minutes the pyschic—a plump, funny-looking little woman—glanced up. When she saw the necklace Greta was wearing, she looked up into Greta's eyes and said, "Your mother's not here."

"My—! How did you know? Who are you?"

"A friend of hers. She's been looking for you a long time. She's looking for you right now."

"Where?"

"On the Showboat. She thought there was a performance this evening. She must have been wrong."

"I'd better go down there and find her," Greta said, staring down at the river.

"Yes," Swallow said, "you should."

Forty-six

Gary called at a little after six to tell me he was back at his place. He was sorry he was late, but he and Kermit had spent the day on the lake fishing, and he couldn't drag himself away.

"I suppose it's too late to go to the fair," he said, not sounding too unhappy about it.

"Yeah, they already went," I said.

"Then how about you coming over here and we'll do Chinese? I know you have to get to work by eleven, but that'll give us plenty of time to eat, et cetera."

"That sounds good," I said, knowing that by "et cetera" he didn't mean opening fortune cookies. "But how about you coming here instead?" I hadn't given up entirely on hearing from Bernie.

"Sure," he said. "Seven okay?"

"Great. Are we celebrating anything, like your buying the Loon Lake *Daily Planet*?"

"Maybe," he said obscurely, and hung up.

So I went around my living and dining room, tidying the place up and practicing what I'd tell anybody who asked when I got to police headquarters that night what I'd done on my three days off. "Thank you for asking! I chased a chimera."

Moonspin, as the late Steadman George's mother would have called it.

Steadman George! I thought bitterly. A drunk living on a boat—what could be more natural than that he'd fall in and drown? But you didn't want to believe it, Peggy O'Neill, did you? Oh, no! The hirsute old goat reminded

. you of your father, so you probably thought you were to blame for his death too, because you wouldn't let him hook you into his struggle against the bottle the way your father had. And you decided to try to weasel out of it by trying to prove his drowning hadn't been an accident, that somebody had killed him instead.

The phone rang again.

"Peggy?"

It wasn't Greta. It was Buck Hansen, a homicide cop I've known a long time.

"What's the problem, Buck?" I asked, because under normal circumstances he wouldn't say "Peggy?" when I say hello.

He cleared his throat, probably another first in our relationship, and asked me if I knew a man named Geoff Seaton.

"Seaton!" I said, surprised, and then I realized what the problem was. "Oh, he's dead, isn't he?"

"Yes." Suddenly cautious, Buck added, "How'd you know?"

"It's okay, Buck. He wasn't a friend of mine, and I didn't kill him. You found my name and phone number in his study, didn't you?"

"Yes."

"I was at his home yesterday," I said. "How'd he die?"

"He probably drowned. It looks like he hit his head on the side of his swimming pool and fell in. There's no sign of a struggle and no evidence of a break-in. But the medical examiner's not entirely happy with that scenario."

"Do you have any idea how long he's been dead?"

"Best guess, sometime yesterday afternoon or evening. His body wasn't discovered until about an hour ago when some friends went over to his place and found him. They'd become concerned when he didn't show up at a ball game yesterday afternoon and a party last night, and didn't answer his phone today."

My heart sank. Seaton must have been killed soon after I left him yesterday. If he told his killer where to find Bernie, the chances were good she was dead now too.

"He was murdered, Buck," I said.

"Why do you say that? What're you involved in now, Peggy?"

I told him the story from the beginning, just the bare bones: Steadman George and the single glass in his cabin, the man I'd seen—thought I'd seen—in George's cabin the night he drowned who was looking for Bernie Knapp; the story George had told me about Bernie and her baby.

Buck listened without interruption. It's possible he was speechless, but he didn't waste any time being skeptical—as I say, we go back a long way, and he takes me seriously.

"How sure are you that this Bernie is Greta Markham's mother?" he asked when I'd finished.

"As sure as I am of the rest of it," I answered glumly. "Greta called me a couple of hours ago and told me she'd talked to her mother and she'd denied it, but Greta's not sure she's telling the truth. She plans to go out tomorrow and talk to her again."

Buck thought a minute. "I don't suppose there's much of a hurry now," he said finally. "If you're right and Seaton was killed by somebody looking for this Knapp woman, he's had well over a day to find her. And if Seaton told him where she was . . ."

He didn't have to spell it out.

"But I'll send Kate Weston out to this Linda Markham's home and interview her," he went on. "If she knows where Bernie Knapp is, Wes'll get it out of her."

I knew Wes—one of Buck's detectives—well enough to know that was true.

It was almost seven when we said good-bye and hung up.

I stood in my window and stared out at the corner of Lake Eleanor I can see from it, paying no attention to the windsurfers darting in and out among the slower-moving sailboats, waiting for Gary to come over with Chinese takeout, the thought of which now nauseated me.

"Where are you, Bernie?" I whispered, leaning my forehead against the windowpane. "Are you still in town, or did you get away before your killer arrived?"

Steadman George hadn't told his killer where she was. Had Geoff Seaton?

Seaton was going to go to a ball game and then see

Bernie afterward. When he'd told me that, he'd said something that had puzzled me a little. What was it? Something about he'd buy her a brat and a beer like they were still sweethearts, and talk over old times.

I'd thought he meant he was going to take her to the game with him, but he'd said he wasn't going to see her until after the game—so where did he plan to take her to get a brat and a beer, if he'd be coming from a ball game, not going to one?

And where she was, he'd said, was on his way home from the ball park.

I was only just starting to visualize the geography between the ball park and Seaton's home when it all slipped into place: the Riverton Mall, half a mile upstream from the University, was about a mile from the ball park. You could get every kind of hot dog at the fair going on there, and beer too.

Bernie sold beads and jewelry for a living at arts fairs and, according to Paula, today was the fair's last day—and Bernie was only going to be in town through tonight!

Forgetting my date with Gary, I ran out to my car and drove over to the Riverton Mall. I briefly considered calling Buck first, but I didn't think there was that much of a hurry anymore. Seaton's killer had had over a day to find Bernie, which meant she was most likely dead now. But if she wasn't, I wanted to meet her and get her story myself before turning the case over to him.

Forty-seven

"Who are you?" Bernie asked again. "What do you want?" Then, in the dim light, she could see the ugly, snub-nosed revolver in his hand as he approached. "If it's sex, you don't have to kill me for it."

"I believe you," he said. "What's the price for your fair special?"

"What do you mean?" she asked, the senselessness of the words overriding her fear.

"I mean I know all about you, Bernie," he answered. "I've been looking for you a long time."

"Me? Why me?"

"How many abortions have you had, Bernie?"

Nothing he said made any sense. "Abortions? None! And how do you know my name?"

" 'None,' " he repeated, mocking her. "Oh, that's right—I forgot—you sell your babies, don't you? You don't get abortions."

"Who are you, anyway? Did Steadman George tell you about me?"

Stan laughed. "Yes, as a matter of fact, he did—almost with his last breath. Your friend Mr. George made a serious error in judgment—and paid for it with his life. He thought he could blackmail my brother."

"Your brother?" Bernie repeated. "Steadman George is dead?"

Stan's face went white with anger, emphasizing the fiery red scratch on his face. "You can stop pretending now, Bernie! You were in it with him. You weren't satisfied with the money Ted gave you for an abortion or the money you got for selling your baby, so you came back for more, didn't you?''

Her eyes grew big with astonishment. "You mean, you're . . . ?''

"That's right. I'm Pastor Ted's brother—and his right-hand man. A jack-of-all-trades, master of one—I kill people. I've done a lot of that in my time.''

He grinned, showing Bernie his yellow teeth. She was reminded of wolves she'd seen in zoos in the Southwest.

"Ted's sorry he can't be here this evening,'' Stan went on. "But it's Sunday—it's his busy day, you know.'' He glanced at his watch. "It's almost time for his television show to start—*Pastor Ted's Fireside Hour.* I'm going to miss it tonight.''

He gestured with the pistol. "Now get up, we're going for a short evening stroll along the river. And don't make a fuss, Bernie. It doesn't matter to me where I kill you, but if I have to shoot you with people around, somebody else might get hurt too. You wouldn't want that on your conscience, would you—especially since it wouldn't do you any good?''

Since it was still light out and there might be people around, his plan was to walk Bernie a short way downstream into the woods beyond the clearing around the Showboat and drown her as he'd drowned George. It would take only a few minutes and it's hard to scream when you're choking on water.

She got slowly to her feet, her eyes never leaving Stan's face.

"But I'm leaving town,'' she protested. "I'm not going to expose Reverend Mason—and I don't know anything about blackmail!''

"I know,'' he said sarcastically, "it's all a big misunderstanding. C'mon, let's go.''

They went up the aisle. She could feel the mouth of his gun poking into the small of her back, prodding her along.

"Push it open,'' he said when they got to the door.

She pressed the bar across one of the double doors, opened it, and stepped out—and almost bumped into somebody standing in front of her, her back to the low evening sun.

"Bernie?"

Bernie squinted to try to see who it was—a young woman with short cherry-red hair and bright makeup.

She thought quickly. "No, dear. My name's not Bernie. It's—it's Greta!"

Greta's mouth fell open. "Greta . . . !"

Something was wrong. Greta's eyes moved to the man behind Bernie. He must be the man Peggy O'Neill was afraid was out to kill her.

"Oh, sorry," she said, and backed away as they followed her out onto the deck. "I was looking for a woman named Bernie. Someone at the fair said I could find her here. I have something for her."

She gave them both a smile as she took off the necklace she was wearing and held it out for them to see. "You don't happen to know if she's on the boat, do you?"

Bernie gaped at the necklace, then at the woman holding it.

With the sun no longer in his eyes, Stan recognized Greta too. He showed her his pistol.

"Don't do anything stupid," he said, "or I'll shoot you both right here. Turn around," he ordered Greta. "Lead the way down the gangplank. Hurry—or I'll shoot your mother right here!"

Greta looked into Bernie's eyes a long moment, started to say something, then did as the man said. Slowly she crossed the deck to the gangplank. As she reached it, she looked up and saw a figure running toward them across the Showboat's parking lot, her bright red hair flying around her head: Peggy O'Neill.

Stan saw her too, and recognized her. "What the hell . . . !" he exclaimed, his eyes widening in disbelief.

Bernie turned swiftly and knocked the pistol aside, stepped into his body, and kneed him between the legs. He screamed and fell to one knee, managed to duck as she swung one of her long legs to try to kick him in the face. She lost her balance, grabbed the gangplank's handrail to prevent herself from falling over into the river.

He staggered to his feet and raised his gun. He could still kill them both, then run to the other side of the boat, jump overboard, and swim away. He'd kill the goddamned cop too! Why not? Nobody'd ever know why they'd died.

"Duck, Bernie!" Greta said, and flung the heavy necklace into his face as hard as she could. He flinched, the pistol went off, and then Greta was on him like a wildcat, clawing and scratching at his face. He fell back against the railing, trying to get the pistol up with one hand while protecting his eyes with the other.

Bernie was on him then too, all flailing arms, blazing eyes, flashing teeth. He jerked the pistol away from Greta and raised it to shoot again, but Bernie grabbed his wrist in an iron grip and twisted, putting her weight into it.

He screamed as ligaments tore in his arm, the pistol dropped onto the gangplank, and then Bernie flipped him overboard as if he were a sack of flour from one of the long-gone mills down the river a way. He landed about where, four days earlier, he'd drowned Steadman George.

Peggy arrived then, out of breath, to find the two equally breathless women with their arms draped around each other's waist, looking down at the man trying to sit up in the river, his face streaming blood and water. He was clutching his shoulder, coughing, moaning.

"Hi, Peggy," Greta said, giving her a little wave.

"Who's she?" Bernie asked.

"The cavalry," Greta told her, as she scooped up her necklace from the gangplank, "riding to the rescue. Where'd you learn those moves you put on him?"

"I took classes," Bernie said. "A woman who lives on the road has to know how to protect herself."

"Cool," Greta said, She turned to Peggy. "Peggy," she said, "I'd like you to meet somebody you've been looking for a long time."

Forty-eight

I never felt so useless in my life as I picked up the pistol and asked Bernie and Greta if they knew who the man in the water was.

"He told me he's the brother of Ted Mason," Bernie replied. "Pastor Ted."

"Pastor Ted!" Greta exclaimed, turning pale. "He's the pastor of my church—why would he want to kill you?"

The look Bernie gave her told her why, if she hadn't already guessed.

"Oh, my God!" she said. "The man confirmed me! You mean he—he wanted you dead and sicced his brother on you?"

"That's what he said," Bernie answered, nodding down at Stan in the water. "I'm sorry," she added.

Greta shook her head, trying to digest that. Then she took a deep breath and turned to me. "Where's the smelling salts when you need 'em?" she asked, trying to be funny. It didn't come off.

"Peggy," she went on, "I need to go somewhere and sit down. Bernie probably does too. Do you mind if we get out of here, maybe walk back to the fair? We've got a lot to talk about. Okay?" It was almost a plea.

"Call the police for me first," I said. "There's a phone in the cabin on the upper deck of the boat. I think Bernie knows the way," I added dryly.

"Yes," Bernie said, "I do."

"And you can sit up there and talk," I added, "until the police get here. There're a couple of chairs on the river side of the boat, and a nice breeze."

As I turned my attention back to the man in the water, trying to pull himself upright, I heard Greta say, "You don't mind if I call you Bernie, do you? It would get too confusing if I called you Mom, because I've already got one of those—and when I think about it, one's all any girl really needs. Besides, she's gonna have enough to deal with for a while without that—and so am I."

"I know," Bernie said. "And I don't want you to call me Mom. Bernie's fine."

"Thanks," Greta said, and started to cry.

Epilogue

I doubt we'll ever know the whole story—Pastor Ted's involvement, for example. He's denied having anything to do with the deaths of Steadman George and Geoff Seaton and the attempted murder of Bernie Knapp. Stan Mason insists he was acting on his own too. One of their old high school teachers was interviewed in the *Tribune* a week or so after the story broke, and said that's how it was when they were kids: Stan always took the blame, even though everybody knew Ted was probably at least as guilty. Some people even thought Ted might have been involved in the crime that forced Stan into the Army to avoid going to jail.

It's not helping Pastor Ted's case any that the church secretary recalls getting a phone call from somebody named George asking about an old babysitter named Bernie, a call she put through to Mason, who rushed out of the church minutes later claiming he was ill. Steadman George drowned that night, of course.

Ted Mason may never go to jail or even stand trial, but his career as a theologian, politician, and cable television personality is over—or, given the times we live in, on hold.

Whatever happens to him, his brother's future doesn't look rosy. He bragged to Bernie that he'd killed both George and Seaton. Maybe her word won't hold up against a charismatic lawyer and a jury that's honed its critical intelligence on talk shows and televangelists, but he left some of his own blood at Seaton's swimming pool, and the knife he'd tried to use on Bernie at the trailer park had a thumbprint on it that matched his.

It's also unlikely that a jury will believe he'd just been taking Bernie for a little stroll along the river and brought the pistol along to shoot squirrels.

Bernie's going to stay in town for a while—at least through Stan Mason's trial. A friend of hers has a house he's remodeling into a furniture-making business and workshop and she's using part of the showroom for her beads and jewelry—she has to earn a living, after all. Her bus and trailer are parked in back.

The crime lab analysis showed that one of the drinking glasses from the Showboat cabin had no fingerprints on it at all. I suppose George could have washed and dried the glass in such a way as not to leave fingerprints, but it would have been hard. Undoubtedly Stan Mason did it after killing George, never imagining anybody would be so suspicious of George's death that she'd look into it that closely.

The marijuana we'd found in George's cabin was laced with PCP—angel dust. Again, there's no way to know if George bought it that way—or even if he bought it—but my theory is that Stan Mason brought it to the Showboat along with the whiskey and gave it to George to smoke, then forced him to start drinking. Or more likely, with the PCP, it wasn't necessary to force him.

My friend Buck Hansen managed to piece together how George got on the trail of Ted Mason in the first place. Sue Ann Naylor admitted she'd told George that Bernie had babysat for a chaplain at the U, and Bernie remembered that when she'd talked to George, she'd let slip that Greta's father was a man named Ted. A librarian at the University, a woman named Sally Pyne, contacted the police to report that George had called her the day he'd died, showing an interest in Ted Mason that she'd thought was odd.

George hadn't needed anything more than those few bits and pieces of information to construct a murder mystery that turned out to feature him as the victim—the first victim.

Nobody, however, can explain why he didn't tell Stan Mason where to find Bernie, since he knew. According to Bernie, she'd told him she'd be at the Riverton Art Fair that week. That leaves me free to believe what I want to about it, and I choose to believe that Steadman George refused to try to buy his own life by giving up Bernie's.

We all need illusions, and that's one of mine.